THE
LONELY
GIRLS

BOOKS BY STACY GREEN

THE LONELY GIRLS

STACY GREEN

bookouture

Published by Bookouture in 2023

An imprint of Storyfire Ltd.
Carmelite House
50 Victoria Embankment
London EC4Y 0DZ

www.bookouture.com

ISBN: 978-1-83790-043-5
eBook ISBN: 978-1-83790-042-8

Ring around the rosy
Lucy thinks she's home free
"Ashes, ashes"
She's going to fall down.

UNKNOWN

He still couldn't believe it had come to this. Best-laid plans, he supposed. He'd prefer things to be less messy. Messiness could lead to mistakes. And he didn't make those.

Lucy made more than he thought possible.

The girl tied up in his backseat whimpered.

He'd never minded the dark. It soothed him, even as a child. While most kids were afraid of the dark, he thrived in it. Nighttime brought everything in his world to life. That's when the girls got what they deserved.

Some of them practically begged for punishment with their tight tops and short shorts and smart mouths. Their defiance had always amazed him. Didn't they understand their purpose?

But their struggle only increased the fun. He shouldn't complain.

"Please." The girl resorted to begging yet again. It bored him. "Just let me go. I won't fight. I won't tell anyone."

That's what they all said. Not a single one meant it. And he didn't care if they did.

The alarm on his watch alerted him the time had come.

He'd scouted the area in advance to find out the best time to slip in and create his message. It had come.

He exited the car and inhaled, taking in the rich scent of the pre-dawn: freshly mowed grass with a coating of dew, accompanied by the heady scent of wildflowers. The sky still appeared black, but the eastern horizon grew lighter by the second. No more time to waste.

He opened the back door. "Get out."

The girl jerked as if he'd shocked her. Perhaps he should have brought the Taser. Seeing her writhe in agony certainly would have been entertaining. "I can't see."

"Use your senses." He leaned down until his lips almost touched her ear. She smelled like sweat and of the dark, moldy place where he'd kept her prisoner. "It's only common sense. Move your feet and step out of the car."

She did as told, flopping about ungracefully. Dark roots had begun to invade the pretty blond dye job he'd given her. Her days in solitary confinement with so little room to move had turned her muscled legs to sluggish stumps. She nearly fell flat on her face before he grabbed her arm and steadied her. She trembled at the contact.

He smiled. "You should always be aware of your surroundings. A girl with your background should have known that."

"I thought I could trust you." Her voice cracked. The lack of sun had turned her skin pasty. Her lips, raw from days of chewing, looked as though a dog had mauled them. The yellowing bruise beneath her eye reminded him of a dagger slashing toward her mouth. Fresh bruising painted her throat. All together quite a colorful canvas.

"You shouldn't trust anyone. First rule of life." He took her forearm and began to lead her toward the building. She dragged her feet, breathing heavily. Her lack of energy annoyed him. He should have fed her more last night. If she didn't fight, he wouldn't have as much fun. "If you take no other lesson from this, remember that."

She looked in the direction of his voice, her breath quickening. "So you aren't going to kill me?"

They'd reached the door. Painted a fading red, it listed awkwardly to the right, as if it had come to the end of its own life.

"Oh, I'm going to kill you," he said. "But what's the point of any experience if we can't learn from it?"

Her body turned liquid, her bruised chin dropping to her chest. A great, silent shudder tore from her starving frame.

He dug two fingers into the tender space beneath her chin and forced her to raise her head. "Don't give up on me now. At least act like you give a damn about your life."

Her rapid breathing told him she was at least making the effort. He'd give her a point for that. Shoving her inside the building, he took a long, careful glance before shutting the door and then securing the lock.

He found the light easily and flipped the switch. Puny track lighting—half of it burned out—streamed over them. Barely enough light to work in.

The foolish girl stood in the middle of the room, cradling her thin right arm. She'd stupidly dislocated her shoulder on their first encounter. Truthfully, given all she'd been through in her life, he'd expected better.

"What happens now?" Her voice fell flat against the grainy tile floor. She kept moving her head, as if she thought he was circling her.

"Now we begin." He took one long stride and slammed his fist into her jaw. The disconnecting crack struck his system like a shot of adrenaline. She hit the floor hard, mewling and begging.

"Much better." He jammed his booted foot onto her fragile chest and pulled the razor blade out of his pocket.

Lucy wouldn't ignore this.

Her pathetic guilt would kick in, and she'd vow for justice. That ridiculous notion would be her downfall.

If she'd only used her head, things wouldn't have to get nasty.

But she'd dug her own grave.

Lucy Kendall would have to decide if she wanted to be buried with the rest of the discarded trash or rise from the ashes like the phoenix he still believed she could be.

ONE

The crimson blood oozed from the tender flesh on my index finger, the first droplet just a tiny globule. A second drop, this one the size of a pearl, was quickly followed by a bubble large enough to splash to the floor. Vaguely aware of the pain, I grabbed a tissue from the box off my desk and wrapped it around the wound. My eyes remained focused on the small box in my lap, the paper—and the reason for my cut—discarded on the floor.

Nothing special about the box: a garden-variety, square, blue velvet thing used by just about every jewelry store in the country. The contents were far more interesting, and I couldn't decide if I felt more fear or curiosity. Two silver dollar coins emblazoned with the image of Lady Liberty standing tall rested inside. I knew enough history to know the "Ellis Island" and the issue year of 1986 made these centennial coins celebratory trinkets for the Statue of Liberty's 100th birthday. My fingers hovered over the coins. If I touched them, I couldn't ignore their existence. I'd have to think about the fact these were the second gift of silver I'd received in the last few months. The set of spoons most likely rested in the Philadelphia landfill.

How had these found me all the way in Alexandria, Virginia?

I snapped the lid back on the box and reached for the brown shipping paper. The paper cut no longer bled, the tissue still clinging to the moisture. No return address.

Postmarked in Washington, DC.

The shudder tore through me without warning, a rapid sensation I'd only experienced during the worst times in my life —the same warning system that alerted me to something being terribly wrong in the house the day I found my sister's dead body. I stuffed the box in my purse and locked it in my desk drawer. The third-floor conference room was just around the corner from my desk, but as I was already late, I practically ran down the hall.

Washington, DC Metropolitan sex crimes investigator Erin Prince had already made herself comfortable in one of the chairs in front of the large, third-floor window overlooking the street. An untouched Styrofoam cup of coffee sat on the table in front of her. Her cropped nails tapped on the table, offbeat with her bouncing foot. Prince was one of a handful of Metro's female investigators and a valuable asset to us. I'd worked with her on two cases since my arrival in Alexandria, and her ability to both compartmentalize the things she saw, as well as communicate with our victims, impressed me.

My main priority as a case manager for the National Center for Missing and Exploited Children—NCMEC to all of us— was acting as a liaison between the family of the missing child and everyone else involved in the case. This meant one voice for the family to trust and one person for law enforcement to work with. As the single point of contact, I had to make sure our resources were being fully instituted in the search for a critically endangered child. Surprisingly, I loved the job. Every day, I had renewed hope I could start over. But my current case was tantalizingly up my shadowy alley.

"Sorry to keep you waiting." I closed the door to the conference room and tried to smile at Prince. "I'm still working on getting the victims into the database."

"No problem." The corner of Prince's mouth lifted in what I assumed was meant to be a friendly gesture. Prince's intensity intimidated much of the staff, but I admired it. She never stopped fighting for the victim, and she didn't mind stepping on a few bureaucratic toes to get the job done.

"I'm happy to help." She said nothing else, and I took my cue.

"Right." I sat down across from her. "I really appreciate your coming out to Alexandria."

She rested her elbow on the table and raised her eyebrow. "I hope it's something I can help with because it took me nearly an hour to get here. This time of year is tourist central."

I couldn't argue with that. Philadelphia was no slouch in terms of traffic and general chaos, but the greater Washington, DC area surpassed anything I'd ever experienced. The area seemed to be busy all the time, the interstates heavy with commuters from Maryland and Virginia, every one of them in a fantastic hurry. The single cab ride I'd taken from Alexandria into DC had moved at the pace of an arthritic snail, and I'd vowed never to do it again. Even historic Alexandria overflowed with people, many of them locals with their heads down, hitting up their favorite coffee shops and going about their lives. But a whole lot more were tourists eager to step back into the past of one of the most richly historic cities in the northeast.

Unlike any place I'd ever been, but maddening at times. I understood Prince's irritation.

Prince yawned, revealing carefully straightened and whitened teeth. She covered her mouth politely—a gesture I wasn't used to from cops. Most of them were blunt and methodical but had no time for gentility. "How are your computer geeks coming along? Did you identify any of the girls in his picture collection?"

Last week, a tip about teenage sex trafficking victims had led the FBI and Metro police to a known pimp and drug dealer holed up in Anacostia, the district's ghetto. Prince was the lead Sex Crimes investigator and had been charged with interviewing the girls in the apartment, as well as locating the dozens of teenagers whose pictures were on the pimp's laptop. She'd called my office for help.

"My team is working hard to do that," I said. "I'm hoping to have something for you by the middle of next week. And your question actually brings me to my favor."

As case manager, I'd received a copy of the digital files taken off the pimp's laptop after the task force's raid. Some of the pictures were years, even decades, old. He'd kept photographic records of his girls, most of them indecent. One of them looked heartbreakingly familiar. I pulled the picture up on my phone and showed it to Investigator Prince.

She took the phone for a closer look. Her carefully controlled expression finally slipped as she briefly closed her eyes. "Damn. She spent too many nights with the needle."

The snapshot told a sad tale. The woman appeared to have been in her mid-forties when the picture was taken, but the evidence of hard drug abuse on her face meant she could be much younger. Several of her teeth were missing, sores caked her skin, and her eyes bore the vacant look of the high. "Since she's older, this woman isn't in any of our systems. I'm trying to identify her. I don't suppose she was one of the girls in the apartment?"

Prince looked back down, her face pinched in concentration. "Nope. All of them were in a lot better shape than this poor thing. From the looks of her, I'd say she was finished. Adonis is a selfish pimp, so if he's got a girl broken in, he keeps them. Once they're too ruined by drugs to attract even the cheap johns, Adonis rotates them into his drug-running business. This woman was probably a mule."

J. Adonis had to be one of the most ridiculous pimp names I'd encountered. Worse than Preacher. Known to run women and teenagers all along the eastern seaboard, Adonis had laughed during the bust yesterday, telling Prince he'd be out in less than twenty-four hours. "Is your buddy talking yet?"

Prince grinned. "He's still trying to comprehend that we've actually nailed his ass this time. I'm enjoying watching him sweat." She handed me the phone. "What's the date on the digital file?"

"Summer, three years ago."

"From the looks of her, she's probably dead by now. Why the interest?"

Because this woman looked like the decade-old mugshot Kelly had dug up of Agent André Lennox's sister, and I wanted to give him some kind of closure in her disappearance. Lennox had given me a glowing recommendation for the job at NCMEC, and he'd saved Chris's life. Probably mine too. Giving him an answer on his sister was the least I could do with the new resources at my disposal. I didn't want to tell Prince that, however. If this turned out to be Jasmine Lennox, I wanted to deliver the news myself. Lennox didn't need to hear it from the law enforcement gossip mill.

"She looks very familiar," I said. "I might have come across her during my social worker days. I worked a few multistate cases, so I hoped she might be one of the pimp's girls you had taken into custody."

"No chance," Prince said. "What about NamUs?"

"That's exactly what I was about to suggest," I said. The US Department of Justice's National Missing and Unidentified Persons Database served as a massive repository of missing persons and unidentified bodies in the country. The Unidentified Persons Database held information about the thousands of corpses across the country that hadn't been identified, including body features and dental information, as well as photographs of any remains.

"I've gone through it, and there were no photographic matches. The only unique body features I can see in this picture are her teeth. A medical examiner with better eyes might see something I didn't. But I don't have the clearance to enter her picture into NamUs."

"And I do." Prince reached for her plain black bag. "Might as well get her into their system. She's probably already dead and lying in a morgue somewhere. But I don't think you've got much of a shot. We don't have her dental records or any real identifying marks." She pulled out a digital tablet and started typing.

"Well, there's one," I said. "If it's the woman I'm looking for, she has a distinct tattoo on her left arm of an angel with blue and silver wings."

Finding Jasmine Lennox's arrest records before her disappearance had been an easy task for Kelly. Her last intake report, dated only months before she'd disappeared, listed the tattoo as well as a gold ring and chain. I doubted those were on her body when she died. She or her pimp had probably pawned them for drugs.

Prince fiddled with her tablet, pulling up NamUs's website. "Let's hope she didn't end up falling into the river. That makes identification twice as hard. But no matter how she died, chances of that tattoo being visible on her body are probably slim." She spoke with the resignation of a woman who'd seen the cruelty humans are capable of inflicting on each other. Like every other good cop I knew, Prince could be both disgusted and removed from the situation.

A trick I'd never managed. I killed the bad guys instead.

Not anymore.

Chris's serial killer mother Mary had insisted killing was my only natural path, that I'd found a way to justify the visceral need because I couldn't accept the truth of what I was: a natural-born killer.

She can't be right.

Prince typed quickly. "This'll take a few minutes. I've got to upload the picture from the seized file. What's the number?"

"225."

More clicks from the tablet. I looked away to hide my impatience. Immediately, my mind snapped back to the silver dollars dangling in my memory like poisonous spiders in their intricate webs.

Someone wanted to tell me something. Who and what, and how did I go about getting those questions answered? The meaning of the coins escaped me, but whoever sent them had a specific message.

The press over the arrest of serial killer Mary Weston had barely died down in Pennsylvania and Maryland. My name had been mentioned over and over, although none of the quotes were direct. Despite my saving her from Mary's diabolical plan, the news reporter from Fox 29, Beth Ried, hadn't been grateful enough not to harass me for an exclusive. In fact, she believed that her kidnapping allowed me to catch Mary finally, so I owed her the interview. Perhaps this was her way of getting me back for refusing.

But what the hell was the point?

Silver had a meaning in symbolism and mythology, but I'd have to do my research for the details. At least I'd have something to do tonight instead of hanging out with my cat, Mousecop. Not that I wanted to socialize. A singular life suited me, at least for now. Some days it took all of my strength not to use the huge amounts of data provided by NCMEC for my own dark gains. I went home utterly exhausted from the effort, but proud. Kelly had been right, at least for another day.

"You met Mary Weston." Prince's hazel eyes watched my

reaction, no doubt cataloguing every facial tic. "And you saved that reporter."

Cold chills swept over me at how Prince had guessed my train of thought. "I was in the right place at the right time."

Prince's grim smile made it clear she wasn't buying it. "I read the case file. Mary Weston asked for you that night. You're friends with her son Chris. We tried to speak with him, but he won't take our calls."

My throat tightened up. "She's crazy, and I'm thankful she's in prison. I haven't spoken to Chris in a few weeks. I wouldn't say we're friends."

Prince glanced at her tablet, frowning when she saw the search hadn't completed. I frowned, too, because her laser-like attention honed right back in on me.

"Her father started it all and passed it down to the daughter. Do you think Mary and her father didn't kill her son because they wanted to bring him into the family business?"

A nerve in my calf rippled with tension. I hoped my skin didn't appear as clammy as I felt. "I don't know. I'm just glad we managed to save Chris."

Saying his name seemed alien. It didn't belong in this place —my new start. As much as Chris had done for me, he was part of my past life. I desperately needed to keep him there. When I'd first moved to DC, his calls and text were frequent and over-whelming. He couldn't talk about anything beyond the torment of his family, and I've got enough dark thoughts in my head without taking on his.

"He's damned lucky to have you." Prince glanced again at the tablet. "Finally. We've got a possible match. The winter after the picture was taken—at least according to Adonis's coding—police found a female under the age of thirty in an alley in Chicago. And we know Adonis had drug business there. Cause of death appears to be a heart attack. Winter cold kept her from deteriorating too badly." She tapped the screen again. "You want to see the picture?"

I was still trying to slow down my heart rate. Her questioning shouldn't have bothered me. The case was sensational and a crime aficionado's dream. But Prince seemed like the type of cop who instinctively knew there was more to everything than the crumbs on the surface. "Yes, please."

She didn't seem surprised by my lack of hesitancy. I was struck by a warm sensation that I'd finally found a place where my darkness actually fit in. Everyone working in this office—case managers, assistants, analysts—had all seen more bad things than the average human being. It was like being in a bizarre club.

Prince turned the tablet to face me. Two morgue shots of the woman in J. Adonis's stable were pulled up on his screen. Her haggard face very clearly matched the picture seized during the raid. But nearly a decade of drug use made comparing that wretched face to the mugshot Kelly had found nearly impossible.

I didn't need it.

Jasmine Lennox's mugshot had been taken in the summer, and she'd worn a sleeveless top. The body in the Chicago morgue clearly showed the angel tattoo still in remarkable condition.

I'd found Agent Lennox's sister.

I promised to keep Investigator Prince in the loop about my Jane Doe, giving her the story that the Jane Doe was a former volunteer at one of the shelters I'd worked with as a social worker. Prince's caseload was heavy enough she gave me the clearance to contact Jane Doe's family—a family I led her to believe I still had access to. As soon as I'd walked Prince out, I took the elevator back to my floor and sequestered myself in my cubicle under the guise of paperwork.

My first call was to Kelly. Her phone went to voicemail, which made me smile. Kelly had made big strides since coming with me to Maryland during Chris's disappearance. She'd started getting out more, taking walks around Rittenhouse Square and even making regular grocery trips. That meant she didn't always answer her phone right away, and that made me immeasurably happy. She deserved the best kind of life. I left her a message about Jasmine Lennox.

It took much longer to get the nerve to call Lennox. After all, I'd stuck my nose in his personal business. Most people took offense to that, especially high-ranking FBI agents who may or may not enjoy basking in the power their position afforded.

But my meddling had been from a completely good place—a new experience for me. I didn't have a single personal motivation; I just wanted to help the man who'd done the same for me.

Dropping the news into a phone message would have been crass and cruel. So when Lennox didn't answer his phone, I just told him I had some urgent information and to call me as soon as he had the chance.

The files from Prince's raid needed to be addressed. My team had possible identifications on two more of the girls, and I needed to put in a request for one of our affiliates to search for an address.

Instead I opened my browser and typed in "1986 Statue of Liberty."

The results came back immediately. As I'd suspected, the coins matched the statue's 100th birthday commemorative silver dollar. They were nearly pure silver—much more than the normal circulation coin. Beyond that, I couldn't figure out any reason why someone would send me two of them.

The Statue of Liberty meant freedom, a new chance at life. I grimaced at the irony. Only a few people knew exactly how much of a new life this one was for me, and none of them saw it as a joke.

Save for one.

I dropped back against my chair hard enough that the front rollers came up. "Her." I hissed the word through clenched teeth.

Mary Weston had taunted me about how foolish I was for not accepting my fate. This was exactly the sort of mental flip-off she'd issue. She could have sent the silver spoons—of course she had! Spoons were her disgusting weapon of choice. Why she chose silver I didn't know, but maybe whomever she had working for her on the outside and sending her trinkets thought they were pretty. Damned if I knew or cared.

I didn't know who would align themselves with Mary Weston when she'd been charged with the murder of two Maryland girls—with more charges pending—but I'd find out. I snatched up the phone and dialed the state correctional institution in Muncie.

My other line beeped, and I cursed. Security calls were priority. Grumbling, I switched the line.

"Lucy Kendall."

"How you doing today?" Bobby, one of the front desk guards, drawled pleasantly. After three months living in the DC, I still couldn't get used to the outright friendliness of most of my colleagues. When I'd made my first visit and interviewed for the position, I'd envisioned grimness, no different than a police station: lots of gray, plenty of Berber carpet and plastic chairs, and an overall feeling of despair for the things witnessed on a daily basis.

I'd been greeted with just the opposite. Walls painted a bright, rustic orange, adorned with pictures and insignias of the numerous law enforcement and political figures who'd worked with the program lined the generous break room area. Smiles on the employees' faces—even the sex trafficking and child pornography units, inundated with filth all day long. These people knew how to function properly, surrounded by the worst life had to offer.

"I'm good, Bobby. What's up?"

"Well, it's kind of strange." The pleasantry in his voice strained into unease. "I've got a criminal investigator from the Park Police asking to see you."

"The Park Police?" Any number of law enforcement officials visited us on a daily basis, and I had regular meetings with various investigators and FBI agents working missing kids' cases. The Park Police worked for the National Park Service, and in the Washington, DC area, its jurisdiction was massive. But I didn't have any cases involving a disappearance from a national park, and nothing had come in on the hotline.

Bobby cleared his throat. "You ought to just come on down. He's pretty antsy."

"I'm on my way."

I nodded at my team, who were all busy but had an ear on everything going on around them in cube land. We rarely exchanged more than general pleasantries, although I knew from their occasional chatter that all three of them had families. One came from a law enforcement background. Another had military experience. They'd stopped trying to draw me into conversations after my first week, but we'd fallen into an easy routine of discussing the case at hand and then figuring out the best way to handle it.

Most days I preferred to work in a private room, but at the moment I didn't want to leave my cubemates. The feeling that something terrible waited downstairs flooded my system. I wasn't sure I wanted to know what it was.

My soft, leather flats felt heavy as I made my way to the elevator, passing the only section of the building where a code was needed to enter. These were the analysts who dealt with child pornography, searching for connections between children and predators. Like all NCMEC employees, they received regular wellness consultations.

I wouldn't last five minutes in that area.

The elevator dinged to a stop, and I stepped out into the lobby. It was large and inviting with natural light streaming in from the windows facing the street. Two male security guards/receptionists held court over the lobby. No one got through without Bobby or Dean clearing it.

Bobby swiveled to face me, his dark eyes worried. His large hand rubbed the back of his neck, leaving pale streaks across his dark skin. "He keeps checking his phone, got that agitated pace going on. Something's not right."

Cold dread washed over me like a spring ocean wave. The investigator's eyes met mine, and I recognized the look of the hunt: dilated pupils, nervous pacing, and an unnervingly calm voice as he finished his phone call.

"Are you Lucy Kendall?" His soft tenor didn't match his height or the way he held himself, coiled and ready to spring.

My heart raced, all thoughts of the silver dollars and Mary Weston draining from my mind. I'd done nothing illegal since moving here. I hadn't even brought any of my poison or drugs, dumping them all in the toilet back in my apartment in Northern Liberties. If this were about Preacher or some other kill, the Park Police wouldn't come for me. I'd be staring at the carefully blank face of an FBI agent.

"Can I help you?" I forced my voice not to shake.

He dropped his phone into the pocket of his dark jeans. "God, I hope so. Investigator Brad King. I need you to come with me."

Now the fear turned into a jagged rock cascading through my belly. My armpits dampened; my lightweight, sleeveless dress suddenly felt unbearably heavy. I forced my hands not to clench into fists and looked him in the eye. "What for?"

King glanced at Bobby and Dean, who watched with brazen

surprise. "It's a private matter."

"These gentlemen are responsible for my safety, as well as everyone else's in this building. I'd like them to hear this as well."

As if it mattered. If this man was about to bring me in, I had little chance of keeping it a secret.

"I suppose you people are used to dealing with horrible stuff," King said. "But the press needs to be kept out of this. We don't know what we're dealing with, and I don't need a panic."

My entire body relaxed to the point my knees weakened. This wasn't about my past. "Of course. What's going on?"

"A young woman's body was recovered early this morning on Oxon Hill Farm in Maryland. We've identified her as a missing person out of Philadelphia."

The damp hair on the back of my neck stood up. "I'm sorry to hear that. How can I help?"

King dragged his hand over his buzz cut. "There was a message written on the bathroom mirror. Your name was in it."

My blood stilled, yet it roared in my ears. "I don't understand."

"The victim's name is Shannon Minor, from Philadelphia. Do you know her?"

This time, my knees truly did give out. I swayed toward the security counter. Bobby caught my arm, and I found my words. "Yes. I was her social worker when I worked for Child Protective Services."

The criminal investigator watched me with the alertness of a bull eyeing a red cape. "He used her lipstick for the message. 'For Lucy Kendall, National Center for Missing and Exploited Children.'" He held out a small plastic evidence bag. "This was clutched in her hand."

The room spun like a Tilt-A-Whirl, throwing my equilibrium into fits. But then I saw Lady Liberty's silhouette above the "1986" on the tarnished silver piece.

TWO

Shannon was dead. Murdered and left with a silver coin just like the one I'd been mailed. What did the connection mean? Had I still managed to get the girl killed even though I'd moved hundreds of miles away? An overwhelming gloom wrapped around me, trapping me inside a dark cloud of sadness that even the bright, hot summer sun couldn't penetrate. Despite the warmth streaming in the car window, I shivered.

"So tell me how you knew Shannon." King wasn't going to do me the favor of leaving me to my thoughts.

"I was her social worker several years ago. She went to a wonderful foster family."

King grunted his acknowledgment. "You guys keep in touch?"

The last time I saw Shannon, my ego had nearly gotten her killed. "Occasionally. She had enrolled at Penn State for their paramedic and emergency medicine program."

Lady Liberty seared into my brain with the force of red-hot fire poker. My coin had been postmarked in DC two days ago. The one left with Shannon looked exactly like it—centennial silver dollars, probably special issue. Mary Weston surely couldn't have found out about Shannon, not from prison.

So who else had a target on my back?

"You doing all right?" King glanced at me out of the corner of his eye as he maneuvered through mid-morning traffic. Shannon's body had been taken to the forensics lab in DC, and King didn't give me the option of taking a cab.

Stuck in the car with yet another unfamiliar police officer, I wished for the Prius and tried to decide how much to share about my coins. My right arm heated up from the invading sun, and I crossed it over my chest. "Don't worry about me. What exactly happened to Shannon?"

I didn't want to know, but I couldn't do Shannon that injustice. I would take in every detail, both verbal and physical, and commit it to memory. Every part of her life deserved to be remembered and appreciated, even her horrific last moments. And I couldn't help find her killer if I didn't know everything.

Is that what I planned to do? Obviously her murder had something to do with me. The police had questions. I could answer them to the best of my ability and walk back to my new life. But how could I shortchange Shannon's memory like that?

"She was taken from a Penn State parking lot after a night class two weeks ago," King said. "No witnesses. Beaten and emaciated, severely dehydrated. That's all preliminary. The autopsy's later today."

"Sexually assaulted?"

"No," King said. "Unless the pathologist finds something else during the autopsy. There were no signs of sexual assault."

I looked sharply at him. "He kept her for two weeks and didn't assault her?"

He nodded. "Why are you assuming it's a man? Shannon's abductor could have a partner, and God knows women do some awful things. The lack of sexual assault means we have to consider both male and female suspects seriously. Shannon might have known her and gone with her. The Philadelphia detective handling her case has considered that an option from the beginning."

Suddenly the sun wasn't the only thing making me feel overheated. This man could have heard the rumors about me from the Philadelphia detective. His voice sounded placid, just a dutiful officer of the law seeking justice for an innocent person. But something more brewed behind his eyes. My imagination had to be playing tricks.

My phone buzzed in my hand. I glanced down at the text and felt the tension further knot in my shoulders. *Chris.* We'd only spoken a handful of times since I left Philadelphia, and we were no closer to an understanding. His texts were always the same: *Just checking in. Miss you. We need to fix this.*

Except I was pretty sure "this" couldn't be repaired.

"You're right," I said. "There are plenty of women in this world who do terrible things. And you could be right about the partnership. But what happened to Shannon sounds very feral, and it's hard for me to imagine a woman working that way. We're much more subtle." Even Mary Weston, one of the worst female serial killers in history, had her subtleties. She didn't survive decades on the run by leaving messages at her crime scenes.

King seemed pacified. "I won't disagree with you. And as bad as this sounds, the lack of sexual assault makes this whole thing a lot scarier to me." He swerved into the inside lane. "Her foster mother spoke highly of you."

I thought about the last time I'd spoken with Shannon's foster mother. She'd forgiven me for the injuries I'd caused Shannon. Would she find the strength to forgive me for this?

I sure as hell wouldn't.

"Did she know you moved to this area?"

"Not that I know of." Our last communication had been before Christmas, with Shannon excited about her grades. I'd been too embroiled in chasing down sex traffickers to respond. Another notch on my list of regrets.

"But whoever did this obviously knew you'd come out here," King said. "Of course, in this day and age, it's not all that hard to track someone down.

"I suppose." I couldn't stop the image of Shannon in that garage, bleeding and waiting for me to help her. I'd barely arrived in time. "A couple of years ago, Shannon asked for my help with a girl she was mentoring. The girl turned out to be mentally disturbed. That information was all over the news. But Shannon may have talked about me too. If the person had staked her out or inserted himself into her life…"

"Right," King said. "He kept her long enough to force her to tell him all sorts of things. Starvation will break even the strongest person's will."

"You're certain she was starved?"

King's mouth twitched. "Her foster mother said Shannon was about 140 pounds, very healthy and fit. Her body weighed 115. The pathologist also found residue around her eyes. She's sent it for testing, but it may be duct tape. If he kept her blind and starved, how long do you think it would take to break her will?"

Sickness swarmed over me. I searched for the button to open the window, desperate for fresh air. King obliged, and I sucked in the smell of sunshine and traffic fumes.

When I was sure the nausea had passed, I sat back against the seat and pulled the box out of my purse, anxious to get rid of the coins. "The thing is, I received these two coins this morning. I'm no expert, but they look like the same ones left with Shannon."

King's round face paled as he glanced at the open box. "Don't touch them."

"I haven't."

He said nothing more as he navigated city traffic. Downtown DC never slowed down. Tourists walked in droves toward the various hotspots in the National Mall. A group stood in front of the FBI building, snapping away on their cellphones. Every block seemed to have a souvenir stand offering Washington, DC paraphernalia and greasy hot dogs. A school bus blocked 4th Street, forcing King to take the long way around to the forensics lab. He drove for several minutes trying to find a space before finally squeezing his sedan into a parking spot.

He dug in his center console, retrieving a pair of gloves, and then carefully lifted the coins from the box. "1986 silver dollar, same as the one found with Shannon. US Mint special issue for the centennial. We're looking into the issue number on her coin, but there were a lot of these. I doubt we have a chance of tracking this creep down with just the silver dollars. I'll need to keep these." His eyes drifted to meet mine, narrowed as if he'd spotted prey. "So the real question is, who have you pissed off?"

I swallowed hard and shrugged my shoulders.

The list was too long to discuss.

The Washington, DC Consolidated Forensics Laboratory on the corner of 4th and E Streets in downtown looked like any other of the office buildings surrounding it. Per District of Columbia law, no building could be higher than the Washington Monument. Because the National Mall was just a ten-minute walk away, I could easily see the monument against the early morning eastern sun, to the west, the top of the Capitol. When I first moved to the area, I'd done the obligatory tourist thing, spending an entire day on a self-guided walking tour of the National Mall. My legs hurt for two days afterward, but I'd thoroughly enjoyed the day. Although I considered myself a history buff, I'd never fully grasped what our nation stood for and just how many people have fought for and died for our country. Despite the crowd of tourists and the constant barrage of vendors selling all sorts of cheap wares, the power and the beauty of the monuments tour overpowered everything else. I often felt like I was the only person making the trek.

A tour of the forensics laboratory hadn't been on my list. I felt small in the large lobby, where an ominous metal sculpture seemed to act as some kind of modern-day statue of Anubis, protecting the dead waiting to enter their next lives. "Why are we here when her body is on a farm in Alexandria?"

"Oxon Hill Farm isn't a farm—it's a national park. That's why it's my case. And because of our budget, we don't have our own medical examiner. The Metro PD was gracious enough to allow us to use the forensics laboratory." King gestured toward the woman in a lab coat hurrying toward us. "Even cops have to have a personal escort in this building."

King nodded at the lab assistant. "Thanks for getting us in so quickly." A rush of homesickness swept over me. Her elfin features and sparkling eyes reminded me of Kelly.

"You're welcome." She glanced at me as if she were assessing my ability to handle what I was about to see. I pretended I could and hoped she bought it. "You'll both need to sign in with reception."

We did as ordered. Dread made my legs feel wooden and awkward. Dead bodies weren't exactly a new thing for me. But this was different. This was the body of someone I'd known and cared for. Someone I believed had a wonderful chance in the world.

Someone dead because of me.

You just can't escape it.

Mary Weston's warning caught me by surprise, her deceptively soft voice floating over me like a ghost, silky and sweet and sinister all at once.

I fell behind King and the lab assistant, barely aware of their muted conversation. Mary couldn't have done this. Or could she? Was this her twisted way of reminding me she was right about me? How could she have done this from behind bars? She'd spent her life manipulating men into doing her cruel deeds. She wasn't in solitary confinement. Could she have charmed a guard? Or maybe a sick, obsessed fan who'd communicated via mail?

My imagination had to be stopped. Her mail would be closely monitored. A prison psychologist was studying Mary, not to mention the FBI's Behavioral Analysis Team.

She couldn't have done this.

Uncertain if I really believed the pep talk, I hurried to catch up with King.

The technician led us down the hall toward an elevator and then punched the number four. It seemed odd. Wasn't there some unofficial rule that said all morgues had to be in the basement? While the technician focused on her electronic tablet, King made conversation. "This place is new with state-of-the-art everything: fingerprint analysis, materials analysis, and even better, DNA analysis. I'm usually stuck going through the FBI lab, which takes forever and a damned day, but these guys can do everything on site, which expedites things. I don't always get to send my cases here, but given the nature of this, I've been accommodated."

I made a noncommittal sound that I hoped resembled interest. I just wanted to see Shannon.

Penance. The word slipped to the tip of my tongue. I swallowed it back but couldn't stop the thought.

Was her death my penance? Or was I completely full of myself?

I didn't want to go to the morgue. No matter how hard I fought it, I'd end up there one day. If not this morgue then another one. How would I die? Would I just die of old age, forgotten among the mothballs? Or would my cruelty catch up to me in the worst kind of way?

I don't want to die. I don't want to end up in a place like this, waiting to be put into the ground.

Like poor Shannon.

I swallowed back the gorge of nerves and followed King off the elevator into a cool, well-lit hallway, where a sign announced we'd reached the office of the chief medical examiner. I realized with a shake that I'd never been inside a morgue. I didn't like the coldness of it, much less the idea of a body being cut open, weighed, and measured like it was nothing more than a vessel. The tech and King bypassed the main entrance and led me down the hall.

"How was Shannon killed?" I couldn't avoid the question any longer. I'd allowed King to bypass the details on the ride from Alexandria, but I needed them now. I needed some way to prepare for what I was about to encounter.

King studied me for a moment, evidently trying to figure out if I was the hysterical type. "Like I said, the autopsy's scheduled for today, but the preliminary cause of death is slashed wrists."

I locked my knees in an effort to keep from swaying. "Wait. Suicide?"

He stopped and looked at me and then looked at the technician, who'd finally brought her nose out of her tablet. "You want to take this one?"

The woman nodded, her black ponytail swishing with the movement. "The deceased was cut vertically on each wrist. She bled out in minutes. From the angles of the cuts, our forensic investigators believe they weren't self-inflicted."

I wanted to grab the pristine lapels of her lab coat and shake the woman. Tell her the deceased had a name. Instead I reminded myself the only way these people could do their jobs was to dehumanize the person on the steel gurney. "Did she suffer?"

"It depends on whether or not she was conscious at the time. We won't know that until the autopsy is complete."

I could dehumanize too. I'd done it many times before; it was how I managed to kill the scum who preyed on children. I turned to King. "That's definitely part of the message."

He nodded. "Absolutely. We just need to decode it."

Shivering from more than the cool air, I wrapped my arms around my waist. "What are the Philadelphia police saying? Do they have any real leads?"

"At this point, no," King said. "But the connection to you changes everything. I'm waiting to hear back from the lead investigator over there. He's tied up in court."

The technician had stopped in front of a locked door marked "Viewing." She inserted a key as King motioned for me to follow her. "You're not going to have to actually see the body. We've got a digital image ready to go."

I stopped short. "Then why did you bring me all the way down here?"

"You think I'm going to email a picture of a poor dead woman to you?" He sounded disgusted. "Have some respect."

He was right, of course. And being at the morgue for Shannon was the right thing to do. But I instinctively knew he also wanted to see my reaction for himself, pump me for information.

King held the door for me, and we entered a small room. Painted a soft tan with very few accents, the room's decor was clearly meant for function. A desk with a computer, as well as comfortable chairs and a box of Kleenex, made up the entirety of its contents.

The tech looked at King. "I'll be outside."

King waited until the door closed and then tapped the keyboard, bringing the computer to life. My palms began to sweat. The roots of my hair weighed heavily on my scalp. I licked my lips. A picture might not have the same impact, but this was still Shannon, the girl who'd had survived the system and had so much life left ahead.

Someone living and breathing whom I'd cared for.

I didn't miss the irony. How many families had I put in this same position? No matter the sick things their loved ones had inflicted on kids, someone still loved them. Someone still grieved.

The image flashed onto the screen. I froze, feeling all the nervous energy drain out of me. I'd expected to see the sort of autopsy photos shown on television, after the body had been washed and prepped. But this had been taken at the crime scene.

Another smart trick by King.

The bathroom in the shelter consisted of the bare minimum: two stalls with wooden doors, a heater in the wall, and two small sinks with a shelf above. The mirror sat above the shelf, the message scrawled in blood-colored lipstick.

I finally made myself look at Shannon.

She stared toward her right, her eyes wide open—a blue that had faded to the color of pond water. Her skin had already gone ashen, and she'd bit her lip as she died. Bruises in various stages of healing dotted her once-beautiful face. Her blond hair, fixed in finger curls, cascaded around her as if she'd lain down in the grass to watch the clouds.

The urge to weep and scream rose. Somehow, I had to keep it together. I needed to look at the photo and glean everything I possibly could to help King find the bastard who'd done this.

My heart rate still doubled, my pulse beating my temples so hard my head ached. Apprehension flooded my thoughts, my subconscious picking up on something I hadn't yet identified. "Why is her hair dyed blond? Is that something she'd done before she was taken?"

"That's new," King said. "She was still a brunette when she was taken."

I kept staring at the picture, trying to see past the eyes that used to be so filled with life and compassion. Finally I whispered for King to show me the next one.

It was a full profile this time. My empty stomach flipped; my mouth tasted like I'd been chewing sand. The blood surrounded her, staining the concrete floor around her as it had flowed from her arteries. Both of her arms were outstretched, and her right fist was closed. I assume it held the silver dollar. I kept looking at the picture, trying to figure out what it was King wanted me to see.

Her wrists. Both of them. Vertical slash marks from the top of her wrists down her forearms.

"Why'd he slit her wrists and then do nothing else to make this look like a suicide?"

"Good question," King said. "I'd hoped you might be able to tell me."

I shook my head "no" even as the feeling that I was missing something crawled over me. I felt like I'd just walked into a massive spider web and couldn't see the way to rid myself of it.

Put it together. A woman with blond hair and blue eyes lying outstretched, looking toward her right hand. Her right knee inched toward her hip, as if she'd tried to curl up. Her wrists cut, but most likely not a suicide.

But the scene was clearly staged. For me. But why?

I studied the picture again, trying to drag the answer out of the dark recesses of my memory. Déjà vu struck first, and then the answer hit me with enough force I staggered into the wall, away from King and from the images of the woman. I gasped for breath, tears brimming in my eyes.

He remained calm, watching me. "What is it?"

"Lily."

THREE

I stumbled into the hallway on weak legs. My fingers skimmed the smooth, cool wall in search of some kind of support. The door closed behind me, King's footsteps following. My eyes stung with tears.

The hair. No one knew about her hair.

"You all right?" King made no offer to steady me, instead stepping around to lean against the wall so he could again see my face.

"Just give me a minute." My tight chest threatened to explode with sobs. I forced the emotion back, and my esophagus felt like I'd breathed fire. Crying would make me weak. Weakness caused mistakes. I couldn't afford to say the wrong thing now.

"Who's Lily?"

The question sparked a burning rage from deep inside me. How dare this monster bring my sister's suicide into this?

Even as the anger flowed, I knew that was the least of my problems. Lily's death could have been found in public records if someone searched hard enough but how would someone know reenacting her death would throw me so far?

Common sense. If a person knew you had a sister who killed herself, using that to get to you is common sense.

But how did he find out about her in the first place? More importantly, how did he know enough to stage the scene?

"My sister." My throat had gone dry. "My mother's boyfriend molested her. When Lily finally got the courage to tell our mother, she didn't believe her. Lily killed herself."

"Damn. I'm sorry to hear that." King shifted from foot to foot. "But you know I've got to ask you some questions about all this."

I nodded. "Can we go somewhere else?"

The lab technician escorted us back to the lobby. I nearly ran out of the building, welcoming the blinding glare of the sun. Staggering and weak, I sat down on the first bench I came to and tried to get my bearings.

I couldn't deny poor Shannon had been a pawn to get to me.

To use my sister's suicide in the message meant the killer's agenda was deeply personal.

King sat down beside me, offering a bottle of water. I gladly accepted it. "Can you tell me about your sister?"

The grief that never really went away rose to full force. The sleepless nights, the long crying jags—a wound that never healed no matter how many times I tried to stitch it closed. "She was fourteen. I was eleven. I didn't realize what was going on for a long time, and then when I did, I told her to go to our mother. It didn't make any difference."

"I assume you were aware of the specifics of how your sister died?"

I tried to stop the shiver. "I found her body. So yes, I'm familiar."

"That's rough." King's attempt at sympathy rang with a note of sincerity. "Can you tell me about it?"

I took a deep breath. "She'd skipped school that day. Our mother hadn't believed her the night before, but I kept thinking she'd come around and realize Lily would never make up something like that." It never ceased to amaze me how clear a memory could be, even after so many years had passed. I could still smell the air in the house, feel the prickly sensation in my spine that something was terribly wrong. "Lily was in the bathroom. She'd used his razors to cut her wrists—vertically. The blood was everywhere. She'd emptied her bowels. Her hair was deliberately fixed in curls as a shot to my mother, and they fell around her like the strangest halo."

King wrote something in his notebook. "The female forensic investigator said her hair looked like someone had used their fingers to make it curl."

Of course a female had noticed. "I saw that too."

King ran his hand over his face. He hadn't shaved, his shadowing beard making him look older. "The estimated time of death is between 5 a.m. and 9 a.m. yesterday."

So few people knew about my sister. Public record only gave basic details. The message on the mirror... I suppose that could have been leaked. It had been sensational. If a person dug far enough, asked the right people, that wouldn't have been a secret. With the exception of Kelly, no one else in my life knew about the message.

"Lily left me a message on the mirror. In her lipstick. 'Sorry, Lucy.' My mother spent more time angry about my getting more attention in Lily's death than she did. So she talked about it to everyone. I suppose someone could have asked around and found out."

King hesitated for a moment. "So this would have been what, more than twenty years ago? I doubt even the best Internet creeper could have found a crime scene photo. The police probably destroyed them since the case was closed. But if your mother talked, that kind of stuff can stay around. I'll buy he might have found it out somewhere." King had very nearly read my mind. "Who all knows the specifics of your sister's death? That you found her, the position of the body, that sort of thing?"

"No one knows about the hair." I cleared my throat. "About the curls. I never mentioned that." That had been the real message, not the note. In my mind, the curls were not only a way of telling my mother to shove it, but of reminding me to stay strong. Self-preservation.

"What about Shannon? Did you ever tell her?"

Had I? I'd used the story of my sister's suicide as a tool to reach more than one of my kids during my social worker days. I wanted them to know I understood pain even if the circumstances were vastly different. But Shannon?

"Her mother died." About a year into Shannon's placement with the Hudsons, her biological mother's alcoholism had finally caught up with her. Shannon had been despondent, and Amy Hudson had asked me to talk with her. "I told her about Lily. I might have told her about finding her, and if I did, I probably told her about the message on the mirror. But not the curls." I wouldn't have given Shannon that detail. I hadn't even told Kelly about it.

"So maybe the bad guy knows Shannon's got a connection to you. That part would be easy enough to find out. And then he pumps her for information, she shares the details, and he uses them against you. The curls could simply be a coincidence, assuming he found out what Lily looked like." He glanced at the hot sun and wiped the sweat off his forehead with the back of his hand.

"So let's get to it. This was a calculated move by someone who knew about your life. The coins are just another part of the message, a tool to make sure we don't miss this murder is all about you. You need to be honest with me if you want justice for this girl. We've all got enemies."

My blood felt cold and slow, my tongue thick. I desperately wanted to help. But I finally had the chance to move forward with my life. How could I give King anything without incriminating myself?

How could I be so selfish as to withhold information?

"Before you showed up, I was on hold with the state correctional institution in Muncie," I said. "That's where Mary Weston is being held. She's the first person I thought of when I received the coins."

King rolled his eyes to the sky. "God help me. You're *that* Lucy Kendall. If you helped take that woman down, you must have a list of enemies and balls of steel. No offense."

"None taken."

"Mary Weston is under maximum security," King said. "As far as anyone knows, her only allies were her father and cousin, who are both dead. Right?"

I nodded. "That's true. Her sons want nothing to do with her."

"So it's hard for me to believe she orchestrated all of this when she's not allowed to talk to anyone but her public defense attorney. Not to mention she wouldn't be able to find out about your connection to Shannon. And she'd have to have a partner who hated you as much as she did. Because you know as well as I do that whoever staged that scene felt it was personal. Revenge."

He wasn't saying anything I hadn't already thought of. Yet I wouldn't put anything past Mary Weston's capabilities. But King had stirred something loose.

"Jake and Riley." The words popped out of my mouth, and relief relaxed my muscles. This actually made sense. If I didn't have such a guilty conscience, I would have thought of Jake

Meyer immediately. My actions had cost his life and resulted in several arrests.

"Who?"

"In January, I uncovered a sex trafficking ring run by Jake Meyer, the aide of Pennsylvania Senator Coleman—who was ironically running a sex trafficking task force. The senator was cleared of involvement, but the FBI discovered Jake found a lot of his clientele through the task force." I explained how I'd ended up in the garage and fought for my life.

"You can get all of the details from the Philadelphia police and the FBI, but Jake killed Riley, and I hit him with the shovel in self-defense." The early stages of a headache banged against my skull. "He died. I was cleared of the charges, but the information found on Jake's computer was a treasure trove for the FBI. Jake sold teenagers and young children for sex in least three states: Pennsylvania, Maryland, and Ohio. His buyers were from all walks of life, some of them with a lot of money and reputations to lose. An entire brothel was taken down in Ohio." Jake's connections had stretched farther than I'd bothered to find out. But King would have access to the investigation.

"And it was no secret you were responsible for Jake's downfall?" King asked.

I took a drink of water, feeling some of the shock wear off. "I refused all interviews, but my name was mentioned in several news reports, in print and on television." Seeing me on television thrilled my mother, as though I had finally earned her attention. She loved to tell her friends she was the mother of the woman featured on Channel 9's lead story. The fact that I'd saved kids from being sold for sex didn't seem to matter.

"Well, aren't you a busy bee." King's head bobbed up and down. "You receive any threats?"

"Not really. A lot of requests for interviews. I was a licensed private investigator, so my business blew up." I hadn't taken advantage of the sudden swell of requests. I'd been too busy wallowing in remorse. "There were a few messages from jerks saying I'd screwed them over or whatever. I passed all of that on to the special victims unit at Philadelphia PD. They were working in conjunction with the FBI."

King scratched his cheek. "I remember that case now, I think. A woman running a fancy salon was one of the fronts for the business, right?"

"Exhale Salon. She knew Senator Coleman. That's how Jake Meyer found her and exploited her financial vulnerability. I'd been working there undercover when she was killed. Her death ended up being completely unrelated. Ex-boyfriend lost it and killed her. But that's what opened the door."

"Jake Meyer didn't do the dirty work, though, if I recall. Seems like the right-hand guy was found dead too. Stupid nickname."

"Preacher." As far as I knew, his murder was still cold. Lennox said the FBI and locals currently weren't interested in finding out who did the world a favor and put Preacher down. I had the distinct impression that my behavior would dictate if that remained the case. "He'd hooked up with Jake at Penn State a few years before."

"Penn State," King echoed. "Not sure I believe the coincidence that Shannon was a student there. Anyone from the school involved in Jake's business?"

I shrugged. "You'd have to ask the investigating team. I can give you the name of the SVU lead investigator at Philadelphia PD. I know they were looking into it, but there were a lot of hoops to jump through. I have no idea what came of it." I could have found out. Although Todd Beckett worked in Major Crimes and primarily handled missing persons and homicides, he'd kept an ear on the investigation. The weeks after killing Riley and Jake were a painful blur for me, full of pity and pretending to contemplate suicide. If Chris hadn't wound up taken by his crazy mother, I'd probably still be holed up feeling sorry for myself.

King jotted down the name of the SVU investigator. "I'll give her a call once I get all this figured out. And we know that your connection with Shannon could have been found from news reports and digging into your history."

"But why choose her? Out of all my foster kids?"

"Because she was vulnerable and easily accessible," King said. "I hope the Philadelphia detective working her case calls me soon. He's Major Crime, but I assume he'll still handle the case. I'm sure he'll want to talk to that SVU investigator and check in with the paramedic and EMS program at Penn State. And I'll check on Mary Weston while I'm waiting for him to call. Won't hurt to make sure she's behaving herself."

A sudden, sinking thought tore through me. *Major Crimes*. "Who's the detective on her case?"

"Todd Beckett. You know him?"

I leaned against the wall, feeling dizzy. "Of course I do." Todd's catching the case was nothing more than luck of the draw. He would have gone through all of Shannon's current and prior contacts. Todd had to have found out I'd been her social worker. Why hadn't he told me?

"Really." King crossed his arms and waited.

My head ached at the idea of explaining how Chris and Justin were half-brothers through Mary Weston, and she'd used both of them as pawns in her game. Todd Beckett was Justin's other half-brother, and the detective who probably knew I'd been killing pedophiles and looked the other way.

"Lots of past history. All professional." If Todd wanted King to know about his brother and all the hell Mary Weston had caused us, he could share. As long as King made sure she wasn't orchestrating all of this from prison, I couldn't see the point in telling him any more.

But what would Todd say when he heard the killer essentially delivered a personal message? He'd long suspected I'd murdered both Harrison brothers. Would he open that can of rotting worms now?

He was a damned good cop. He'd know the Jake Meyer angle was the most logical. He'd chase it first. But he wouldn't leave anything unchecked. Especially when the victim was an innocent girl.

I looked at King. "Did you tell Detective Beckett that Shannon had asked for me?"

"No," King said. "I left him the information that we had her body and for him to call me right away." He stood up. "I'm going to leave him another message now and let him know the new information. You need to keep thinking about who else would have a big enough grudge against you to do something like this. And if you've got any close friends or family, you might want to warn them. If this guy can get to someone like Shannon Minor, he can sure as hell find someone else you care about."

Kelly's face flashed in my mind. Panic rose in my chest. I sucked in a deep breath.

"I need to make a phone call."

FOUR

Feeling thick and unwieldy, my fingers jabbed through my contacts. I smacked Kelly's name and hit send. She had to answer.

She's probably busy.

She's going to tease you for freaking out and then get to work helping figure this out.

She'll answer.

The call went to voicemail, and my knees weakened.

I tried again.

Same result.

Barely able to breathe, I scrolled to my next option. Hopefully Todd would answer his cell even if he had King on the office line. He didn't, and my call went to his voicemail.

God Almighty, what if this bastard already had Kelly? It was the logical step. If he'd researched me, if he'd found out about the recent Mary Weston arrest, he might have found out about Kelly's assisting the FBI and traveling with me during Chris's disappearance.

Beth Ried. That reporter. She knew. How easily could she be bilked for information?

My heart threatened to beat its way out of my chest. The sun felt unbearably hot, the crowded sidewalk like a trap. My right leg jerked with the instinct to run.

But to where? I was too far away to protect Kelly.

I needed to go home.

Not Kelly.

My phone rang. It took three tries for my shaking hands to answer. "Todd. I need your help right now." I must have sounded like an idiot, breathless and crazed. But I could barely think straight enough to speak a full sentence.

"Lucy." Todd's wary voice did nothing to ease my nerves. "I know you're pissed at me, but I had a reason for not telling you about Shannon's disappearance. I'll explain—"

"I don't care about any of that right now. I need you to check on Kelly. She's not answering her phone."

Todd hesitated. "I'm sure she's fine."

"I'm sure King told you Shannon was taken as some sort of revenge toward me. That the scene was staged to resemble my sister's suicide. Kelly's a logical target, and I'm telling you, she should have called me back by now. Something is wrong."

"She's fine," Todd said. His voice sounded strained. "I promise you."

"How could you possibly know that?"

"Because she's with my brother."

I let the words sink in, trying to make sense of them. "Justin? Why would she be with Justin?" Kelly might have been making major progress, but she didn't go do things with other people, especially ones she didn't know.

"They met a while ago," Todd said. He cleared his throat. "I really didn't want to be the one to tell you this. It's Kelly's decision."

Everything clicked into place. I backed against the wall of the forensics building, away from the foot traffic. "Kelly and Justin are dating, and she didn't tell me."

"She was afraid you'd be worried about her, with both their backgrounds. But it really makes sense, if you think about it. Both damaged and abused like they were. They get each other. I know it seems like they could be a detriment to each other's recovery but Justin's doing great, and I've checked in on Kelly just like I promised. She's happy."

That's not why Kelly hadn't told me. I didn't care about her dating Justin because of any of that. I cared because his brother was a cop, and if Justin found out my secrets, what would he do? Would he really care?

"How did they meet?" I asked.

"Justin was with me when I stopped by to check on her a couple of months ago," Todd said. "I asked if he could come up. He wanted to meet her in person and thank her for the help with getting his record fully expunged. They hit it off."

I couldn't even be angry with Todd for not telling me, at least not right now. Kelly's safety was too important. "So how do you know she's safe right this minute?"

"Because she and Justin were going to a movie. They're not supposed to be back until this afternoon. But I talked to Justin less than an hour ago, right before they went into the theater. He's with her. She's fine."

I tried to breathe normally again. Justin could keep her safe. She wasn't alone. But I couldn't risk Kelly not knowing she might be in danger, even if the truth set her recovery back. "I believe you, but whoever this guy is found Shannon at Penn State. He could find Kelly or Justin. So could you please call Justin and tell Kelly to call me as soon as you're done with King? Let them know what's going on."

"Of course," Todd said. "I'm trying to get my lieutenant to approve travel so I can see the crime scene and do my own questioning. But he's a pencil pusher whose main agenda is keeping the political machine going, so he won't want to ruffle the Park Police's feathers."

The idea of seeing Todd made my stomach do a strange flip. Todd paused, and I realized he was waiting for me to speak. I swallowed the nerves. "I hope you can come down."

More awkward silence until Todd cleared his throat. "And yes, King did tell me about the staging. How are you doing?"

The concern in his voice almost brought me to my knees. "I'm okay. But if I talk about how I'm feeling, I won't be."

"All right," Todd said. "Just know that you can talk to me when you're ready. Because this is really personal, and it's okay for you to need help."

"I know that," I said. "But right now, I want to figure out who went after Shannon. He's still out there, and sooner or later, someone else is going to get hurt."

"You realize you are an eventual target? Even if he's trying to make you suffer, make you run scared, he's going to try to take you at some point."

Let him. It would be the last mistake he ever made. "And I promise I'll be careful. What about Beth Ried? Remember her?" *I'd still like to kick the reporter in her perfect, white teeth.* "She could easily be this guy's source without even realizing it."

"Good point," he said. "Make sure you mention it to King. As much as the Harrison theory"—he cleared his throat—"is a possible motive, I agree that a connection with Jake Meyer is the first place to look."

My throat tightened. "Thanks." I didn't want to say anything more, but the words forced their way out. "Todd, there's something else. Lily's curls. That's something I never told anyone about."

"The killer could have found out from a source," Todd said. "You know how easily people can find just about anything now."

"It's not that." My throat locked up. "I took the curls as a dig at my mother because Lily hated her hair that way and our mother always wanted her to wear them. But I never told a soul that."

"Are you sure?"

"Positive."

"Then the killer must have known what her body looked like. But how? And what about the message on the mirror? Did you tell anyone about that?"

"Kelly's the only person who knows about the message. And she wouldn't have told anyone."

Helplessness draped over me. I pushed away from the hard wall before I slid down into a heap. "I thought the old life was behind me. But I guess I'll never escape it. My road less traveled is no longer an option."

That was as close as I'd come to admitting my bad deeds to Todd. He didn't know the things Mary Weston had said, that she'd told me I was destined to be a killer no matter how much I tried to deny it. That I killed because I wanted to, and my justification was no more than an illusion.

A part of me had feared she was right. So I fled to my new life in Alexandria, thinking that keeping myself away from the old haunts would change things. So far, it had worked.

But maybe it didn't matter. The bad deeds of the past were going to hold me accountable.

"Stop that right now." Todd's harsh voice felt strangely soothing. "You control your fate. As long as you keep fighting to take that new road, you will leave the old life behind you. But if you let yourself get sucked back in, then that's on you."

I couldn't talk about it anymore, or I'd end up telling him everything just to ease the burden of guilt. "Please tell Justin to have Kelly call me right away. I need to hear her voice."

King drove me back to Alexandria, spending most of the drive on the phone arguing with someone about who should do what in the multi-state investigation of Shannon's murder. I tuned him out. I couldn't see anything but Shannon's body arranged to mock my sister's death.

King parked in front of the NCMEC building on Prince Street. "If you think of anyone else, call me."

"I will." Asking him to keep me updated on the case would be pointless; he wouldn't be allowed to share the kind of details I wanted.

Feeling as though I'd gained a hundred pounds in the last few hours, I walked into the lobby, barely acknowledging Bobby and Dean. Thankfully, the elevator was empty.

As the floors dinged by, I thought about what a mistake this bastard had made. I assumed his organization and ability to dig into my life meant he was intelligent. So his mistake had to be ego-driven rather than stupidity. Which meant his arrogance was his weakness—a weakness I would use to discover his identity.

My private investigator's license was still valid. I'd have to work the case in my spare time. Kelly would need to dig deep into her resource bank. We'd keep looking until the case was solved.

What if we found him before the police did?

As I stepped out of the elevator, my phone vibrated in my clenched hand. I heaved a sigh of relief when Kelly's number popped up on the screen.

"You're all right?"

"I'm fine." Kelly's voice erased some of the tension in my shoulders. "I called as soon as I got Todd's message. I'm so sorry about Shannon."

"Thanks." I'd sworn I wouldn't make her feel guilty, but the words had a mind of their own. "When you didn't answer your cellphone, I panicked. I thought he had you too. Thank God Todd knew where you were." My skin heated with shame at the note of accusation in my voice.

Silence invaded, the tension palpable despite the distance between us. I walked over to the nearest window and watched the clutch of tourists hurrying down the sidewalk.

"I'm sorry I didn't tell you," Kelly burst out. "It sort of happened out of nowhere. Justin and I just got to talking that night Todd brought him over a while ago. I know we've both been through different traumas, but he can understand on a level most people can't. When he asked for my number, I gave it to him without thinking. Can you imagine?"

"I understand." Something that felt an awful lot like jealousy welled up inside of me. I didn't want to be replaced, especially when I hadn't made any real friend in my new life. "And I'm thrilled you're dating. That's an amazing step for you. But Justin... it's just..."

"He'll never find out." Her voice had dropped. "I swear. He'd have to hack into my laptop, and unless he's a computer genius like me—and trust me, he's not—that's not happening. He doesn't even know where I hide it."

"But what if you tell him? What if you slip up and implicate yourself?" I wanted to bang my head against the wall.

"I won't," she said. "But do you really think he would care about what we've done to those monsters?"

The truth was, I didn't. Justin probably wouldn't blink an eye, and he was loyal to me. But I didn't want Kelly getting in trouble.

My ego knew there was more to it than that. But I'd deal with that problem later. Shannon was dead; Kelly might be in danger. And she was happy. Who was I to mess with that?

"Just promise me you'll be careful," I said. "And not just with that information. With yourself. Don't do anything you don't feel comfortable with, no matter how small it seems."

"I won't," she said. "We're taking things slowly. But I'm happy."

A pang shot through me. "Then I'm happy for you. I just

need you both to be careful. Todd's going to check on you every day."

"I won't go anywhere alone," she said. "And I definitely won't let anyone in the apartment. You know me. But I think I have something that will make you feel better about my safety."

I couldn't imagine what it might be, unless she'd already discovered Shannon's killer. "What?"

"I've got a tracking application on my cellphone," she said. "Mostly because I kept losing it in the apartment. But I can add you to the account and make you an admin. If you can't reach me, you can log in and see where my phone is. That way you'll be able to tell I'm somewhere safe and won't have to worry."

"Are you sure you won't feel like I'm stalking you?"

"It's fine," she said. "I'll feel better knowing you have access because you'll be less stressed. And you can't access any of my personal information anyway."

I couldn't match her teasing tone. "Thank you. That makes me feel a little better."

"But what about Chris? Are you going to call him?"

The answer caught in my throat. I hadn't thought of him as a target, even after his text. Shame heated my face. After Mary Weston's arrest, our personal relationship had become public knowledge. "Of course."

"You guys are talking, right?"

If you wanted to call infrequent and short texts talking, then yes. "Sort of. He's still upset with me, and I can't blame him. How's he doing?"

"Justin saw him a few days ago," Kelly said. "Chris still doesn't want to have any kind of deep relationship with Justin, but the guy can't stop trying. Chris told him he's been taking on as many extra shifts on the ambulance as they'd let him. He seemed okay, I guess."

"I've shut him out the last few months. After everything

that happened the past winter, all the secrets he'd kept... I can't deal with him. Not if I want a clean start."

"You had to do what was best for you," Kelly said. "It was the right thing."

Until today, I'd actually believed that. I sucked in a breath that made my throat burn. "Did Todd tell you about the way Shannon's body was staged?"

"God, yes," Kelly said. "You're sure there's no one you would have told about those things?"

"I only told you about the message on the mirror." Energy sparked in my saturated system. Old habits wrapping around me like a favorite blanket. "Don't you remember?"

"Of course," Kelly said. "But I didn't know you thought she'd curled her hair to piss off your mother."

"No one did. That's got to be a coincidence."

"So let's talk this out," Kelly said. "We know I'm the only one you told about the message, and I've never shared that info. So it's got to be someone your mother told or someone who either witnessed the scene or saw photos."

"My mother bitched to everyone who would listen that Lily thought of me when she died instead of her. So that pool is too big to search. And that was over twenty years ago. Even if someone remembered her blabbering, the chances of this guy tracking the pictures down are pretty slim. He wouldn't even know where to start."

"Unless your mother told him," Kelly said. "You're going to have to talk to her and see if she can think of anyone."

I'd rather spend the rest of my life in solitary confinement. I kept my head down as I made my way to my cubicle. "What about crime scene photos?"

"Lily died in the early nineties," Kelly said. "The Internet was in its infancy and pretty much the Wild West. A pretty, dead teenager—it's possible the picture made it online."

I rubbed my temples and then dug into my desk drawer for

aspirin. "I think we're making this too complicated. And giving this guy too much credit. I can buy him finding out about Shannon from doing his due diligence, but I think she told him about Lily. She knew about her. Maybe I described the scene in detail."

"Down to her hair?" Kelly sounded doubtful. "It's one thing for you to have told her about Lily, but it's another for you to give her intimate details. That's not something you do unless you're really close to someone."

She was right. I popped the aspirin and swallowed them dry. They raked down my throat and left me feeling as if I'd inhaled a bug. "Then he finds out about Lily from Shannon. Because she's terrified and telling him everything he wants to know. Then he gets the details somewhere else."

"If Shannon gave him Lily's name, and he had a year or location, it's possible he could have found crime scene photos. Any number of people from the police department have access to the files. Whoever took them may not have been a creep. Some people just like to collect crime scene photos. Maybe they were making some sort of remembrance site and thought their freaky efforts would be appreciated. So the picture makes it online and then the creep comes along. You know as well as I do that once it's out there, it's there for good. I'll go digging. See if I can find it on the sites. Unless..."

"What?"

"Unless you just want the police to handle this. They're going to look at all the same things."

I looked around, lowering my voice. "Someone sent me two 1986 silver dollar coins this morning. And another one was found with Shannon. Don't tell that to anyone."

"Silver dollars?" Kelly's voice rose in surprise. "So this guy is trying to tell you something else beyond what he wrote on the mirror."

"I have no idea what, but I don't see how I can just sit back and do nothing."

"That's not what I'm saying," Kelly said. "I think you should communicate with Todd, tell him all your theories. Tell him to talk to your mother so you don't have to. And you let him do his job while you keep to yours."

"I don't understand," I said. "This is what we do. We can find this person. You know we can."

"Maybe. But then what? What will you do when you find him? You think you'll just be able to call the police and move on?"

I tried to keep my tone even. "I assume Justin isn't within earshot."

"I'm at my apartment, alone."

"Small favors, I guess."

"Don't be like that." Kelly spoke as if she were coaxing a small child out of her hiding spot.

"Why are you pushing me away from this?"

"Because I'm trying to protect you," she said. "Going down this rabbit hole is too close to all the things you're supposed to have left behind. It's a mistake. Especially with all the information you have at your fingertips now."

I sat up straight in my chair as Kelly's words slammed into my sluggish brain. "I guess you're right. I should just let Todd and Investigator King handle this."

"Thank you," Kelly said. "I just can't stand the thought of your getting caught up in something that will drag you back down."

As if I were an addict. And maybe that was the truth because I had just lied to my best friend.

FIVE

In a normal missing or endangered child case, NCMEC employed a very structured plan. My job as case manager meant facilitating everything, including any communication with law enforcement and the missing child's family.

But it also meant I had unlimited access to our private search engines.

Sitting in my cubicle in plain sight of everyone else, I couldn't start searching the intricate web of child pornography sites. NCMEC housed a private section for those jobs, with meticulously screened employees. But I didn't think photos from Lily's crime scene would have ended up on a child porn site.

She'd been fully clothed. A small subset of pedophiles did enjoy looking at dead kids, but the pictures were usually staged and sexually suggestive. I didn't need the child porn sites. I just needed the dark web in a safe place.

Kelly was right. Crime scene buffs liked to gather every damned thing, and the Internet was their storage reservoir.

As my colleagues said goodbye and left for the night, I hunched in front of my computer. More than half the lights in our section had been shut off and the blinds were all closed, leaving me in a dusky room with the white light of the computer shining on my undoubtedly pale face.

Search parameters came easily—I'd been right next to Lily, crouched in her blood. I knew what to look for.

Still, I didn't expect results to come so quickly.

But they beamed out at me like a gaudy neon sign. Not scene-specific details like "wrists cut," "suicide," "blond hair, teenager," but by name.

I didn't need the dark web after all.

I could have googled my sister's crime scene. Six photos had been scanned and uploaded on a site called Mourning Our Young—Gone Too Soon.

My chest grew heavy as if I'd stayed underwater too long and was only seconds away from my mouth bursting open and sucking water into my desperate lungs.

God, I didn't want to look. I couldn't look. I couldn't see her again.

But I had to.

The first picture nearly destroyed me. Someone started crying—a deep, painful yowl of a wounded animal.

Me. It's me.

The black and white quality of the picture only enhanced its brutality. The blood surrounding Lily seemed darker, thicker. Her skin even whiter than I'd remembered.

Her small hands open and slack. Submissive to her death.

And the eyes—the opaque, vacant look that haunted me every night of my life.

I wanted to be angry. But the emotion wouldn't come. Instead the very same shock and sorrow that had struck me that night over twenty years ago attacked. I pushed my chair back, stumbled away from my desk.

Everyone had gone home.

No one around to hear my anguish.

. . .

The sun was setting by the time I finally left the building. Completely drained and dried up, I robotically set off on my walk home. Normally I enjoyed the walks. I lived close enough that driving seemed silly, especially when I spent the day sitting on my butt. Usually, I made it to my place in less than fifteen minutes. But my legs moved slowly as if they were tied together at the ankles. Other people gave me a wide berth, averting their eyes.

I couldn't decide which cut more deeply—seeing the pictures or reading that five years ago, Joan Kendall had been the one to upload them.

My mother had an entire sympathy thread discussing the terrible suicide of her daughter, with complete strangers fawning over her unimaginable suffering. Joan ate it up, even discussing at length how she'd felt so hurt that her daughter chose to reach out to her sister in her final moments instead of the mother who'd sacrificed so much for her. The message. Joan had talked about the message from Lily to me on the message board.

Not a single word about why Lily had killed herself. Each time the question had been asked, Joan deflected like the master she was, bringing the conversation back to her.

She'd exposed my sister for the entire Internet to feast on and couldn't even tell the truth about why she'd died.

A hatred unlike anything I'd ever known rushed through me.

I should have known. The biggest betrayers were always the people who were supposed to be closest to you. Only the people who've witnessed your worst moments and tasted the same pain and fear can use those things against you.

Joan would answer for her lies this time.

. . .

I reached Royal Street in Old Town without remembering the route I'd taken to get there. The historic heart of Alexandria hadn't been my first choice to live in considering it was also among the most expensive places to live in the area, but the location was near great restaurants and shops, and even more importantly, within walking distance to both work and the bus station.

The brilliant sun from today had disappeared, replaced by bulbous clouds. The earthly smell of distant rain followed me as I drifted down Royal Street to the renovated building that now housed eight apartments. I lived on the ground floor—not ideal, but slightly cheaper, with the bonus of the small patio surrounded by the fenced-in communal courtyard on the corner of Royal Street. After a long day of work, I loved to pop open a bottle of wine and sit in the tiny space, listening to the sounds of my new city.

Tonight I just wanted to burrow in and think.

Plan.

Pretend that I could actually kill my own mother.

Mousecop's yowl welcomed me home, with the fat cat zigzagging between my feet and then theatrically flopping to the floor. I tossed my things in the nearest chair and dropped to my knees to rub his belly.

Tonight even my apartment felt like an enemy. Original, slightly scuffed hardwood floors no longer held character. They were just old. The updated kitchen pretentious, the bay window with its cozy seat a miserable trap. The same furniture I'd had in Philadelphia no longer vintage and chic but just cheap crap I'd bought on consignment.

I hated it all.

And now I was stuck in a new life I wasn't meant for. Because if I was meant to change, then why had the urge to drag my mother into the street and beat the hell out of her consumed me? I could do it. I had the means to kill her and make it look like an accident.

My stepfather would move on.

I dragged my short fingernails through my hair, feeling it come loose from the bun. What did I do now? How did I go back to my regularly scheduled life knowing what she'd done?

The apartment had gone completely dark when Todd called. I still sat in the same spot, revenge and confusion paralyzing me.

"Hello?" Did my voice sound different? It must, because I was different now.

"No dice on the trip," Todd said. "My lieutenant caved into the jurisdictional pressure. Personally, I think he was intimidated to be dealing with National Park Police. King's going to work the murder, and we'll work the stuff from our end."

The disappointment rushed over me with the force of a tidal wave. No words could escape my swelled vocal cords. The idea of seeing Todd had been the only thing getting me through the day.

"Lucy?"

I finally managed to breathe. The next step was forming words. "I really wanted to see you."

He must have caught the change in my voice. "What's wrong?"

"My mother. That's how the guy found Lily's death photos. She somehow got her hands on them, and now they're online. All he had to do was google her name."

"Jesus." Todd's disgust did little to appease my anger.

"She uploaded them five years ago. Has a whole message board of people feeling sorry for her. And since the last entry was just a few months ago, I wouldn't be surprised if she's communicating with one or more privately." Talking about what Joan had done helped to unclutter my head.

"One of them might even be our bad guy."

"I wouldn't be surprised. Joan's too self-absorbed to catch on to something like that."

"Any chance you can take a couple of days off and go with me to talk to her?" Todd sounded shy, and I pictured the blush on his plain face and the way he tugged at his lip when he was nervous. Had he grown his mustache back? "She might tell me more if you're there."

He wants to see me too.

She wouldn't. But that wasn't the issue. "I can't."

"Yeah. Probably too soon for you to take personal days." It was his turn to sound deflated. I didn't even take the time to wonder if it had more to do with the case or with the chance to see me.

"That's not it. I can't see that woman, Todd. Nothing good will come of it."

"I understand."

"No, you really don't." How could he? His parents weren't the best life had to offer, but his mother had been good to him. Joan had no maternal instincts. "But that's okay. You're just going to have to talk to her by yourself."

"I'm sorry about all this," Todd said. "I should have told you Shannon was missing. But I didn't want to distract you. Not when things were going so well."

"Afraid I might go down the wrong path?" I didn't care how rude I sounded. We both knew it was true.

Todd didn't answer right away, and I started laughing. The bitter sound rattled through my dark apartment and pushed me further toward the edge. On hands and knees, phone tucked against my shoulder, I crawled to the end table and flipped on the lamp. The yellow glow did little to pacify me. "What can you tell me about the investigation? Do you have any leads?"

"A few," he said. "A couple of friends of Jake Meyer's who made vocal threats against you after he died. I don't think they're involved, but we're checking. Beyond that, we're waiting for the task force to get their shit together and get us the data. We're going to have to cross check every known contact on that list, and it's going to be a bitch."

"Then you definitely need to talk to Joan. She might be able to give you something to narrow things down."

"I'll go over there first thing in the morning. You talked to Kelly?"

"She's going to be careful," I said. "I told her you'd have a car drive by and keep an eye on her building."

"I'll do my best," Todd said. "But her building is secure, and she's very cautious."

"And she has Justin." Did I sound jealous? I didn't want to be jealous. Kelly had a right to have someone other than me in her life.

He sighed. "Are you upset about that? Because I'm telling you, it's a good thing."

"I hope so."

Seconds ticked by, and I couldn't think of anything else to say. My mind had drifted too far down into the dark temptations I thought I'd let go. Try as I might, I couldn't shake the idea that had taken root earlier.

"I'm sorry I won't get to see you." Todd's voice sounded gruff. "Even if the reasons for the trip are shit."

"Me too." I wanted to say something more, but anything else felt too personal. No matter how much I wanted to see him, Todd needed to steer clear of me. Bad news all around.

He promised to call if he heard anything.

After he hung up, I spent more than an hour in the same spot, fighting the temptation.

I couldn't do this terrible thing. It was immoral and went against everything I'd convinced myself I stood for.

Everything I'd put in the past.

But I could no longer allow Joan to escape the accountability of what she'd done to Lily. Not just to her life, but her memory.

Tomorrow morning, Todd would interview her.

And then I'd come out of the shadows and put the fear of God into the woman who'd ruined my and my sister's lives.

SIX

I called my boss at home that night, and he graciously gave me the time off to grieve for Shannon. I called Kelly next, hoping her excitement at my visit soothed some of the anger.

"Okay," she said when I finished. "I'll be here."

"Wow. Don't get too worked up."

"Sorry." Her far-away-sounding voice told me she had the phone balanced on her shoulder. "I'm excited, I promise."

I curled into a ball, jamming my head into the pillow. "Is Justin there?"

"What? No. I'm just working on something."

"It must be a juicy case if you're this distracted." Kelly's job as a consultant for the Philadelphia Police Department usually came second to our work. But I supposed my leaving changed all that.

Kelly laughed. "No. Just a bunch of fact checking on a backlog of robbery cases. I want to get it finished. It's a nightmare."

Pacified, I told her goodbye. "I should be there by noon tomorrow."

"Perfect. I'll be back from the grocery by then."

It still sounded odd to hear her talking about going out alone, but it put a small smile on my face. Two Tylenol PMs and a shot of bourbon gave me a few hours of sleep, and by seven the next morning I was on the road to Philadelphia. Home.

I even left a message for Todd letting him know I was coming into town. But he could go ahead and talk to Joan without me.

As the miles passed, futility began to set in. Who was I kidding? I wouldn't be able to confront my mother. She was the one monster I'd never been able to stand up to. I'd storm into her perfect house and demand to know how she'd gotten the photos and why she was so selfish. And then she would start in, making herself the victim. I'd anticipate each move, but I wouldn't be able to counter it. Some sort of twisted sense of duty or respect for my elders. No matter how they'd treated me.

By the time the Philadelphia skyline began to emerge from the horizon, I felt stupid. I didn't want to see my mother. Nothing would change, except my own feelings of inadequacy would triple.

The trip wasn't a waste, I reminded myself as the thunder-clouds began to roll in from the west. I'd see Kelly and regroup. Maybe even spend a few hours with Todd. Pretend all was normal.

Five miles outside Philadelphia, the rain unleashed. Kelly had mentioned excessive amounts of rain this summer, so I should have expected it. The weather hadn't let up by the time I reached the Rittenhouse Square area and found a parking spot. My umbrella was no match for Mother Nature, and my sandals were drenched by the time I rushed into the entryway of Kelly's building and rang the buzzer.

She didn't answer. Paranoia slashed through me, but I was

several hours early. I thought about calling Justin, but then I remembered the Find A Phone application. She'd emailed me directions on how to use it yesterday, but I hadn't gotten around to setting up my account. Five minutes later, I had my username and password and access to the location pinging from her SIM card.

She was at Whole Foods, one of her favorite places.

I'd just have to make us a fresh pot of coffee while I waited for her to come home.

The familiar smell of Kelly's apartment set me at ease. Her vanilla candles had been recently blown out, and the vague scent of her perfume lingered. I dropped my things onto the counter and wandered to her fridge. A child of habit—an essential part of her recovery—she kept her weekly list on the refrigerator. Today's afternoon meant the walk to the corner health food store, and true to her routine, the list was gone. I sat down on her couch to wait, relaxing against the comfortable cushions and taking in the normalcy of Kelly's apartment. Her desk area was its usual mess, covered in files and loose sheets of paper, with Post-it notes lining her computer monitors.

To hell with confronting Joan. Being with Kelly was good therapy. Even though I'd needed to start over, the isolation that it brought had taken its toll. I didn't long for friends. Just the good ones I'd left behind. Maybe one day Kelly would be healed enough to leave Philadelphia altogether. Start over with me.

But now she had Justin, and that complicated things. In a good way, I reminded myself. Jealousy still pricked at me, like picking at a scab that wasn't ready to come off. She needed someone. She deserved someone. And Justin could very well be that person. He had the capacity to understand her. God knows I wasn't the right person to discuss any sort of romantic relationship with. I couldn't remember the last time I'd been with a man, let alone considered dating one. Too busy using my excuses to save the world.

Except for Chris. He had a way of stripping me bare without moving a finger. And part of me yearned for real intimacy with him. But I didn't have time to think about that right now.

Rain still pouring, thunder cracked outside, loud enough the lightning must have struck somewhere in nearby Rittenhouse Square. As a kid, lightning had scared the hell out of me. Lily used to tell me it was God pissed off and smiting the bad people. I'd been foolish enough to believe it and made sure to be extra good. Storms still set me on edge, as if the lightning acted as some sort of key to open a well of bad memories. The first storm I'd endured in Alexandria, I wound up beneath the covers in a cold sweat, deluged with all the mistakes I'd made after finding out about Lily's abuse. I gritted my teeth and hoped this one would pass soon.

I rose from the couch and paced to the window near Kelly's office area. It would do me no good in spotting her; it faced Rittenhouse Square. The trees, lush with summer foliage, bent in the rising wind. I could almost taste the scent of rain and storm, earth and heat in a disgusting cocktail. Kelly had recently talked about taking a cab. She wasn't ready yet, but she thought the time was close. Maybe she'd done so today. Or maybe Justin had taken her. Or she'd walked, thinking she could beat the rain. At four blocks away, the trek to Whole Foods was a short walk.

I'd wanted to surprise her with my early arrival, but now the plan seemed stupid. Kelly would panic at the sight of someone unexpected in her apartment—even if it turned out to be me. I should warn her. Better yet, tell her to wait at the store and I'd pick her up. She didn't need to be walking in this.

I saw the lightning streak by this time, jabbing straight down out of the sky and making contact somewhere in the park. The accompanying thunder came less than ten seconds later. Way too close.

Kelly still didn't answer her phone.

Surely she was on her way home, probably rushing through the rain lugging her groceries.

I logged back into the phone tracker account. The connection seemed slower than it had a few minutes ago, and long seconds ticked by as I waited for her location information to come up.

Phone cannot be found.

I tried again. The same result.

Brittle panic rose in my mouth. Her phone must have died —no tracking application or GPS could work if the phone was off. She'd forgotten to charge her cell, and it had died.

Rain pelted the window. Rolling my neck from side to side, trying to stretch the muscles that had once again tensed up, my gaze landed on her computer. Not the laptop she kept our secrets in, but the desktop provided by the Philadelphia Police Department, the one she did most of her consulting work from. Both monitors were dark, but the one directly in front of me had a Post-it note with my name written on it. I hadn't noticed it before because of Kelly's habit of sticking Post-its on everything within eyesight.

I collapsed into her chair and shook the mouse until the screen flashed alive. The scream built in my throat and then stuck. Kelly's terrified face, her eyes wide and teary, with a gag in her mouth, stretched across the 22" screen. The box asking for a username and password rested on top of her forehead.

I don't know her password!

Panic sucked my throat dry; I rocked in the chair. Another flash of lightning, followed by thunder, both accompanied by the slashing rain.

Her username was Kelly. I typed that in and then sat staring at the picture, into her frozen eyes as if they would tell me what to do next.

The Post-it.

I typed my own name into the password box. After three shaky tries, I finally managed to hit the right keys. The box disappeared, and Kelly's desktop appeared. Along the right were the usual files and programs from the PPD. The center video, obviously cued up for me, captured my attention.

I dragged the mouse to the arrow and clicked.

First, black video. And then Kelly, tied up, right in this chair. Duct tape on her mouth. The video had been taken on her computer's web camera. Sweat beaded on her forehead. Her eyes jerked from the camera's focal point to just a few inches above it. Each time, fresh fear filled them.

"Lucy Kendall." A disembodied, electronic voice. Was he using her microphone? Kelly used one to dictate reports. I didn't see it anywhere. Had he taken it to protect against fingerprints?

"I heard you'd be visiting today," the voice continued. "Things couldn't have worked out better." He made a clicking sound with his tongue. "Poor Shannon Minor. No wonder you've come to visit Kelly. You're drowning in guilt and fear." Whatever the man used to disguise his voice made him sound like a heartless robot. He sighed into the microphone, the sound coming out like a horrific whoosh. "You ruined everything for me. So now I have to set things straight. You need to be punished. Kelly too."

Kelly stared directly at the camera, her eyes wide and desperate.

I could practically hear her screaming at me to help her.

Don't let this happen to her again!

Kelly suddenly tried to make a noise through the duct tape. I turned the volume all the way up and leaned forward, but I only heard her terror. The man laughed. Shivers ratcheted through me at the strange, robotic sound.

"Here's where the real fun starts," he said. "Kelly's only got forty-eight hours. Can you find us before she runs out of time? I have rules, of course. No cops. If you say anything, I'll know. I've been digging into your life for years. I found Shannon. I found your pathetic sister too."

He started laughing again. "I assume you got that message. That was truly fun, I admit. But I'll know if you go to the police, and Kelly will die. That shouldn't be a problem for you. After all, keeping the police out of your life is a special skill of yours. See you in forty-eight hours." He paused, another soft laugh that made gooseflesh burst on my arms. "We left you a clue, though, didn't we, Kelly?"

She nodded, staring into the camera again, words I couldn't read in her eyes.

"Say goodbye, Kelly."

Kelly tried to scream again, and the video ended.

I sat there panting like a thirsty dog. Sweat dampened my armpits, and my fingernails had drawn blood on my legs.

Her phone pinged at Whole Foods less than thirty minutes ago.

SEVEN

Four blocks.

Rain beat at my skin as I sprinted around the few people brave enough to be outside in the deluge. My black T-shirt and denim shorts were soaked; the cheap flip-flops I'd chosen for comfort on the drive oozed with water, my feet constantly slipping inside them. A single thought fueled me to ignore the cold rain and lightning streaking nearby: whoever took Kelly had her phone, and he might still be at Whole Foods.

Water blurred my eyes as I jerked open the heavy, glass door and slid into the small grocery. I stopped, gasping for air. My hair felt like a wet blanket had been thrown over my head; my knees hurt from running. A cashier in a bright green apron gaped at me from her register.

"Was there a strange man in here with a phone in the last hour?"

The young cashier glanced around as if hoping someone else would talk to the crazy lady. "Um. Pretty much everybody who comes in has a phone."

"He wouldn't have been using it." Futility began to sink in. I had exactly nothing to go on. "Just sort of hanging around, killing time."

She must have told him about the application, hoping she could change his mind. How else would he have known?

"I haven't seen anyone." The cashier started scanning items again, averting his eyes. "But my manager is stocking shelves. He might have noticed."

Retrieving my phone from the relative dryness of my pocket, I took off for the nearest aisle, my flip-flops squeaking louder than the pounding of my heart. I checked the Find A Phone app. Kelly's phone remained dark.

Aisle by aisle I stumbled, looking at the floor, checking beneath the shelves and searching for the manager.

This is stupid. Waste of time. He's long gone.

"Can I help you?" Another man in a green apron stood in the middle of the essential oils and other smelly things aisle. He was much older than the cashier, his round belly straining against the green material.

I still couldn't catch my breath, could barely form a coherent thought. "I'm looking for a man with a cellphone. He would have just been loitering around. Killing time."

The portly manager set his box down. "Can you describe him?"

No! I can't do a damned thing!

"No. But he might have seemed edgy. Like he was afraid someone would make him leave or question him. Looking over his shoulder."

"Honestly, I don't remember anyone like that. If you had a description or a picture—"

A picture! I did have that. I skimmed through the pictures on my phone until I got to the first one of Kelly. "Was she in here today?"

Now the manager smiled. "Oh, I know her. Such a nice girl.

Quiet, though. Very routine—comes in at the same time every week." His eyes narrowed as he caught on. "Except for today."

Now he examined me more closely, undoubtedly taking stock of my pale face and the shock in my eyes, the raw fear rolling off me. "Did something happen to her?"

He'd call the police. And the kidnapper said no police.

And he's watching. He had to have been watching. That's how he knew to turn the phone on.

"She's sick," I said. "But she thinks her phone might have been stolen."

"Ah." He nodded, seemingly pacified. "Well, it's been very slow today. I didn't notice anybody strange. But if I happen to see her phone, I'll keep it in my office until she's able to come in and pick it up."

"Thank you." I left him staring and took one more trip through the aisle. No men in the store. No one who looked concerned about my dripping presence.

So cold. The air conditioning made my wet shirt feel as if it had come from the freezer. Wiping my face with my still damp hands, I exited the store.

More rain slamming into the top of my head, each droplet like a tiny nail being hammered into my skull. No more impulse decisions. Whatever new life I'd managed to create in Alexandria would go to waste. *That* Lucy didn't have the right mindset to find the bastard who'd murdered Shannon and taken her best friend.

My family.

But the real Lucy did. She was capable of cruel, desperate things.

And she would find Kelly before time ran out.

But finding Kelly alive wouldn't be enough.

Mary Weston had been right after all.

EIGHT

Kelly's apartment no longer seemed like a refuge. I couldn't stop thinking about the fear she'd experienced, and in the place that had been her safe zone. I slammed the dead bolt into place and walked to her desk with lead feet.

Her kidnapper said forty-eight hours, but how much time did I have now? My fast-food breakfast threatened to come back up at the thought of watching the video again, but I had no choice. I needed to have a better idea of when the clock had started ticking.

Now that I knew what to expect, I steeled myself against the fear and despair dripping from Kelly and focused on the small details. Her attacker was smart; he stayed behind the computer monitor the entire time. No chance of catching his reflection. He'd even made sure to move the fat, ceramic lamp that usually sat on the coffee table. I hadn't even noticed it was out of place.

I watched Kelly's eyes as they flickered between the camera and the man. I caught the pattern on the second replay. A fast glance to the man standing behind her monitor and then a hard, pointed glance directed into the webcam.

At me.

I played it again. Kelly's attempt at speaking still made no sense; I couldn't tell if she said one word or two. But she leaned forward as she said it. *For emphasis.* And when the man laughed at her, she looked at him with a hatred unlike she'd anything she'd ever displayed.

What is she trying to tell me?

I still had no clue when Kelly had been taken, but she'd been safe last night when I called, so this had happened after midnight.

Unless he'd already been here.

No, Kelly would have found a way to give me some kind of warning.

The computer's desktop. The wallpaper had been a capture from the video. I searched the screen, hoping to find the time had been part of the capture, but found nothing. How the hell could I know how much time she had if I couldn't figure out when she was taken?

I'd have to assume she'd been taken just after midnight. It was 11 a.m. now. Kelly had likely lost at least twelve hours, if not more. I had thirty-six at the most.

More questions railed at me. How had the man gotten into the building? Had she let him up, or had he charmed someone into believing he'd forgotten his key or code?

She wouldn't have buzzed him into the building unless she knew him. And the only men who might have come by were Todd and Justin.

What about the police? Or someone posing as a cop? Shannon's killer knew enough about my life to know about Todd Beckett. Which meant he'd known that I would have asked for extra protection for Kelly. He could have pretended to be a police officer with urgent information.

Would she have bought it?

I needed to see the building security cameras. I went to the address book on her computer and found the super's number. Somehow I managed to feign calm when his tired voice came over the line.

"Yeah?"

"This is Kelly Swan in apartment 3C. Is there any way I could see the security cameras from last night?"

"Why? Someone try to get inside your apartment?"

My heart hammered against my ribs. I didn't want to say anything that would make him call the police. "No. Someone knocked on my door really late, and I just wondered how he got into the building. Could I see them?"

He'd have to email them to me, I realized. Or I could try to convince him I was too emotionally distraught and would have a friend come down to the office.

"I can't just show you the video for privacy reasons," he said. "But I know everyone in the building. I can tell you if anyone different came inside or if anyone brought a friend. That would at least give you a starting point."

It was the best I could do. "Well, I'm not sure what time it was. I know I went to bed around 10 p.m., and I was dead asleep when I heard the knock."

"Did you look at the clock?"

"I don't have one," I lied. "I use my phone, and I'd left it in the other room. Too lazy to get up." Did my laugh sound even remotely genuine?

"Okay, well, I can look between ten last night and what time this morning?"

"Four a.m." If I'd taken Kelly, that would be the absolute latest I'd try to get into the building. People were moving around by five, early rush hour geared up. The guy was too smart to be seen.

"Give me twenty minutes, and I'll call you back."

I gave him my cell number. At the silence signaling the end of the call, panic threatened to steamroll me. Saliva pooled in my mouth; my nerves felt like they'd been lit on fire.

I clutched at the back of my neck, hoping the pain would clear my head.

This had to do with revenge. Jake Meyer's pedophile ring was still the best option. This had to be someone associated with it, but how could I get that information without help from the police? And in time to find Kelly before he killed her?

Her kidnapper said he'd left me a clue. No, that *they* had left me a clue. Everything else revolved around the computer, so why wouldn't this?

I clicked on the portal from the Philadelphia Police and was immediately asked for a username and password. The combination of Kelly and Lucy didn't work this time, and I didn't dare keep trying. If the account locked up, the system might notify the administrator. Someone would call Kelly to check, and then she wouldn't answer. Would the police be concerned enough to send someone? Kelly had access to sensitive data, so it was possible.

Her other files were reports that made no sense, analyzing information given to her for various cases. None of them looked to be associated with the Jake Meyer case. But there were so many players involved, how would I recognize the name? Still, nothing looked like anything worth using.

There was only one place left to check.

My legs ached as if I'd been sitting for much longer than an hour. I dragged myself to my feet and then to Kelly's bedroom. I'd never been inside, and I felt like I'd completely betrayed her trust by crossing the threshold. But I needed the laptop.

Every old building has a good hiding place, and this one was no exception. I shimmied partially underneath the bed and started knocking on the floorboards until the hollow one made itself known. My nails caught on the jagged seam as I struggled to remove the board. Finally, it came loose and banged against the bedspring. The eleven-inch laptop, safely in its protective sleeve, was tucked inside. I slipped it out and squirmed out from beneath the bed. My head pounded from the change in position as I sat up. Or maybe it was the stress taking its toll. Either way, I closed my eyes against the pain, my face pinched until the wave subsided.

With the laptop open, I typed in the username and password combination. This one Kelly had given me because the laptop contained our secrets—just in case.

Another desktop popped up, this one with different browsers and files. I knew she was also allowed to access the dark web from her work computer, but she rarely did so in case she found information we could use. Instead she hooked the laptop to the extra monitor so we could actually see what we were looking at.

I squinted at the small screen and started skimming files. It didn't take long to find what I was looking for. She'd labeled it clearly. Perhaps too clearly? I had no idea if she'd done this with the aid of her attacker, but it was the best I had to go on.

Meyer Trafficking Case—Suspect Tesla.

Thunder continued to roll outside, the room even darker as the center of the storm enveloped me. In Kelly's usual style, the file was done in a series of entries, with double spacing between them.

Robert Tesla (no relation to the physicist, bummer).

Penn State grad student who knew and communicated with scumbag Jake Meyer.

One of suspects tracked down by task force. No clear evidence but plenty of innuendo in messages.

Daddy is chair of fundraising at Penn State.

Assistant district attorney wants to prosecute.

Why did the cops back down?

Tesla's reputation damaged from investigation.

Prior hidden sex assault accusation brought up.

Grad program dropped him.

Police still claiming not enough concrete evidence. Task force detective and FBI agent disagreement, ADA trumped by boss.

DA taking orders from the FBI now?

Why had Kelly been researching the Jake Meyer prosecution? I knew she'd been following the case through her contacts at the department, but this was taking it a lot further. If the task force and the investigating agent had butted heads over it, that news would have spread. Kelly could have easily heard about it. Cops liked to talk, especially when it came to complaining about other agencies. But this... why had she kept this from me? To protect me?

Even more, why had she dug in so much further?

The next entry offered a possible answer.

Found address. Lives in Daddy's guesthouse in Chestnut Hill.

16 Marstan Road. Big freaking spread.

Justin and I followed the guy today.

Why is it always the pretty boys who get away with everything?

She'd told Justin she was researching this case. Or had he encouraged it? Had he been the one to suggest she follow Tesla? What if that had been the final trigger for this bastard's action? If he was part of the investigation, he would have easily heard my name. For all I knew, Kelly and Justin could have made contact with Tesla. Neither one of them were experienced in this side of the work.

Why the hell would Justin let her do something so stupid?

I couldn't worry about that right now. I had a lead and very little time.

My cell rang. The super.

Please let him have something for me to see.

"Nothing," he said. "Only three people came in during that

time, and they were all residents. One was a guest, but it was a female and I've seen her around. They live on the first floor. You know anyone down there?"

"No." Kelly didn't know any of her neighbors. She had no desire for anyone to poke into her business. "You're sure?"

"Positive. Maybe you were just hearing things. Or one of the other residents on three came knocking. Either way, I don't see how I can help you."

"Thanks for trying." Kelly's captor hadn't come into the building through the front door. The back entrance required a special key—one that only the super had. I knew the man was over seventy, so I didn't think he'd be a candidate for Kelly's abduction. But he might be easy enough to dupe and steal from. "Listen, your keys haven't gone missing lately? Just for a few hours?"

"What are you saying?" His indignant voice hurt my ears. "I'm not too old for this job. This building is one of the safest around, and I keep it that way. Nothing happened."

My heart dropped. The super would have no clue who took his keys, and I didn't have the time to jog his memory. Tesla was the best lead. "Of course. Thanks for your time. If you think of anything else—like maybe someone hanging around who shouldn't have been—please call me."

He grumbled something and hung up. I got to my feet and headed for my bag. I'd have to change my shoes if I was going to be out in this weather.

NINE

After disposing of all the cyanide and other drugs before moving south, the only weapon I had left was the Glock. Thankfully, I'd brought it with me from Alexandria. I secured it in my handbag and changed my wet flip-flops into sneakers. I had an umbrella in the car, along with a flashlight if I needed it.

As soon as I stepped outside of Kelly's building, the skies seemed to recognize me. A fresh deluge of rain came down, and I was immediately soaked. Rain had slowed the traffic. Half of Rittenhouse's residents were walking yuppies. I turned in the direction of my car, resigned to being wet the rest of the day.

"Lucy!"

The jubilant voice sparked fresh panic. Rooted in place, rain still bombarding me, I watched Justin run across the street, umbrella in hand and a silly grin on his face. Was he supposed to meet Kelly today?

Holding the umbrella over us, he grabbed me in a warm, one-armed hug. My face jammed into his neck. "What are you doing standing here in the rain?" Still lanky and his hair once again too long, he smiled down at me with the exuberance of someone newly in love. "Kelly didn't tell me you were coming."

My brain caught up to the situation. Justin hadn't talked to Kelly after I had. She'd probably gone to bed.

I needed to get rid of him.

No cops. If I told Justin, he'd freak out and call his brother. I'd never be able to convince him not to. I couldn't risk Kelly's life like that.

And you're still jealous.

"It was a last-minute decision." I kept my voice steady and cold. Intimidating people and getting them to do what I wanted fit me like a second skin. I knew Justin well enough to push his buttons and easily dispatch him. "Kelly's not here right now."

His smile faded. "Really? We were supposed to go to lunch." He scratched behind his ear. "You're mad at me, right?"

Justin sounded like such a little boy I felt even worse for what I was about to do. "It's not me you need to worry about."

"What's wrong?"

I gritted my teeth for resolve, knowing I looked angry. Justin's fears dangled from him like a talisman. So easy to twist things to my side.

"You pushed her too hard, Justin. She's not ready for this."

Now the real worry flickered in his eyes. "I don't understand."

"Clearly not. She's a mess. Not ready for everything a relationship entails."

"Did she tell you that?"

I rolled my eyes. "Why do you think I'm here? She called me last night crying. You've pushed her too far." I'd fix all of this later when I had Kelly back. Justin would understand.

"No," Justin said. "That can't be. I'm not interested in sex." A blush tore over his face. "No, I don't mean that. Of course I am. But I'm letting her make that decision. She's got the lead, always."

"I know," I said. "You've done nothing wrong. Not intentionally, at least. Kelly's just... for all the terrible things your mother inflicted on you, what she went through is even worse."

He seemed to draw himself up straighter. "She told me."

I hadn't fully anticipated that. "Everything?"

"She told me about how her stepfather kept her chained in the basement so he and his friends could rape her, that he kept her hungry and thirsty so she'd be weak. She told me about how it all made her feel. Emotionally."

They had bonded. I saw it in his eyes, felt it in the way he spoke of her. Until now, she'd told only me the details of her captivity. Pettiness drove me forward. Clock was ticking.

"She's had a setback, then," I said. "It happens with people with PTSD like hers."

Justin looked up at the building. "Let me talk to her. I need to see her."

"She's at her therapist. When she called me last night, I made her an appointment and got into the car."

"What time last night?" Justin asked the words I needed him to. "She was fine when I left at ten."

I'd spoken with her after that. She'd been taken after midnight.

"About half an hour after that." I fixed my hardest glare on his sad face. "And were you guys researching someone named Tesla? She mentioned the name."

Justin blinked. "We followed him one day. She thought he might have been connected to the trafficking ring you helped bust, but nothing came out of it." He glanced down at the ground, scrubbing his eyes.

I pretended not to notice his tears. "Look, I'm sorry. She needs space from you. Give her a few days, and let the therapist and me handle it."

He stared at me, his chin sagging and his eyes hurt. "Are you sure? I'll do whatever Kelly needs, I promise. I just want you to be sure."

Justin trusted me. I'd helped end his nightmare, put my neck out on the line for him.

"I'm absolutely sure." I kissed him on the cheek and walked back into the rain, hoping it masked the tears starting to roll down my face.

16 Marstan Road in Chestnut Hill lived up to its reputation. One of the oldest areas in the city, Chestnut Hill boasted million-dollar homes from nearly every generation. Some were brand new, some were mid-century modern, and even more were nineteenth century restored. Past Germantown Avenue and historical downtown, I wound up the gracefully sloping hill toward Marstan Road. It reeked of newer money. Lined with established trees that dipped into sweeping yards and impressive flowerbeds, the street's homes were nearly all newer construction. No matter how big the lot or how intricate the landscaping, the newer homes were easy to spot. No amount of windows and soffits could replicate the character of Philadelphia's historical homes.

The official Penn State title of Robert Tesla's father was Chair of Development and Alumni Operations. Meaning he was in charge of bringing in millions of dollars a year for the prestigious school. No wonder the task force had been divided on him, especially if the evidence had truly been circumstantial. The Tesla home reminded me of every single newer-construction luxury home I'd seen: gray siding, a couple of dormers, a grand entryway with white pillars, and lots of windows. That much I envied. Natural light was my only form of therapy.

I parked the Prius a few blocks down from the Tesla estate and started up the hill. The property had to be well over an acre, with the guesthouse having its own small quadrant, complete with private entrance and garage. An expensive, red car was parked outside, as if to remind the neighbors of the family's deep pockets. When I finally made it up the looping drive, I recognized the Mercedes emblem. The vehicle was pristine outside and in.

Focusing on getting to the house had kept the adrenaline at bay. Now it roared through my ears and veins, reminding me of exactly what was at stake here: Kelly's life, and my own, if I were being completely honest.

I quickly surveyed the guesthouse: two stories, curtains drawn on all the windows, quiet. Almost as if the place were in mourning. The edge of a cement patio peeked around from the side of the house, so Tesla had a back exit. No sign of a basement, and I assumed that would be unlikely in a guesthouse anyway. With the storm finally passed, humidity had settled in, bringing a different kind of wetness, like a soaked towel had been thrown over my face. Still, thick air added to the unnerved feeling creeping over me.

I'm rusty, that's all this is.

I could handle Robert Tesla. Just like any of the other greasy, sweating scum I'd killed. They were all cut from the same rotten piece of life. And nothing stood in my way when I wanted something.

I smoothed my hair, taking comfort in the heavy feel of the weapon in my bag. What if Kelly were trapped somewhere inside, and she heard me talking to Tesla? Would she be able to give me some kind of warning? Would I hear it?

A few feet away from Tesla's door, and my phone vibrated in my pocket; Todd's name flashed on the screen. My blood froze. I'd left him a message about coming to town, and he was supposed to talk with my mother this morning. He probably had an update and wanted to meet up. I couldn't deal with lying to him right now and decided to let the voicemail pick up.

No more delays. I knocked on the door, a familiar calm settling over me. I excelled at this part. Tesla would be eating out of my hand in minutes.

He answered the door half naked. Purple board shorts hung on a slim physique, brown hair that looked as if it hadn't been brushed in a couple of days, and dark eyes so clouded over he might have been blind. The butt end of a joint stuck in the corner of his mouth. Altogether a pretty picture had he been sober.

"Yeah?"

"Are you Robert Tesla?"

He took the joint out of his mouth in a languid motion and snuffed it out on the doorframe. "If you're a cop, you need a warrant."

"You answered the door with the marijuana in plain sight," I said. "No warrant necessary. But I'm not cop."

"Then who are you?"

"Lucy Kendall."

The haze in his eyes cleared. Recognition swept over him, every muscle tightening. His anger made him even better looking, making his jaw more pronounced and his lips thinner. His biceps flexed, his stomach pulled in, shoulders taut. "I know you. You bitch."

I smiled. "You recognize me."

He raised his fist, but I held my ground. "I know how to defend myself. That's your only warning."

"You think I'm afraid of you?"

"I think you should be."

Tesla Jr. ran his tongue over his mouth, too high to stay angry for long. "Feisty. I like that."

"That's not what I heard. Don't you prefer little girls?"

Tesla's lips drew into a sneer, exposing expensively white teeth. "That's a lie. Your investigation ruined my life."

"Asking a sex trafficker to hook you up with twelve-year-old brunettes ruined your life."

"I never said that." He spread his arms wide, his shorts dropping far enough to expose the trail of hair on his abdomen. "You'll notice I'm not in jail."

"Because the police couldn't get a strong enough case. Penn State evidently disagreed. Even with Daddy's money."

His jaw twitched. "School's freaked out over everything now. I'm a victim."

My turn to sneer. "Right. It's always someone else's fault."

"What do you want?" He backed up, reaching for the doorknob. "I'm busy."

"Shannon Minor was a friend of mine."

Tesla cocked his head. "The girl who got dumped in DC? Too bad for her."

Admitting he'd heard about her was a bold move since Shannon's death hadn't made the national news, but he was high enough to make a stupid mistake. Still, had this guy orchestrated Kelly's kidnapping? Stolen the super's keys and made a copy and then got inside without anyone knowing? Killed Shannon and taken the time to stage her body? I couldn't judge his intelligence, but if he were more than a recreational marijuana user, it was hard to believe he'd be alert and organized enough to pull this off.

But people surprised me every day. "I think she might have been killed out of revenge against me."

"Enjoy your guilt, then. I hope it eats your heart away."

"Trust me, I've got more demons than you can possibly imagine. My heart's spoken for." I stepped forward, allowing my hand to drift over the bag that held the gun. "Which makes me dangerous. Or hadn't you heard?"

A flicker of fear in his eyes, followed by an exaggerated smirk. "Nope." He took a long, arrogant look at my legs and then let his eyes drift over me. "You look like a nice piece. Maybe you want to make up for all the trouble you've caused me."

"Too old for you. Tell me about Shannon."

He snapped his mouth shut. "I already told the police I didn't have nothing to do with her. I didn't even know her."

So the police had beaten me to Tesla. He must have been one of the suspects Todd had mentioned last night. "I don't believe you. You might not be in prison, but you still lost everything because of me. You threatened people, said you'd make everyone pay for ruining your life. Instead of being a big shot, you're sitting around getting high in Daddy's guesthouse. Not exactly the life you dreamed of."

He sneered. "You don't know a fucking thing about me."

I pushed close enough to smell the sweet stench of pot and body odor rolling off him. "I know your type. You think the world owes you something. That you should be able to do whatever you want without any consequences. You can't deal with anything less. You're burning inside, aren't you? I bet if I agreed to take you up on your offer of making things even, you'd beat the hell out of me as soon as the door closed."

He said nothing, but the straining cords in his neck spoke more than enough. "I know your kind, Robert. One black heart can spot another."

"You're crazy."

"Most likely. What about Kelly?"

"Who?"

"I followed the clues you left. Now tell me where she is." I hated playing the card, but I didn't have time to keep up the waltz, as much as I enjoyed the verbal sparring.

"I don't know a Kelly. And I didn't leave you any clues. Crazy bitch."

"Sure you do. She's my family. And she helped me bring Jake Meyer down. So you came into her apartment and took her. Now I'm here to get her back."

A sickening smile spread over his face. "Now that's interesting. Maybe I've got something you want. Why don't you come in, and we'll see who wins?"

The challenge dripped from his tone, his breathing heightening the way a predator's does when its dinner is close. The haze had never returned to his eyes. Instead they were flat brown, cold and measuring. He had the physical advantage. I'd have to get the gun out of my purse, and I had no clue what waited for me in the guesthouse. If he had Kelly, he probably didn't have her inside. I just couldn't see him keeping her on the property, not when anyone could come calling.

He had to have her somewhere else.

If he had her at all.

Tesla Jr. was angry, for sure. Desperate and wanting vengeance. Most likely a pedophile. Or at least fantasizing about being one. But was he really capable of something so violent? My desperation to find Kelly might have blinded me. Her having information on Tesla could have been a coincidence. He was a natural suspect in Shannon's murder. But most pedophiles lived in the cracks of society. Anyone who survived the task force's investigation of Jake's contacts most likely would have gone further underground.

Had I made a terrible mistake?

My scalp felt sticky with sweat, my eyes suddenly blurry, as if an unseen force had literally sucked the confidence right out of me. If I was wrong about Tesla Jr., Kelly had lost two more hours.

"Where'd you go?" Tesla Jr. waved his hand in front of my face. "You thinking about all the things you want to do to me?" He leaned against the door, hip cocked, arms around his chest. That fake smile again. A rich, good-looking college boy so used to getting everything he wanted he couldn't deal with being held accountable.

I smacked his face before I registered the thought. "You're a liar. You want little girls, but you don't have the guts to seek one out—yet. Not after Jake failed to come through. So you stand here posturing for me, pretending to be interested when the truth is, you wouldn't know what to do with me. I bet you couldn't even get it up."

His reaction came swiftly. Stronger hands than I would have expected closed around my upper arms, his fingertips digging into me. "Why don't I bring you inside and teach you a lesson?"

Fear pulsed through my body at an exhilarating pace. Danger. I'd forgotten how intoxicating it could be. How much fun it was to match wits against someone and twist him all up inside. Killing a piece of trash like Tesla might actually be fun.

Kelly's running out of time.

"Detective Beckett's supposed to meet me here. You sure you want to do that?"

Tesla Jr. hesitated and then released me with a hard shove. "Get off my property. If you come back, I'll call the police. My father will make sure you're thrown in jail."

"Daddy takes care of everything, right?"

The predator appeared once more, cocky and taunting. "Silver spoons, bitch. It's a good life."

TEN

I collapsed against one of the willow trees lining the street and forced myself to catch my breath. The extravagant homes passed in a blur, my chest so tight I thought I might pass out. I didn't even realize I'd stopped running until I felt the rough bark beneath my fingers. Bright spots swarmed in front of me like giant, mutant glow bugs. I leaned my forehead against the tree. The bark scratched my forehead. My fingernails dug into the oak, skinning away tiny slivers of the tree's protective covering.

I'd wanted to kill that arrogant little prick. I could have done it with my bare hands. Rage would have overcome his physical advantage. I'd have gone for his eyes first, jamming my thumbs into the sockets until the wet, squishy orbs popped out into my hands. Knee in the crotch, another in the stomach. He would have begged me for mercy, and I'd have pretended to give it until I had Kelly's information.

And I'd turned on my heels and run like a coward.

I'd never done that before.

His words had rocked me.

Silver spoons.

That nasty reminder had come with an oily smile so broad his face might have cracked open. His ego lighting him up from the inside of his sick soul.

How long had he been watching me, planning this? How much of my real life did he know about?

I hadn't killed anyone since that cold night in Jake's garage. The younger Tesla couldn't know that. Which meant he'd underestimate me. That would be his fatal mistake.

But how did I figure out where Kelly was?

I still didn't think she was in the guesthouse. But could I be certain? The answer was simple: I'd go back and find a place to wait and watch. As soon as he left, I'd break in and search. But what if Kelly wasn't there, and he'd left to go to her, and that was my only opportunity to find her?

Do I follow or do I search?

Robert Tesla Jr. had to be the only real suspect, didn't he?

But I'd hurt other people too. Some of the men I'd killed had been disowned by their families, but a few of them still had people who cared. What if one of those people had somehow found out about what I'd done?

The chances were remote, even with the Harrison brother running his mouth. But to go to these lengths amounted to such personal revenge.

I didn't know what to think anymore.

My head started to clear, my blood pressure easing down. I pushed away from the tree, brushing the bark off my face. One of my fingers had started to bleed.

The sight calmed me.

I had to trust my instincts, and every one of them insisted Tesla wasn't involved. I must have missed something on Kelly's computer. My only option was to go back to her apartment and look all over again, wasting more precious hours.

I needed help. I needed police resources and manpower. I

needed someone to stand with me and promise me everything would be all right.

Todd would understand the need for secrecy. He'd worked undercover before. There was no reason to think he couldn't do it again. We could pull this off and find Kelly together.

Heat burned the back of my neck, my stomach rolling with waves of nausea. I moved to the shade of the tree, barely aware of what I probably looked like to the occasional car passing by. I should get something to eat and drink. I'd do that after I called Todd. We'd meet somewhere safe and figure it all out.

A tiny ray of hope began to bloom in my heart as I pulled out my phone. My fingers trembled, scrolling over the contacts.

The phone rang. "Unknown caller" flashed on the screen.

Dread swept over me. I felt quivery and very much alone, even though it was broad daylight in one of the safest areas of the city.

"Hello?"

"He wants to know who you were going to call." Kelly's quivering voice made my legs buckle. I grabbed onto the tree to keep from falling down.

"Oh Kelly, thank God you're alive. I'm so sorry."

"He's got a gun to my temple, Lucy. He says if I say anything that might help you, he'll kill me. I believe him."

My breathing accelerated to near hyperventilation. I fought to calm down, and then Kelly's original question hit me like a mallet. I whipped around in search of them. Was she this close? It had to be Tesla. She was in the house, and he was taunting me.

"He wants to know who you were calling." Kelly seemed to struggle to speak.

"No one."

"He says you're lying."

"Can I talk to him?"

Kelly didn't answer right away. "Kelly? Are you still there?"

"He says no."

A terrible suspicion crept over me. The hollow sound of Kelly's voice, the canned answers that sounded forced and unlike her. "Kelly, what's my biological father's name? I told you once. I know you remember."

Another delay. "I have to go now."

The call ended. I clenched the phone until my knuckles felt ready to break. He'd recorded her. She could be dead by now.

He was watching me. The call had been a warning.

The phone vibrated with a text. The caller was still unknown, but I had no way of knowing if it came from Kelly or her kidnapper.

Kelly's stashed away safe and sound. You should hide before the kid sees you.

I didn't waste time questioning, dropping to all fours and crawling into the rhododendron bushes flanking the tree.

He had to be messing with me, I thought as I looked in one direction and then the other. Where was he?

Stupid. He could be watching from anywhere. The house across the street was for sale. Had Kelly's kidnapper broken in and taken up watch, knowing I would come here? Or was Tesla playing a game?

A familiar car rounded the corner. My brain felt like it might burst wide open as I realized exactly who the caller had been warning me about.

What the hell was Justin Beckett doing here?

ELEVEN

Justin drove up the long drive, and I followed his path without a second thought. Keeping low, I eased up the lawn, using the shrubbery as a barricade. I settled behind a giant Atlas cedar tree, which gave me a decent view of the doorway.

Justin got out of the car wearing a ball cap and carrying a backpack. His shoulders slouched more than normal as he strode up the walk to Tesla's door.

Sweat burned my eyes. My fingernails dug into the dirt around the cedar tree. The overpowering scent of the needles teased my allergies, and I fought back the sneeze.

Tesla opened the door.

Justin shook hands with him.

My entire body jerked forward into a runner's crouch; I barely stopped myself from sprinting across the lawn and accosting them both.

Patience.

Justin went inside the house. Rage shuddered through me.

I could wait.

Justin would give me answers if I had to bleed them out of him.

. . .

I didn't stay behind the tree. Instead I sat down on the curb at the end of the drive, where the sloping hill and landscaping gave me enough cover. Tesla couldn't see me approach Justin. He'd call the police, and then I'd really be in it.

So I'd have to stop Justin on the way off the property, without being seen. I wondered if Kelly's attacker still kept tabs on me, or if he'd been satisfied with his earlier show.

I tried to remember if anyone followed me from Kelly's, but the truth was I hadn't been paying any attention. I thought briefly about trying to trace the call, but it would have been a waste of time. Even the most advanced law enforcement systems were useless against a pre-paid cell, and that's probably what the caller used.

Had he known Justin would eventually show up?

Forty-five minutes later, the old beater clunked down the driveway. I spotted Justin's open window, his perspiring face pinched in concentration. At least he'd made it easy for me.

"Hey." My loud, abrupt voice made him slam the brakes. His head whipped around. He stared at me with terror in his eyes. Caught red-handed, but doing what?

Justin didn't have the kind of sick psyche it took to become involved in murder and abduction. In spite of all the terrible things his mother had made him endure, he still had a naïve and good heart.

But whatever he'd gotten into might have dragged Kelly into a terrible mess, so I no longer cared about keeping the peace or protecting Justin from who I really was. Kelly didn't have time for charades. The weight of the gun in my right hand, partially hidden by my T-shirt, spurred me forward. I flicked my wrist, making sure to draw his attention.

"You drive around the corner"—I pointed in the direction of my Prius—"and then you park behind my car. You get out and get inside. And then you start talking."

He glanced to his right, obviously thinking about taking off. His hands tightened on the wheel.

"That's a big mistake," I said. A coldness entered my voice. I recognized the detachment, felt the desperation swarming over me. "I don't give a damn who you are. I *will* get answers."

His pupils widened to the size of broken pebbles. "Lucy, you don't understand what's going on."

Hand still on the gun, I stepped to his window, dropped my face to his level. Stared at him with eyes I knew were deadly cold. "You're right, I don't. But that's why you're going to tell me."

Justin's eyes flashed toward the gun. "You wouldn't really—"

"Don't test me. Not today."

His Adam's apple jerked up and down. The scent of nervous sweat and old car wafted through the window. "All right. I'll talk."

"Good choice."

I tucked the gun back into my shorts and followed him as he drove around the corner and parked behind my car. Standing at the bumper, I waited as Justin unfolded his long frame and stepped outside. Killing time, and possibly killing Kelly. Probably running over his story, trying to decide what lie I might believe.

Too bad he still had no real idea who he was dealing with.

We faced off. I pretended to be calm. "You realize that Robert Tesla is connected with Jake Meyer's pedophile ring and that he's a suspect in Shannon Minor's murder?"

Justin held up as his hands. Scared and defensive. "Todd said they don't think he had anything to do with her murder. Tesla's got an alibi."

"I'm sure he does. Daddy to the rescue."

"You don't understand." Justin's voice gained urgency.

I gritted my teeth. This boy... I'd fought for him too. But that no longer mattered. If he decided to remain an obstacle, I would forcibly remove him. "Explain."

Justin looked like he might vomit. "Kelly's been investigating Tesla on her own, and I've been helping her. I posed as a drug dealer." He flushed and looked at the ground.

"Look at me when you're talking." Why hadn't Kelly told me? Why would she investigate on her own? "I don't have time for that embarrassed, poor-me bullshit. Tell me why."

"Because he talked more when he got high," Justin said.

"Not about the pot. Her investigation. So Kelly was trying to get him to confess to being in Meyer's trafficking ring?" What the hell was she thinking?

"No," Justin said. "Robert Tesla's innocent."

I rolled my eyes. "You can't be that naïve. Not after everything you've lived through. I haven't seen the emails, but if he was investigated for it, the task force had reason."

"I've seen them," Justin said. "Kelly showed me. She got into the files."

And she hadn't told me. A flash of hurt nearly sucked away my anger, but I recovered. "Then you know he's a creep. He's out for revenge against me, and he either killed Shannon or had her killed."

He's not organized enough.

Someone else has Kelly.

"You're wrong," Justin said. "It's not him. It's his father."

"Oh my God." My patience snapped. "I know we both have mommy issues, but not everyone has parents who are monsters."

Justin rocked back and forth on his heels, a battle raging in his eyes. I very nearly pointed the gun at his forehead and told him to get on with it.

"I shouldn't tell you any more. Kelly wouldn't want me to."

I rested my hand on the gun. "Someone I care about is dead. Kelly's not talking right now. And you're here."

"I'm looking for her." He closed his eyes for a brief moment. "Tesla Sr. is one of the men who raped Kelly when her stepdad kept her in the basement."

My legs weakened. Could it be true? Only her stepfather had been arrested. The others had disappeared. "How did she find out?"

Justin wiped the sweat off his forehead, pushing his hair back. "She didn't want you to know. You should ask her." He paused, taking a deep breath. "Since she's not talking to me."

Hell if I would trust him now. I had zero qualms with keeping Kelly's abduction a secret. And even less worry about Justin's feelings. He never should have allowed her to get involved in something like this. He'd helped her step right into harm's way and kept the one person who could protect her in the complete dark.

"Can you blame her?" I said. "Why did you let her dig into this? It obviously set her back. She's reliving it all."

His nose scrunched up like he might cry.

"Save the pity party." I pointed to my car. "You get in there and tell me everything. You understand me?"

"I know you're angry," he said, "but this isn't you. You don't lose your cool and threaten your friends."

My laughter tasted even more bitter than it sounded. "Justin, this is exactly who I am. Everything else is just fluff. I don't care if we're friends or how good of a guy you are. A girl is dead, and Kelly's been digging up dirt where she shouldn't have been. She could be in danger." My voice cracked on the last word. I hoped he took it as anger. "Her safety trumps everything. I will not allow anything to happen to her. So your feelings? They don't matter."

But something's already happened to her.

And you're a stone-cold bitch.

He still hesitated. Fury at myself, at Kelly's kidnapper, and even at her own foolishness boiled over. "Do you believe the stories about me? Because I think you do. And if they're true, how close to the edge do you think I walk?"

Justin stilled. "You... I don't understand."

"Yes, you do." I took the safety off the Glock. "Do not underestimate me."

Instead of fear, anguish darkened his face. He'd just have to get over it. "I'll get in the car because I want to help Kelly. If she could be in danger, then I'll do whatever I can. But I'm not scared of you. You're not the evil you want to me to believe."

My affection for Justin fought to burst from the dark place in which I'd stuffed it. "Keep telling yourself that."

TWELVE

I didn't turn on the car. Even with the windows down, the humidity was stifling. But I wanted to stay here for now, keep an eye on Tesla's house. I didn't have any other viable leads. Hopefully that was about to change.

Justin tried to make himself small in the passenger seat, leaning away from me. "Right before you moved, Kelly saw the name in a report. She thought she recognized it and started searching. She found Tesla Sr.'s pictures easily enough. She had no doubt he was one of the men her stepdad allowed to rape her."

As a teenager, Kelly had survived years of physical and sexual abuse from her stepfather. He kept her locked away in a crude basement room and shared her with a group of friends. It had taken a year's worth of tips before Philadelphia Child Protective Services finally saw fit to investigate.

"And she didn't tell me." I had no right to feel betrayal. Kelly carried this cross, and she owed me nothing. But the notion had already taken root. After Jared Cook—Kelly's stepfather—had lied to me about her whereabouts, I'd returned to the house with a warrant and two police officers.

The basement made the hairs on the back of my neck stand up. As soon as I stepped onto the first step, I knew something horrific waited for me.

In the farthest corner, an L-shaped wall butted up against the foundation. A putrid smell emanated from the room. One of the officers broke the padlock, and I saw Kelly for the first time.

She was lying on a filthy cot, curled up in the defensive stance of a wounded animal. No restraints needed—Cook had already broken her down. Immediately realized the cause of the smell: the combination of Kelly's inability to wash and the plastic bucket in the corner that served as a toilet. Later I would find out she was only allowed to bathe before men came over.

Kelly blinked as though she wasn't sure if she was awake. "Who are you?"

Her voice sounded grainy, weak. Unused.

"My name is Lucy Kendall." I stayed at the doorway, motioning for the male officers to stay back. "I'm with Child Protective Services, and I'm here to take you away from this place."

Her head whipped back and forth, her dirty, long dark hair going with it. "You're a liar."

I inched forward. "No I'm not. I promise you're safe. And I'll keep you safe." I wasn't prepared for the fierce protectiveness that welled in my chest at the sight of this damaged girl. I knew then I'd do whatever it took to keep my promise.

Kelly drew her knees tighter to her chest, her dull eyes squinting at me as I came to stand at the foot of the cot.

"But I understand why you don't trust me. I'll wait here until you're ready."

More than an hour later, she finally uncurled her legs and took her first step toward freedom. From that moment on, I vowed to help her heal, no matter how long it took.

Damnit, Kelly. We've been in this together. Why didn't you tell me?

"You were moving. Starting over." Justin cut into my memories. "She thought it was your only shot at getting a normal life back. If you knew about Tesla, you wouldn't have gone."

I'd have tracked him down and killed him. Kelly's gang of abusers had always been on my list, but she didn't know their names. Had she been lying, or did seeing Tesla's face jog her memory?

"When we met, she was already investigating Tesla. I think she just needed someone to talk to. For some reason, she chose me." Emotion colored his words. I kept my eyes on Tesla's driveway.

"You said you've seen the emails between Tesla and Jake Meyer," I said. "They were sent from the son's account."

"His Penn State account, which is really stupid," Justin said. "The school owns that account and can dig into it whenever they want. That's probably what got him kicked out. Kelly says it would have been easy for his father to use it."

"And the son would know he'd been used." That aspect didn't surprise me. A man like Robert Tesla Sr. had money and a reputation to protect. People threw their kids away for far less.

"That's our theory. Robert Tesla might not suspect his dad, but we wanted to find out. That's why I was selling him pot. Keeping him medicated made him easier to talk to."

But Kelly wouldn't have trusted Justin with getting the information. She'd want to do it herself, make sure all of her questions were asked. "And who did the talking?"

"Kelly." Justin's mouth twitched into a smile. "She pretended to be interested in him and tried to get information. She wasn't as good as you are, but she's learning."

I twisted in the seat, torn between betrayal and pride in her actions. "You're telling me Kelly went into that house alone?"

He glared at me. "No way! She wasn't ready for that, and I didn't want her to. She'd meet him for dates in public places."

"And what did she find out?" My stomach felt antsy. Insight

into Kelly's life would only help if it gave me a location to search.

"He hates his father," Justin said. "His mother does too. Robert's pissed his daddy didn't keep him from getting kicked out of Penn State. He told Kelly his dad laundered all sorts of money and a bunch of other conspiracy theories." Justin shrugged. "She didn't know if the laundering was true, but she said she'd try to find out in case he didn't get hauled in for the trafficking."

"The statute of limitations hasn't passed on her rape. It started when she was fifteen. In Pennsylvania, child sexual assault victims born before 2002 have twelve years after their eighteenth birthday to file charges."

"We didn't talk about that," Justin said. "She just wanted to get enough to put him in jail now. I don't think..."

"She didn't want to testify about the rapes." That was the main reason her stepfather had gotten away without naming any of his co-conspirators. No one blamed Kelly, and I couldn't hold it against her now. She shouldn't have to relive that in front of a jury, especially if she had to go against well-known and respected men like Tesla.

"What about Jake Meyer?" I asked. "Did she bring that up to Tesla?"

"Yesterday," Justin said. "They went to a movie; I hung around outside. She finally got the conversation headed that way, but she didn't really get enough. He did say someone framed him, but she couldn't get any information on his dad."

"A movie." A stinging sensation echoed through my chest. She'd lied to me. "That's the movie she was at when I called after Shannon's body was found."

He twisted around, trying to look contrite. "You would have come straight back here. You were already worried about her. And you would have done something bad." He looked down at his constantly moving hands. "She was afraid it would be something you couldn't come back from."

"So she put herself in serious harm's way with no experienced backup." God, I wanted to be angry. But to hear how far she'd come, to know she was ready to take on something like this, putting herself out there... I felt only pride.

"That's why you should go back to her place and ask her," Justin said. "She wouldn't want me telling you all of this."

"I can't ask her right now." I frowned at him, making sure my expression looked as disapproving as possible.

"Why?"

The lie came deliciously easy. "She had a breakdown and checked herself into a mental health center. No visitors for three days. I'll let you infer what caused the breakdown."

I should have thought of that earlier. No matter. He'd believe it, and I had time without him breathing down my neck.

His head dropped to his chest. "You're kidding. She seemed okay—more than okay. Every day, I asked her if she was handling it. If she needed to stop. She promised she'd tell me if she did."

"You can't seriously be surprised." My jealousy pushed the issue. "She's got PTSD, and she just jumped into this. You should have called me."

"She's stronger than you think," he shot back. "You can't control everything."

We glared at each other, the throbbing in my head making me see spots. My control issues were none of his business. "What was her endgame?"

Kelly didn't have any poison that I knew of. But after hearing all of this, I had no doubt she would be resourceful enough to get it.

"She wanted to gather as much evidence on Tesla as possible. She said that her stepdad let several different men down there, but there were three main ones, in addition to him. She remembers them sounding like friends."

"I know. Like a gang of pigs." Kelly's stepdad had denied all the allegations of allowing other men to attack Kelly, but he'd pled guilty to her rape and imprisonment. Because of Cook's refusal to name co-conspirators, the only hope was if Kelly testified. And it was a slim one.

"Please tell him I can't do it," Kelly had begged me. "I can't get up there and talk about it in front of a jury. And I don't know their names. Please, Lucy!"

I'd spent an hour arguing with the prosecution, and the attorneys finally agreed not to ask Kelly to testify.

"So she wanted to try to find them all and then give my brother the evidence," Justin said.

Of course she did. She was better than me in so many ways. "But Kelly has been on this property?"

Justin nodded.

So Tesla Sr. very easily could have recognized her. She was a threat to him, and he could have decided to eliminate her. But where did Shannon come into all this? Or the aspect of revenge against me? How did it all tie together?

"Has she had any contact with Tesla Sr. or her stepfather?"

Justin pulled on his earlobe, looking down at his lap. "No. But she's got the names of the other guys. Through one of the programs she has access to."

"What program?" Surely not something associated with the police department. Too risky.

"It's some kind of analyst program," he said. "I guess there are companies that aggregate personal information for profit. Addresses, jobs, phones, car info, some financials. Basically they follow consumer trends and catalog them, and then they sell the information to marketing firms."

I couldn't believe what he was saying. Justin had just described the case analysis team at the National Center for

Missing and Exploited Children—a place that had some of the best online security protocol I'd ever seen. The only way Kelly would have access to the information was through me, and I hadn't given her any of my login info.

And then I remembered the day nearly a year ago, when we'd needed to get into Brian Harrison's computer.

It's easy to put a Trojan into someone's system. You just send them an email with something you know they'll click on, and then you've got access. You can even get usernames and passwords if you know what you're doing.

And Kelly definitely knew what she was doing.

Kelly had discovered Tesla shortly before I'd left. We'd had lengthy discussions about the resources at NCMEC.

She'd stolen my access information.

I couldn't stop the smile creeping over my face. Justin looked even more nervous, inching away from me.

"Go home," I said. "I've got something I need to do."

THIRTEEN

My laptop battery crapped out as soon as I opened it. Time continued to sail by, each new hour bringing with it a fresh image of Kelly and the horrors she could be going through.

Had she been raped again? The thought made me sick enough I would have vomited if my stomach wasn't already empty. But Shannon hadn't been raped. Just mentally and physically tortured. Another thought slithered around the recesses of my consciousness.

What if Kelly survives all of this?

How did someone come back from a second time of being held prisoner? All the trust she'd gained toward the world would be obliterated. What would be left for her?

Entertaining the thought got me nowhere. One horrific thing at a time, and right now, I had to get into NCMEC's system.

I hated the thought of leaving the Tesla estate, but after hearing Justin's information, I had little hope of finding Kelly on the property. If the elder Tesla had managed to evade authorities all these years, he wasn't stupid enough to hide her anywhere near his private oasis.

My eyes kept straying to the rearview mirror as I drove down the hill and into the lifeline of the Chestnut Hill area. Had the man followed?

With the Tesla property disappearing in the rearview mirror, I felt like I'd abandoned Kelly.

But none of the information added up. I couldn't reconcile Kelly being taken by Tesla for his own personal gain to the cool, controlled ego of the man who'd taunted me on the video. He'd made it very clear this was at least in part about me. And he'd referenced Shannon. But why would Tesla go after Shannon or me? The idea of me as a threat to him now made little sense. If Justin's story was true, then Kelly was the threat.

Was Shannon's reference just a diversion?

Very little surprised me anymore. But I'd be shocked if a wealthy, prominent and most likely very paranoid man like Robert Tesla Sr. broke into Kelly's apartment. If he was behind the abduction, then he had help.

And that might make more sense. Perhaps Tesla had found some twisted thug to do the hard stuff. Someone with experience scaring the hell out of people. Maybe Shannon's abduction had been completely unrelated, and Tesla had just used it to his advantage to taunt me in the video.

But two people with connections to me being taken within weeks of each other? No chance for a coincidence. Both abductions had to be connected. I couldn't allow both to end up in murder.

More than half the day was gone now, and Kelly's hours dwindled. Every single second ticked off like a bomb in my chest. If my count was close, she had roughly thirty-two hours left. My only hope was figuring out what she had gleaned from my NCMEC access.

Germantown Avenue in Chestnut Hill on a busy summer afternoon wasn't the ideal place to work, but I didn't have the time to search for a more secluded area. I ducked into a coffee shop on the lower level of a centuries-old building, quickly ordered a coffee and a pastry, and then found the nearest charging station.

I wondered if the man followed me or if he'd left the area after sending his cryptic text. One by one, I stared down every patron in the small coffee place. They were all women, some teenagers. The lone male in the place looked older than my stepfather and decidedly unhealthier.

I didn't bother with Kelly's computer. Whatever information was there would be hidden deep within her hard drive, and I wasn't skilled enough to find it with any sort of speed. Instead, I logged into the NCMEC portal on my laptop and began going over the search history. Since I'd only been working there a few months, the search for Tesla's information showed up quickly.

I'd never noticed it before because I wasn't looking, but my lack of attention to detail bothered me. Maybe if I'd noticed, I would have caught on to Kelly's plan and stopped everything before it started.

Staring at pages and pages of data that went back decades, my eyes quickly blurred. I'd always known privacy was a myth, especially in the digital world, but seeing the sheer amount of information tracked from search engines, public records, and our digital footprints never ceased to amaze me.

The information the companies stored barely landed on the side of legal, and they were amazingly efficient in their collections. Which meant figuring out the specific information Kelly had taken from the search would be tricky.

Four addresses came up for Tesla. The system's history showed Kelly had found them as well. He'd owned the estate in Chestnut Hill for five years, with his previous address being in Society Hill, another historic area with plenty of wealth. Tesla had been living there during the time of Kelly's imprisonment. Society Hill was at least a twenty-minute drive from the northeastern neighborhood where Kelly had endured her torture. Zero evidence of a connection to her stepfather.

How did a prestigious fundraiser for one of the city's top universities hook up with a lower-income jack-of-all-trades like her stepfather?

Jared Cook had been working at a rental car company when I discovered Kelly locked in the basement. I tried wading through the information for a sign of Tesla using the rental company, but found nothing.

Doesn't mean that's not how they met. Penn State could have paid for the rental. Or another company. It's still a viable possibility.

Next came cellphone carriers, local phone companies, charity donations. Useless data after useless data. All pivotal when searching for a missing kid, but no help for me.

What else would Kelly have been looking for?

More names, obviously. When she finally began to talk about her time in the basement, she said there were three men who returned week after week, but she didn't know their names, and she felt guilty.

"Another girl is going to go through the same thing because I don't have the answers." Her head dropped to her hands. She'd cut her hair, and the stylish bob suited her.

I touched her shoulder, careful of her boundaries. "Listen to me. None of this is your fault. There's nothing you could have done differently. And Jared Cook made all of this happen. He's in jail."

Kelly wiped a tear. "But what about those other men?"

"Hopefully they're too scared of getting caught to hurt anyone else." It was the first and only time I'd lied to Kelly.

I had no doubt that as soon as she made the connection to Tesla Sr., she would have wanted to find their names and find a way to tie them to Tesla.

And then deliver the information to Todd? She had to have more of an endgame.

A few more minutes in the search history gave me the names.

Hours after Kelly searched for Robert Tesla Sr., she'd searched for two more men, one right after another. Dr. Adam Barton and Brent Johansen. She must have dug much deeper into Tesla's information to find them.

I'd forgotten about the pastry and coffee. I took another bite and then combined the men's names and entered a new search.

The page took ages to load. My noisy brain ran scenarios, determined to connect the dots between these men and the need to lash out at me. What had I done to them?

The simple answer was that I'd taken away Kelly and their private playground. Her stepdad would have known my name. But that had been so many years ago. Was he still in contact with the others? From prison? I doubted it, since all of that information would be logged by the correctional facility in Greensburg where Jared Cook was serving his sentence. Too bad I didn't have the time to request a visit.

So my crusade against Jake Meyer had put Tesla's name on the creep radar. He tossed his son into the storm, effectively covering his tracks. Then Kelly came around. I could buy he'd abducted her to silence her.

But Shannon and the revenge angle against me still didn't ring true.

The page finally loaded. My search called up phone and address information for Philadelphia Renovations. The company appeared to be in the business of gentrification, working with the city to restore the decaying historical homes. Several names were associated with the company, all of them day-to-day operations people who would only be able to give me the run-around. But tax records showed the company was co-owned by Dr. Adam Barton, a successful pediatrician with a twenty-year-old practice; Brent Johansen, a civil engineer; and Robert Tesla Sr. Kelly must have searched each man individually. Had she found pictures? Would she recognize them?

My fingers felt lifeless as I clicked on the company website. Their opening slideshow was impressive: before pictures of dying, old homes and after pictures of dazzling renovations. Contact information for the same operations people I'd already bypassed.

Company history.

The pictures loaded one by one as if the Internet had decided to break the news to me slowly. Tesla came first. He looked like an older, more distinguished version of his pot-smoking son.

Next came Dr. Adam Barton. A pale reed of a middle-aged man with thick, unruly hair, Barton's bio described him as a pediatrician noted for his successful practice and easygoing demeanor. Kids and parents loved him.

Of course they do.

Brent Johansen was an African-American man with lovely green eyes. His work as a civil engineer took him into all areas of the city, and he claimed to have a passion for saving the city's grand old homes.

No mention of how the men had met. Just a shared passion for history and making their beloved city better.

I nearly puked into my coffee.

More than a decade had passed. But images like that were seared into a person's soul.

She would have known.

How had Kelly felt when she saw these pictures? Despondency momentarily paralyzed me. I could not imagine how she must have felt, sitting alone in her apartment, looking at the faces of these monsters. Most likely anger at first, and maybe fear. But then Kelly's goodness and nurturing would have kicked in. She would have known the men hadn't stopped their sick games and that every new business venture gave them a brand new list of potential victims.

I wished I'd been there to comfort her.

Especially when they described their renovations as "turning Philadelphia history into your family's future."

Come, buy our restored homes. Bring your children. Teenage girls preferred.

Familiar rage descended. The table began to shake, my fisted hand repeatedly hitting the wood. I tasted blood in my mouth. I'd been biting my tongue to suppress my anger since Lily's funeral.

What had Kelly done with this information? Had she gone to their homes? Sought out their family members as she'd done with Tesla? Somewhere along the way, she'd made a major mistake. And one of the men made her pay for it.

None of this gave me what I really needed to know: where did Kelly's captor have her?

Vacant properties. Philadelphia had hundreds of them. How many would qualify for the gentrification Philadelphia Renovations pushed?

Most of the old homes that had been gentrified belonged to the city. They were condemned and left to rot or had been run down by public housing. None of these were safe places to hide Kelly. Too many drug addicts and homeless looking for shelter.

A vacant property privately owned by Philadelphia Renovations and in the midst of renovations would be the perfect place to stash her.

The company had dozens of homes in their records, but only two were listed as currently vacant. Pictures showed one in the middle of reconstruction, with the other waiting its turn.

I packed up my now charged laptop, took a couple of bites of the dry pastry, and then grabbed my cold coffee.

I'm coming for you, Kel. God help anyone who stands in my way.

FOURTEEN

He leaned against my car, obviously waiting to see which business I came out of, although he should have known I'd have been in the coffee shop. Knowing Todd Beckett, he wanted to avoid a scene.

He looked safe and inviting, and I had the silly urge to rush into his arms. Heat warmed my face, and my heart rate ramped up. I wanted to believe it was because I had to lie to a police officer's face about Kelly, but I knew that was only a fraction of the issue. No time to deal with that now.

His usually pale face had a reddish tan, his forearms looking more muscular. His black sunglasses hid his eyes, but the set of his mouth gave away his irritation.

"You haven't answered my calls."

"Sorry." I kept my distance, hovering near the Prius's bumper. "Trying to get caught up on everything. What happened with Joan?"

Fresh anger roiled through me at my mother's callous betrayal of my sister. And if she'd somehow managed to set this entire mess in motion by drawing the attention of a killer... but those photos had been online for five years. And what would I do? I'd never been able to do anything as far as Joan Kendall was concerned—the grand villain of my tragic life.

Todd's mouth twitched. "She's really something, isn't she?"

"The Wicked Witch of the East would have been a better mother. At least her hate would have been straightforward." I briefly wondered what life would be like if I didn't carry the burden of hating her. But I couldn't fathom that existence. "Let me guess. Joan denied everything and then tried to make you feel like a terrible person for believing a grieving mother could do such a thing?"

"Boy, you have her pegged. Basically," Todd said. "She admitted to talking with a grief support group about Lily's death a few years ago. But she denied uploading the images."

"Did you tell her we had proof?"

"I didn't get the chance. She told me if I had any more questions I could come back with a warrant. Which is what I'll need if I want to get on her computer."

I shouldn't have been shocked. I certainly shouldn't have allowed the anger to course through me until I wanted to pound my fist on the car. But Joan never had to be accountable for anything. Why didn't someone make her admit her own wrongdoing? I stood rigid, my fingernails digging into my palms. My jaws locked. I studied the jagged crack on the sidewalk.

"I'm not sure it matters." Todd's voice softened. "I'll get the warrant because I want to see if she communicated with anyone, but I doubt we will get any sort of lead from it. Not for Shannon Minor's murder."

Or Kelly's disappearance. My mother had just made mentally torturing me easier for the bastard.

Todd remained against the car, his long legs stretched out so that passersby had to step over him. "So you're not even going to mention Kelly?"

My head snapped up so fast pain shot across my neck. "What do you mean?" I glanced around. Had I been tracked here? Did he see me talking with Todd? I needed to get out of here.

"I talked to Justin. He's a wreck."

Damn. "Well, it's the truth. I didn't want to lie to him."

What a terrible person you are.

Had Justin said anything about Tesla? If he had, Todd would have been all over me about it by now. Then again, he liked to work up to things and then pounce at the right moment. I appreciated that about him.

"You're sure he can't talk with Kelly?"

I felt my throat tightening. "They told me no calls or visitors. I don't know what else to do."

"What's the name of the facility? I'll see if I know someone; maybe I can pull some strings." His gaze searched mine, trying to find the lie. I refused to break.

New raindrops landed on my nose, trickling down my face. "No. Don't you see? Overstepping Kelly's boundaries is what put her there. You can't keep doing it. She has to have the control."

I wished he'd take off those stupid glasses so I could read his eyes. A muscle in his cheek worked quickly, but he nodded. "I suppose you're right."

"Thank you." The rain fell harder, dampening my shirt.

Finally, he pushed the glasses on top of his head. I wasn't prepared for the rush of emotion at finally getting to truly see him. If I could only tell him everything, we could find Kelly together. He had the resources and the skill, and he'd stay right by my side until it was all over. And then what would happen?

I couldn't take the risk.

Or maybe I was just too damned proud to admit I couldn't do it.

You just want to kill the person who took her.

That too.

He stood up straight, shifting awkwardly from foot to foot. I realized he wanted to hug me. I couldn't allow it. I would break if he did.

I took a step back and around the bumper, toward the driver's seat.

Todd flinched, and I warmed with shame.

"No other updates on Shannon's case?"

He shook his head. "They've got about as little as we do. He might have created one hell of a scene, but her killer didn't leave much physical evidence. He's not a first-timer."

Which meant that if Tesla and his crew were behind Kelly's kidnapping, they'd likely hired someone.

"You know what's really interesting?" Todd put his sunglasses back on, the business tone back in his voice. "One of the guys we identified as being affected by the sex trafficking bust and possibly having a grudge against you doesn't live far from here. Just up the hill, really. His name's Robert Tesla."

I snorted. "Like the physicist? How kind of his parents."

I hope the rain hides the sweat on my face.

"I just think it's kind of fascinating you're in his neighborhood."

I tried to smile. "Chestnut Hill is one of my favorite places. I think you can chalk that up to coincidence."

Todd didn't take the bait. "Nothing you do is coincidence. You've obviously decided to investigate on your own. I can't stop you, but I don't think Tesla's got anything to do with Shannon Minor. He's a pothead living on Daddy's name. But he's not a killer. And he's got an alibi."

"Good to know."

Daddy's the one you need to worry about.

"So I guess I'll get going." He still hovered around the passenger side. "Unless you wanted to make plans for tonight." His cheeks turned the color of a sunrise, and I suddenly wanted to close the distance between us and step into his arms. Some childish part of me still pretended that one day, Todd and I could be together, a normal couple with normal things to talk about.

I shook my head, wondering when those feelings had taken over. They needed to be shelved, because Todd deserved normalcy.

"Let me call you later. I'm not sure what's going on tonight." Another lie. At some point I wouldn't be able to weed out the truth.

"Yeah, all right." He smiled again, this time genuine. "You look good. Alexandria was the right move for you."

"Thank you." I got into the car before I lost the rest of my resolve. By the time I had entered the address of the first property into my GPS, Todd had disappeared.

FIFTEEN

I spent the entire drive to the first address waiting for another contact, but nothing came. Either he'd lost his tail on me or decided he'd had enough fun at the Teslas'. Either way, I couldn't keep worrying about it. If he called, I'd deal with him then.

Dismissing building one turned out to be easy enough. A construction crew crawled over every inch of the row house in Center City west, tossing trash and worn-out building materials out of the top floor of the brick structure. More hardhats hauled rotting wood and bags of trash out of the bottom floor, throwing all of it into a rapidly filling dumpster. Apparently Philadelphia Renovations hadn't updated its website, and these guys had decided to take advantage of the break in the weather.

Nearly an hour and the downpour passed by the time I arrived at the second property in a largely vacant area of northern Philadelphia. The abandoned commercial building sat across the parking lot from an abandoned power plant. The apartment's name had long since disappeared off the front door. The fuzzy black mold on the plywood covering most of the building's windows only made the place more of a health hazard. A thick chain and padlock ensured no squatter entered through the front door.

Darker clouds drifted into the horizon, with thunder grumbling in their wake. The entire street appeared to be abandoned, but I had no way of knowing if the other boarded-up properties were home to transients. I made sure both computers were safely in my bag before slinging it over my shoulder and leaving the safety of the locked car. They made for a heavier trek, but leaving them in the car was out of the question. Both had information I might need, and I wasn't risking a robbery. The pressure of the Glock against my tailbone did little to boost my nerve.

Following the chain-link fence line, my shoes sinking into thick mud, I checked each section for a weak spot big enough to crawl through. I found it in the back of the property, where the base of the fence had been cut away.

A shiver of unease came over me, as though someone standing far behind me had called my name. I whipped around, desperately trying to get my bearings. My sense of smell provided the first clue: a fishy odor competing with the stench of rotting earth. My heart suddenly tried to crawl into my throat. Nearby, the Delaware River drowned Monterey Cemetery, a casualty of bad planning and the city's post-industrial age. From this distance, only a few crumbling vaults at the top of the hill were visible, but they were enough to hasten my step.

The Delaware reclaimed the Victorian garden cemetery, and the city responded to the health risk. Most of the bodies had been removed, with only the vaults on the hill remaining untouched by the water. Not all of the monuments had been taken away, however, and now their tops peaked out of the water like ancient reptiles.

Even with the rain making me feel wrung out and wilted, I shivered before turning my attention back to the cut-away hole in the fence. One last check for any onlookers and then I shoved my bag through the hole. Shimmying through on my belly proved harder than I thought. My elbows dug into the dirt and the back of my shirt snagged on the jagged fence edge. By the time I slipped through, mud covered my clothes. I snatched the Glock out of my shorts before it got caught and wormed the rest of my body into the courtyard.

Shouldering the bag and gun, I crept toward the back of the lonesome apartment building. Every window boarded, same as the front. But the back entrance descended into the ground, and three sub-level window wells looked like perfect places to break and enter.

The plywood covering the basement windows appeared bright and clean—wet from this rain, but not weathered like the other windows. Someone had recently boarded these up. Just Philadelphia Renovations being proactive or something worse? No way would I be able pull the boards free without some kind of tool. I didn't have anything other than a spare tire in the trunk and a lock-picking kit.

The wind kicked up, bringing with it the scent of summer heat and stinking sewer. I doubted many of the surrounding buildings had working plumbing, but any person calling them home still had to relieve themselves. I searched the yard, desperately hoping for something I could use to pry one of the boards away. Nearly everything in the small courtyard was trash: broken bottles, fast-food wrappings, and discarded drug paraphernalia. No sign of a screwdriver or anything I could use to wedge between the boards.

The brick exterior appeared to be cracking, with shards of brick and masonry littering the ground. I grabbed a jagged piece of broken brick and hurried back to the window well. All three window wells had trash floating in the standing water. Thank God I'd changed into tennis shoes earlier.

I eased into the nearest well, shivering at the cold water and filth, slipping down into the small space. The water went up to the middle of my calves.

The brick piece barely fit between the plywood and the window frame, but I managed to wedge it down and started to pry the board away. The brick's saw-toothed edges scraped my hands, drawing blood. I kept trying, using my weight as leverage.

More thunder stormed in the west. I pulled again, and the shard snapped in half.

"Damnit!"

The remaining remnant was smaller than my hand, but I had to keep trying. Sweat soaked the roots of my hair, my back ached, and my hand kept bleeding. My nerves built with every pull, desperation making me lightheaded. Kelly might be inside. I had to get through this window, had to find out. Tears and sweat mingled on my face as the frustration threatened my sanity.

The plywood splintered, and a palm-size piece flew into the pile of filth at my feet. My bleeding right hand left bloodstains on the wood as I braced my feet and broke away more sections until I finally had a big enough space to crawl through.

Pure darkness awaited me, and I didn't have a flashlight.

I fished my phone out of my back pocket and used the light app to shine a bright, blue-tinged stream of light into the basement. I noted a boiler in the corner, along with an ancient water heater. Much of the ductwork had been ripped away, and I guessed the copper piping had been stolen to pawn as well.

I strapped the heavy bag to my back while I slipped feet first into the unknown. My shoes hit the concrete floor with a dull thud, and I whipped around, aiming my phone. My heart felt like it had become a growth in my throat. I retrieved the bag and secured it on my shoulder and then pulled out the Glock and the silencer Chris had given me months ago. Until now I hadn't seen fit to use it, but I didn't want to draw attention if I had to defend myself. I wrestled on the silencer and faced the darkness.

My eyes stung, and I wiped the sweat away. After only a few minutes inside, my thin shirt stuck to my back, and my sinuses felt blocked from the heat and dust. My shoes scraped the floor as I forced my legs to move.

Safety off, gun in front of me, I eased toward the boiler. It looked to have been defunct for years, but these old buildings had often been built with various side rooms in the basement, for equipment and maintenance offices. So I checked that side of the basement.

Nothing.

My chest hurt, and my head felt uncomfortably heavy. With no air and the high humidity, the building was a baking sauna. I took a deep breath and focused on the building's layout. Rectangular, longer than it was wide. So I needed to move straight ahead, sweeping from side to side. Clear the basement first and then go to the first floor. Kelly could be in an apartment.

The streaming light from the phone caused the dust in the air to sparkle like freshly dug diamonds. A piece invaded my eye, and I struggled not to scrub it out. I skirted more forgotten junk in the basement, probably storage of long-gone residents. A rat scurried away from the light. Cobwebs rained down from the ceiling. My hair and the back of my neck suddenly felt as if tiny, quick legs scurried over my skin. I brushed away the sensation, trying to pretend the spiders had vacated along with the residents.

With the basement cleared, I shouldered open the door to the stairs. The scent of urine nearly gagged me. I pulled my shirt over my nose and listened for any sign of life above my head. If Kelly was here, did her kidnapper stand watch?

I could only hope, because I had plenty of rounds in the Glock's magazine.

Up the stairwell and onto the first floor. Perpetual dusk reigned inside the boarded-up building. I blinked as if the hallway would suddenly become brighter. Three apartments on the left, three on the right. A couple of doors stood open. Flattening against the wall, I edged on tiptoes toward the first open door. Was something moving around inside? I tried not to breathe, but my lungs refused to cooperate. The air moving through me sounded like it had been run through a compressor. On the other side of the wall, more movement.

More rats?

I forced my outstretched arms to steady, taking aim with the Glock's sight.

Just when I'd gathered enough nerve to bust into the room, something large ran across my feet, its cordlike tail streaming behind it.

I shuddered so hard I nearly dropped the gun.

The adjacent room was empty. So were the next two.

Forty-five minutes had gone by, and I had several more rooms to search. Time to stop being afraid.

I approached the first closed door, grateful I'd thought to bring my lock-picking kit. The lock snapped quickly. I pushed the door open before my imagination took over with all the horrible things I might find.

Empty.

I moved on to the next.

And the next, my despair increasing with every step.

Kelly wasn't here.

I didn't know where else to look, and I couldn't call for help.

"Damnit!" I threw my bag onto the floor, the lock-picking kit scattering. I beat my fists against the door of the last room until I drew blood. Helpless. No, useless. I couldn't do anything to save my family. And that's just what the bastard intended. He wanted me running in circles until I gave up.

"I won't give up," I shouted into the darkness, reaching for my weapon. "Even if time expires, I'm going to keep looking. And I will make you pay for what you've done." I snapped the safety off and pulled the trigger. Bullets sprayed into the opposite wall. Every pop felt like an accelerant to my anger. I kept shooting until the magazine was empty.

Out of breath, I dropped to my knees. The impact from the hard floor traveled all the way to my chest, but I barely noticed.

You've got to get yourself together.

You just wasted time and bullets.

But it felt damned good.

My phone buzzed, the light an ethereal glow in the dank. Ready to pass out, I scrambled to my bag and grabbed the phone. What if he called again?

It wasn't a phone call. The subject of the email message froze me in place.

The software Kelly installed on her phone had sent me an update. The phone was on, and the service had immediately tracked it. My fingers trembled as I opened the email and clicked on the attached map. I recognized the address immediately.

It was the same one I'd been keeping watch over earlier.

SIXTEEN

My hand finally stopped bleeding, but I clutched the wheel so tightly the cut burned.

Had Kelly's phone been at Tesla's the entire time? Or was someone playing more games with me?

Night descended on me as I raced back to Chestnut Hill. Perfect. I'd done much of my dark work in the dead of night. I knew how to blend in and move through without attracting attention.

But creeping down a manicured lawn with a semiautomatic weapon tucked in the back of my pants was a first for me. Most of my previous assaults were carefully planned out. Even the truck-driving pedophile I'd killed with an overdose of insulin had been meticulously planned. No time for that now. I'd wasted away nearly half the day on a wild goose chase. I should have stayed with my instincts.

I parked farther down the street and headed toward the house, my hidden gun reloaded and ready.

If Tesla had used his son's email like Kelly believed, then using his house to hide Kelly wasn't that much of a leap. And maybe the son was involved, groomed by his father.

Except Kelly was an adult now. I shrugged off the thought and kept moving forward.

Body low enough to smell the cloying scent of healthy grass, I stalked up the property toward the guest house. Lightning danced in the horizon, but no thunder or scent of rain followed. Still, the heavily clouded sky made the muggy night extremely dark—a small advantage for me.

I ducked behind the same Atlas cedar tree I'd hidden behind earlier. The tree's width had to be at least thirty feet, giving me ample hiding space. The evergreen's silvery needles looked ghostly in the darkness, their tips making my arm itch as I crept around for a view of the guesthouse. The application couldn't pinpoint to the exact area, but it was able to tell me Kelly's phone was somewhere within a fifty-feet radius, meaning the search area included the house and part of the surrounding landscaping. Had Tesla left the phone there and taken her somewhere else? Why turn it on now?

I'd just have to ask him.

A flashing blue light on the guesthouse's lower level glowed into the landscaping on the side of the structure. Television, I realized. Maybe Tesla had passed out with his joint and would be an easy mark.

I slipped forward, eyes on the various windows. In this heat, they were all shut and most likely locked. I could try one but risked making too much noise, not to mention setting off the alarm system. Good thing I knew how to pick a lock.

The front door stood ten feet ahead and to my left. I dropped lower, damned near crawling. My knees skimmed the cement as I hit the entrance. I leaned back against the recessed area, catching my breath. Even with his private entrance, Tesla must depend on his parents' security system for protection.

His time had come. Daddy's boy was going to give me answers.

I slipped the pick into the lock and twisted.

A sound behind me. A twig snapping?

Frozen from the inside out, I forced myself to turn my head and checked the vast expanse of property. Nothing to see. I couldn't even make out the mailbox.

Something above me buzzed. My head jerked up, eyes watering.

A security camera.

My desperation had made me careless.

That was probably why I didn't sense the blow coming.

A heavy fist connected to the tender spot at the base of my neck, propelling me forward. I slammed against the door hard enough pain shot across my forehead.

I reached back for the gun, but he was too quick, snatching my arm and twisting it tightly enough I thought it would break free of the socket.

"I knew you'd come back." Tesla's breath stank of pot and whiskey. "I just didn't think it would be tonight. But I'm happy to see you." He shoved his pelvis against my back. "What's this?"

Tesla pulled the gun from my belt. "Were you going to shoot me?"

"Not until you told me where my friend is."

He pulled my right arm harder. It would break soon if I didn't do something. I summoned all my strength and drove my left elbow backwards, but he'd anticipated it, dancing out of the way. He caught that arm too, trapping both of them behind my back and pressing me against the front door. "I don't have your friend. But I'll take you."

"No you won't. You're not interested." Any excitement from this came from his need for revenge, not to have me.

He laughed, his hot breath teasing my ear. "I'll work something out."

Where had he put the gun? He must have it on him.

"I'll kill you first."

"You're awfully cocky for a woman trapped like a rat."

My mind tripped and raced trying to figure out what to do next. "I just know what I'm capable of."

He laughed, the sound almost seductive in my ear, and then pressed his erection into my back. "I like it when girls fight back."

"What about the little girls?" I tried to bait him. "Did you like making them cry?"

Tesla wrenched both my arms until I cried out in pain. "I don't like little girls. You've got things all wrong."

"Then tell me about it." I still didn't know if Tesla had been used by his father or enlisted to act as his guard dog. Either way, I needed to bring him down.

"Waste of time. You won't believe me. Neither do the cops. But they don't have enough to charge me. Just ruin my life."

He pressed his face into the curve of my neck and inhaled. "You smell sweaty. Why don't we take a shower first?"

I gritted my teeth. As long as he had me in this position, I was helpless. I had no choice but to make him act. "Why? I'm too grown up for you. You'll just be standing there like an idiot, limp and useless."

He twisted both my arms and pressed me harder into the door, his knee jammed between my legs. I should have expected the blow, but Tesla was quick. He yanked me back and slammed my head into the glass front door. I heard the pane of glass crack, felt the trickle of blood on my forehead. Pain fragmented across my face and down my spine.

"Is it your father?" I gasped. "Are you covering for him? If you know something, tell the police. He deserves to pay for what he did."

"And you deserve to suffer." Tesla's spittle landed on my cheek. "Fucking bitch. You need to learn to mind your own business." The combination of his breath and fluids and my own blood threatened to make me sick.

"Believe me, I suffer every day." I couldn't allow this to continue. But he had my body nearly locked down.

I jammed my foot into his right knee as hard as I could, smiling when he howled and his body buckled. His grip weakened, and I managed to slither around and bring my knee into his groin as hard as I could.

He anticipated me once again and brought his arm up to stop me. I loved the sound of his wrist breaking as it snapped back. Now my arms were free, and I started hitting him. "Where's Kelly? Her phone is here."

"I don't have anyone's phone." He lunged at me, but this time I moved faster, ducking low. My legs didn't want to move, but I forced them across the lawn, toward the safety of my car.

You're going the wrong way. You need to get inside the house. You can't help Kelly if he takes you too.

My legs slogged forward, feeling as if I'd gained fifty pounds.

I should have taken the silencer off. I didn't hear the shot.

I only felt the bullet searing into my flesh. I staggered forward, nearly falling to my knees. I dug my teeth into my bottom lip to keep from screaming, but I kept running. Tesla fired again, this time hitting one of the ornamental light posts. The glass shattered, the bulb exploded, the sound like fireworks. Shards sprayed the lawn. Lights in the big house flashed on.

I kept running for the car that was parked too far away. Warm wetness dripped down my arm. Would the blood leave a trail? Would the police test for DNA? How much would Tesla tell them?

His father would have me in jail. He'd rob me of my last few hours to save Kelly. Had that been the plan all along? Is that why the phone had come on?

I could call Todd from jail, but the kidnapper had assured me that would result in Kelly's death. What if I was on the wrong track? Or what if the police descended on Tesla, and he couldn't leave the house to take care of her? How long could she survive without food and water?

I slammed against my car hard enough to bruise my ribs. Blood stained my arm and dripped onto the hood.

Tesla screamed in the distance.

I couldn't stay here.

But where did I go? Who could I turn to for help?

SEVENTEEN

Once I'd escaped the Chestnut Hill area, I pulled over to assess my shoulder. I hadn't lost a lot of blood, but enough to leave the back of my arm feeling wet. The car bumped to a stop against a curb, blocking a bicycle lane. My head felt light and somehow stuffed full all at once. Suddenly I realized eating only half of a dried-out pastry all day had been a very bad idea. How much blood could I lose before I passed out?

I snapped on the dome light and gingerly examined the part of my shoulder I could see. No exit wound. But the bullet had embedded just beneath my skin. It felt like a tiny pebble, except it was still blazing hot and burned harder every time I moved.

I couldn't leave the bullet. Infection would probably set in within hours. If I were less squeamish, I could dig it out myself with some tweezers and a lot of whiskey.

But Chris kept his EMT supplies in his apartment.

Don't call him. Don't ask for his help after the way things have been.

I wouldn't be able to keep my secret about Kelly. And then he'd want to help. Together we might find her, but what would the consequences be?

The thought sent chills down my back.

Kelly was the first priority, and to help her I needed to be healthy. Going to the emergency room was out—too many questions and far too much time lost. And reporting gunshot wounds to the police was mandatory.

My phone's battery had drained to less than 10 percent. I knew Chris's number by heart.

My heaving stomach rebelled, pleading with me not to call him. Just before I hit send, another face flashed into my memory. I hung up and searched my bag for something to wrap around the wound, but I had nothing other than the laptops and my wallet.

A safe place to regroup. That's what I needed. I couldn't go back to Kelly's. What if Justin had showed up?

Fresh panic set in. Did he have a key? What if he went inside and saw how I'd torn the place apart looking for a clue? All he had to do was move the mouse, and the monitor would come to life. He'd see the desktop and call his brother.

I couldn't worry about it right now. I needed help, someone who could take out the bullet and wouldn't ask questions I didn't want to answer.

Someone who'd be understanding about not calling the police.

It was time to tell my stepfather I knew his secret.

For years I wondered how my stepfather dealt with my hateful, manipulative mother. And then I started paying attention. The only time he ever really put his foot down with her was about his poker nights. Two nights a week with his buddies. The stipulation was that Mac would never hold a game in my mother's house. He agreed, and peace was kept.

But I discovered poker night didn't exist and quite by accident. Less than a year ago I'd been tracking the pedophile who eventually kidnapped Kailey Richardson, and I saw Mac go into the bottom apartment of an ancient row house in West Philadelphia. In the middle of the day? My imagination had reared. Was he having an affair? My mother would have been devastated. The idea of having such a juicy, cruel secret to cling to every time she belittled me was too tempting. I'd abandoned my target and followed Mac's trail across the street.

The truth proved to be far less scandalous but still satisfying.

On poker nights, and sometimes during his lunch break if his construction crew was close enough, Mac came to this apartment. No one else lived there. Kelly found out it was rented in his name.

No one showed up for poker night.

Mac sat alone in the old recliner my mother had forced him to give to Goodwill and watched sports.

He rented the apartment to escape my mother.

Once I stopped laughing at her expense, I felt immensely sorry for him. And yet he'd made the decision to stay, although I suspected it was simply easier not to divorce. She'd take everything he owned, for one. And she'd make his life a living hell.

So I didn't rat him out, and I didn't cause him the stress of telling him I knew about his secret place.

But I needed his help now.

Mac waited on the steps when I parked in front of the row house. The neighborhood was lower middle class, mostly safe, and the late hour made it relatively quiet. The drive had taken longer than it should have, especially since I continued to feel more lightheaded.

He pulled himself to his feet, the plastic drugstore bag heavy at his side, and hurried over to meet me. The past year had taken a hard toll on his health. Atrial fibrillation and high blood pressure meant he took a cocktail of medicine. His weight loss seemed to have stopped, but he was still much thinner than he'd been before he retired from his successful general contracting career. I hated seeing him so weak.

"Lucy." He yanked the door open. Worry darkened his eyes as he gazed at my bloodstained arm. "You should go to the hospital. And where have you been? You're covered in mud."

"I can't." I didn't know if the bleeding had stopped. My shirt clung to the back of the seat as I leaned forward and took Mac's outstretched hand. "It looks worse than it is. And the bullet is right at the skin. You can take it out."

Mac hadn't asked any questions when I'd called. I didn't know what excuse he'd given my mother, but he'd left the house immediately. I shouldn't have dumped the stress on him. But I had no one else—not with Kelly's life at risk. And I couldn't just walk into a drugstore and get the supplies I needed.

Keeping his arm around my waist, Mac guided me up the steps and into the apartment. His living room looked exactly the same as it had last year when I'd spied on him—just the recliner and television with the rickety side table for his cigars and drinks. He'd closed the blinds. The overhead light made the room look yellow and old.

Mac blushed. "I need you to take off your shirt."

I sank into the chair, long past modesty. "Can you help me?"

Together we maneuvered the shirt off, Mac trying his best to keep his eyes on my arm. The blood had begun to dry, and the material peeled away with a wet, sucking noise.

"The blood loss isn't that bad." Mac trained as a medic in the National Guard, and he'd stayed current with emergency care during his construction career. He claimed it made people feel safer to work with him. "Which isn't uncommon for a flesh wound." He pulled his glasses out of his pocket and continued to examine my arm. "Since the entrance is so close to the outer part of your shoulder, I don't think the bullet went through any muscle. It wouldn't have risen to the skin if it had." He gently touched the raised spot on my arm where the bullet had lodged, in the soft part of flesh near my tricep.

"I picked up some tweezers," he said. "But I've also got needle-nose pliers if we need something bigger."

I felt suddenly lightheaded but found the energy to nod. The sooner we finished, the faster I could get back to looking for Kelly. She had roughly twenty-seven hours left.

Mac grimaced. "You still need to go to the hospital. You'll need an antibiotic."

"I can get one."

He stared at me, the suspicion deep in his eyes. "Are you going to tell me what the hell's going on?"

Drawing Mac into my mess wasn't fair, but I needed to talk to someone. My overwhelmed brain could no longer make sense of everything that had happened in the last few days. A new point of view might help me spot something I'd missed. And Kelly's abductor never said anything about help, just the police.

Mac wouldn't make me go to the police. He'd understand.

I nodded, trying to think of where to start and what I'd have to omit.

"I'm going to clean the wound first." He took peroxide out of the bag, along with a pack of cotton balls. "You can start with why you're back from DC and running around getting shot."

The peroxide didn't sting, but his touch, no matter how gentle, hurt. I spoke through clenched teeth. "Yesterday morning, one of my former CPS kids was found murdered in Maryland. The scene was a message to me." I told Mac the theory that I'd made enemies when I'd discovered Jake Riley's sex trafficking ring. Mac and my mother had come over the day after I'd escaped from the garage. The police had accepted the story I'd killed Jake in self-defense. Instead of being distraught that she'd nearly lost her remaining daughter, my mother had been humiliated and furious at the terrible thing I'd done. I'd brought her name down. How could I have done that?

Mac took me to lunch and listened to as much of the story as I could tell him. When I'd finished, he'd said he was proud of me.

"So after Shannon's murder, I knew I had to come back and check on my friend Kelly. Do you remember her?"

Mac had never met Kelly, but I'd talked about her frequently over the years—to him, not to my mother. After I'd removed her from her stepfather's basement, Mac became my outlet. Kelly's situation was—and remained—the most horrific case of abuse I'd personally witnessed. Images of her emaciated body, along with the tomblike feeling of the basement, had haunted me for weeks. Mac was the only person I could talk to about the experience, and I'd kept him updated on her healing progress.

"Of course."

"Someone took her." No more easing into things. The words poured out of me, half babble mixed with anxious sobs. "I thought it was a man named Robert Tesla. He's a person of interest in Shannon's murder. Kelly had a file on him. But then I found out she'd discovered Tesla's father was one of the men who raped her. I think she went looking for the rest of them, and they've taken her. I've been given forty-eight hours to find her, and that's nearly half gone."

"Jesus. Why haven't you called the police? This is beyond your skillset!"

"Whoever took her knows things about me," I said. "He staged Shannon's body to look like Lily's." I nearly stepped off course and started ranting about my mother's betrayal of putting Lily's photos online but caught myself. That didn't matter right now. "He warned me he'd know if I called the police, and I believe him."

Mac held a small knife, the blade wet with peroxide. "I've

got to cut in order to get to the bullet. It won't be very deep, but it'll hurt. How'd you end up getting shot?"

I tried to slow my breathing even as my heart raced, my gaze on the shining blade. "Kelly put a tracking program on her phone. I was searching for her at one of the properties Tesla Sr. owns when her phone came back on. The app said she was within twenty-five feet of the son's guesthouse. Oh shit!" The knife pierced the already swollen skin on my arm. I dug my fingers into the worn chair.

"Deep breaths," Mac said.

I did as he said, trying to think about Kelly and the pain she must be enduring. "I planned to confront him, but I screwed up. He got the gun, and I ran. Thankfully he's a bad shot." Another stab of pain, and I bit my lip, tearing the flesh.

"There it is." Mac put the knife down and started with the tweezers.

The digging was much worse. Almost like a bug that had rooted itself inside my flesh and was making its home. I refused to cry.

"Got it." Mac held the bloody bullet fragment under the light.

The searing pressure subsided, and then I felt slightly faint. "Thank you."

He cleaned the wound again and then applied butterfly stitches to both the entry and to the incision, followed by a dressing that would need changing in a few hours. "This is going to scar, and you have to get it checked out soon."

"I have to find Kelly first."

Mac reached into the plastic sack and pulled out a dark blue T-shirt. "This is a size medium. It's all they had. I hope it fits. And I got you a sandwich and some water."

Now my eyes flooded. "Thank you."

Woozy, I went into the bathroom and cleaned up, washing the mud off my shorts as best as possible. I didn't look at my reflection. When I returned, Mac sat in a folding chair. His skin looked gray, and his fingers shook.

"Are you all right?"

"I'll be fine." He popped a pill into his mouth and dry swallowed. "Sit down and eat."

The vending machine turkey and cheese sandwich tasted like heaven.

Mac watched me eat. I could see the wheels turning. I didn't want to further upset him, but I couldn't go to the police. He had to understand that. Allowing the police in would open Pandora's box for both Kelly and me. She would be implicated in my crimes, and Kelly wouldn't make it in prison. She would take her own life before she served a day.

"You know I think you should tell the police," he finally said. "Explain the situation and ask for their cooperation. But I also know you're not going to do that. This is your penance. Always has been."

I wasn't sure I'd heard him correctly. I finished the sandwich and then the water. "I don't understand. What penance? I'm trying to find my friend."

Mac's indulging smile reminded me of the way he dealt with my mother. "Did you ever wonder why you got so attached to Kelly?"

"Have you forgotten how I found her in that basement?"

"Of course not," he said. "I still can't imagine how awful it must have been. But do all social workers form these kinds of bonds with kids they've helped?"

My jaw tightened. "This is different. Most social workers don't encounter a case like that. Thank God."

"It is different, but you've never been able to accept the real reason why," he said. "Even now, you've taken the weight of saving her life onto your shoulders, and you're letting that cancel out your better judgment. Common sense, even."

I didn't have time to decipher whatever message he wanted to impart. "Can you please just lay it out in black and white?"

Mac leaned forward, resting his calloused fingers on my knee. "Honey, this all goes back to your sister. You couldn't save her, but you saved Kelly. Now she's in danger, and you're going to get yourself killed trying to fix what you see as some kind of personal error. Your penance is that you've convinced yourself your own life isn't worth much because you didn't save Lily."

My spinning head had little to do with blood loss. I didn't want to hear any of that, regardless of how right he might be. I didn't have time or strength for introspection. If I allowed myself to stop and think about everything Mac had said—and all the things he hadn't—I'd never get out of the chair.

His single nod told me he understood all the turmoil inside me better than I did. "So you're going to do what you believe is right, and I can't stop you. But is there anyone who could help you? Someone you can trust to watch your back? I'd do it if I could, but I'm not as tough as I used to be. I'd only slow you down."

I tried to ignore the mounting pressure in my skull. If those emotions unleashed, I'd never rein them in. This man had been the parent I'd needed, and he'd do anything for me. I'd never fully appreciated that until tonight.

"Because that's the condition," he finally said. "It goes against everything I know, but I have faith in you. The things you've done—taking down this ring of filthy child molesters—that means something. It matters to a hell of a lot of people, good and bad. I also know you've got a life no one knows about it. There's darkness in you, Lucy. I saw it as soon as we met. I used to worry it would get you into big trouble. And I still do. I've just accepted there's nothing I can do to change things." He smiled wryly. "So I know you can take care of yourself, but I can't let you walk out that door alone. As a father, I need to know you've got help."

I couldn't speak. The emotion closed up my throat and made me feel as if I'd been sucked dry. Mac waited, his patience and understanding nearly overwhelming. Finally, I nodded. Because I loved my stepfather, I agreed to speak to the one person I'd vowed I wouldn't involve.

"There is someone. I'll call him."

EIGHTEEN

Chris's sharp voice went right to the anxiety rumbling in my gut. "Lucy, I'm just getting off shift. Why are you calling at one in the morning?"

Is that what time it was? That meant Kelly had less than twenty-four hours.

I looked at Mac sitting next to me, his hands in his lap and looking frailer than he deserved. How much stress had I brought to him tonight?

"I need your help. Can you meet me in southwest Philadelphia?"

After I took some ibuprofen for the pain, Mac and I drank instant coffee he'd found in the cabinets while we waited for Chris. I'd blurted everything out about Kelly over the phone, and he was in his car before I could finish the story. I couldn't count the number of hours since I'd slept.

We sat out on the front step, listening to the night sounds. A city like Philadelphia was never truly quiet. Stray cats fighting over the trash in the dumpster down the street, a party going on a few blocks down. Mac watched a cab drive by before turning to me. "How'd you find out about this place?"

"I was on a case," I said. "Tracking down an adulterer so his wife could cash in on her prenup. I saw you come here in the middle of the day. At first I thought you might be having an affair, but I figured out pretty quickly that you just needed an escape from Joan." I couldn't help the bitter smile. I'd decided to spare Mac from knowing what Joan had done with the crime scene photos, but I'd be damned if I forgave her.

"I love her, Lucy," Mac said. "But loving her takes a lot out of me. I just need my own space every now and then."

"I'm glad you have this place." Any compassion I had for my mother had evaporated my last day in Alexandria. "I wish you'd just leave her. Then I wouldn't have to see her again."

"You don't mean that." His sad tone made it clear he knew that I meant every word.

"Of course I do. And it would give her yet another sad story to use, so she'd benefit too."

"I know your mother's—"

I drew the line at listening to him defend her. "She's a cold, manipulative woman who has always put herself first. She doesn't deserve you, Mac."

He sighed, setting his cup down on the step. "She's made mistakes. With you and your sister. She knows that."

"Really? Because that's news to me."

"I think telling you would really force her to face it—to relive everything again. She can't handle it." He actually believed what he was saying. I had an entire lifetime that proved otherwise.

I made a sound of disgust. "God forbid Joan feel uncomfortable in any way."

"All this anger and resentment, it's poison." Mac's tired voice made me feel even more hopeless. What had I done, bringing him into this? How could I be so selfish? "If you can't find a way to get rid of it, you'll never be happy."

I accepted that happiness wasn't in my destiny a long time ago, but Mac didn't need to hear that. I'd caused him enough stress. I squeezed his hand. "I'll try. Promise."

A sleek, black car came around the corner, driving slowly. My lungs suddenly forgot how to work. Why had I made that promise to Mac?

He pointed to the car. "Is that your friend?"

All I could do was nod. My insides churned, my skin hot and cold at the same time. My skull felt heavy, as if it were squishing my brain. I tried to breathe slowly, but my lungs continued to revolt against me, sucking in air as if I'd been underwater for too long.

The Audi parked behind my rental, its gleaming black exterior illuminated by the streetlight. The car looked utterly out of place here, which could have been the perfect metaphor for Chris.

I thought about running into the house.

Chris's shoes appeared first, new red running shoes with a black swoosh symbol. And then he stepped out of the car and looked directly at me. My heart lurched into my throat.

Nothing much had changed. He was still tall, still broad shouldered. His beard had a day's worth of scruff. Despite the distance between us, I felt the piercing warmth of his striking eyes.

Mac stood up first and then helped me to my feet. "Please be careful."

I wrapped my arms around him, thinking once again he was too damned thin. "I promise I will. Thank you for helping me. For everything."

"You know I love you just like you were my own, right?" I'd never seen my stepfather cry or get very worked up about anything. He was always even-keeled and rational—a calming influence on freight train Joan.

"I know," I said. "I love you too."

Mac turned to Chris, who'd been watching nervously. "Take care of her."

Chris smiled now, that grin that always made me feel off-kilter. "I swear to it."

I looked away, focusing on his shiny shoes. "You've got a red spot on your shoelace."

Chris glanced down and scowled. "I knew I shouldn't have worn these to work. Gunshot wound tonight." He shook his head. "But that's not important. Luce, let's go find Kelly."

Old habits are easy to fall back into—especially if someone's life is at stake. I settled into the familiar passenger seat, feeling the leather wrapping around me with the warmth of an old friend's hug.

"I made some calls," Chris said. "To a friend in 14th District—that's Chestnut Hill area. There's been no reports from the Tesla residence. Apparently he didn't feel like calling the authorities. Guess he figured he's on their radar for enough. But does he still have your gun?"

I hadn't even considered the full ramifications of Tesla having my gun. Even though I still believed Tesla's involvement in Kelly's abduction would keep him from talking to the police, the gun could have ruined everything. I needed to get my head in the game before I started missing more important things. "It's still unregistered." I'd felt like a hypocrite buying the gun last year on the black market. But I knew anonymity would come in handy one day. "It can't be traced to me."

"But did he know who you were? He can say you were on his property." As usual, Chris was the stalwart voice of worry.

"And I can also say he shot at me." I couldn't change any of that now. "And that he threatened to rape me. Considering he's already a suspect in the sex trafficking case, I'm taking the chance he won't bring up my name. And no one knows I'm back in town except you and Justin. And Mac. He won't say anything."

"Justin?" Chris glanced at me, the familiar edge in his voice. I had no interest in dealing with his resentment toward his younger half-brother.

"He and Kelly have been seeing each other. He stopped by yesterday as I was leaving. He thinks Kelly had a relapse and checked into a facility."

"He'll tell his brother he saw you," Chris said. "If Todd hears Tesla's accusations—"

"I can't worry about that right now." I double-checked the cellphone application. "Kelly's phone is still pinging at Tesla's place."

"She's not there," Chris said. "He wouldn't have her there."

I agreed. But I also thought Tesla enjoyed the power of tormenting me. I hoped Kelly's phone would have some kind of clue as to where he'd stashed her.

"So tell me exactly what you think is going on," he said. "Because I'm not exactly sure how the murder of your former CPS kid correlates to Kelly being taken. Or how they're both tied to you."

I hadn't told Chris about the message on the mirror at Shannon's crime scene or how her body had been staged. I needed to keep something back, for reasons I couldn't explain. "The man in the video made it sound like both Shannon's murder and Kelly's abduction were the result of something I'd done. The National Park Police and the Philadelphia PD are investigating that angle in Shannon's murder. The assumption had been that someone screwed over by the sex trafficking ring investigation blamed me. Tesla was one of those people, and Kelly had a file on him."

Chris exited onto the freeway. "All right, but you said something about being all wrong."

I yawned widely enough to break my jaw. "Justin told me Kelly had been investigating Tesla because she found out his father was one of the men who raped her. I found out she put a Trojan on my computer and got my login information for NCMEC. She used their system to find the names of all three of the men who regularly assaulted her, along with her stepfather."

"Did any of them know she was investigating them?"

"She was pretending to date Tesla's son for information. She's been on the property, so there's a good chance the father saw her and put it all together."

"And she never told you any of this?"

I closed my eyes. "She was protecting me. She wanted me to have my new start in Alexandria."

"Damn." Chris's hands looked tight around the wheel. "Well, she's obviously learned a lot from you. And she's tough. She'll make it through this."

I said nothing, fighting to keep the panic from taking over. Time moved too quickly.

Chris headed northwest, toward Chestnut Hill. My eyelids drooped, heavy, refusing to stay open. I turned the air conditioning on high.

"When was the last time you slept?"

The answer took some thinking, and I wasn't sure if I'd done the math correctly. "Roughly twenty-four hours."

"You're going to need to rest."

"Not until I find Kelly." I shivered against the blasting cold air.

"What about your shoulder?"

"Mac took care of it."

"You know I have to look at it."

"Later." My eyes wanted to close again.

"Traffic is light," Chris said. "But we're still looking at twenty minutes at least. Give me Tesla's address and take a catnap."

My exhausted body gave me no other option.

I woke up completely confused. My head felt so heavy I wasn't sure I could stand up; my shoulder screamed in pain. Grotesque figures loomed out of the Audi's window, waving in the darkness. Some seemed to reach forward, as if they were determined to yank me out of the car and prevent me from getting to Kelly.

I blinked, my eyes sticky. My vision cleared enough for me to realize we'd parked down the road from Tesla's, and the figures were just trees.

"I let you sleep a little bit. Just an extra fifteen minutes." Chris held up his hand before I could argue. "You needed it. You're no help to Kelly if you can't think straight. But we can't just be sitting in the car in the middle of the night. If we're going to look for the phone, we need to move now."

My legs felt even more wooden than my head. I looked at the application again, wishing it gave a more precise location. I led the way onto the Tesla property. "It's within twenty-five feet of his address. It hasn't moved since it came back on." Which meant it had likely been tossed. A diversion? What if I'd gotten too close at the old apartment building and the phone had been dropped here by one of the men?

"Do you think we should just try calling the phone?" Chris said as he fell into step next to me.

"No way," I said. "Not with that bastard all stirred up. Too risky."

Chris made a low noise in his throat. "That's true and lucky for him. If I get the chance to put my hands around his throat for shooting you, I'll take it."

I dropped low, my knees almost touching the damp grass. "Thanks, but it's not worth it. I need you out of jail."

"If Tesla or his father searched," Chris said as he ducked down and moved quietly forward up the sloping lawn, "and it was out in the open, they'd have confiscated it."

"So it's probably hidden. But not necessarily close to the house."

"Why don't we split up and sweep this side of the property?" He glanced at me, heavy creases between his eyebrows. "If you can make it on your own. I thought you didn't lose much blood?"

"I didn't," I said defensively. "But I'm tired, okay? I'll be fine." I stalked to the east side and started looking for the phone. The case was green, but Tesla might have taken it off. Most of the land leading up to the house was dotted with trees and sculpted gardens, and every single one looked the same in the dark. I checked the lilies first, crawling around on my hands and knees. Nothing but dewy grass and flowers that smelled so sweet I wanted to choke.

Keeping low, my knees and palms damp, I found my way back to the Atlas cedar tree. Surely the phone wasn't here. I'd hidden behind the thing twice and hadn't spotted it. I moved the prickly branches away from the ground, searching for the black phone that would no doubt blend into everything.

The blinking blue message light caught my eye.

I was right next to it earlier.

My fingernails dragged in the dirt as I reached for the phone and pulled it out. Her password was easy: her birthday.

She had several text messages from Justin, begging her to call him. I skimmed those and went on to the text from a blocked number. The message consisted of an image. My finger shook as I clicked on the download button and waited.

When it finally loaded, my legs gave out and I landed on my ass in the dew-covered lawn. And then I started dry-heaving.

Chris must have heard me because he was suddenly by my side, helping me to my feet.

I handed him the phone without a word.

"Coldhearted bastard." Chris stared at the image. "And ballsy. He's showing you his face. Maybe we can get into one of Kelly's databases and get a name."

I took long, cleansing breaths. I would not throw up. Or panic. Or collapse into some kind of sniveling heap. Not when this stupid pig had just made such a mistake. He couldn't possibly have known the kind of person he'd chosen to torment.

"I don't need any help from a database." I stood straight, a familiar cold calm taking over. "That's Jared Cook, Kelly's stepfather. He's supposed to be in prison."

Chris looked again at the image, his nose curled as if he could barely stand it. I snatched the phone from him. I wouldn't look away this time.

Kelly was in a small, dark room, naked and chained to a twin bed. Leaning next to her and obviously taking the picture was Cook. One of his eyes sagged, and a dark red scar ran down his cheek and into his neck. Child molesters never fared well in prison.

"Did you know he was paroled?"

I kept looking at the picture. The smile on Cook's face made me want to beat someone. I would kill him slowly.

"No, but I bet Kelly did." I put the phone into my pocket. "Which means Justin probably did too. And he didn't tell me."

I started back down the hill, no longer tired. Chris hurried after me, nervously glancing behind him. "I notice we aren't hiding that we're trespassing now. What are you planning?"

"I need to get online."

NINETEEN

It was too early for the sunrise, but the fat, dark rain clouds stretching over the entire northeastern side of the city indicated we were in for another nasty day. Chris turned on the Audi's interior light as he drove toward Center City while I fumbled for my laptop.

Kelly had taught me how to gain Internet access using the Bluetooth on my phone. After a few miscues, I managed to get a strong enough signal to log in to the Megan's Law website. Having the offender's first and last name made the search much easier, as long as Jared Cook wasn't a transient offender. Being on parole meant he could be in a halfway house or a shelter or a friend's, or even worse, he could have gotten lucky and been assigned an overworked parole officer who hadn't made sure Jared registered.

I drummed my foot on the floor mats as I waited for the page results to load. "We don't have time to stop."

Chris turned too sharply onto his street in Center City. "You can't risk not getting an antibiotic. You're no use to Kelly if you spike a fever." He eased into the parking garage and into his rented spot. I hated to think how much it cost him.

"How do you have an antibiotic?" I asked. "Paramedics don't carry that sort of thing, do they?"

He looked sheepish. "I had a sinus infection last month and stopped taking it when I felt better. I've got a few pills left. That doesn't mean you get to skip going to the doctor. It just buys you some time."

"Whatever." I leaned back in the seat. "Just hurry."

Results began popping up, separated by last name. There were several Cooks registered in the state, but only one Jared who was the right age. Because the state believes even sexual predators are entitled to the right to privacy, the Megan's Law site only provided address information as well as identifying marks. Jared Cook had several identifying scars, including one circling the back of his skull that he'd probably earned during a prison beating.

The system had serious problems, but none of this added up. As a Tier 3 violent sex offender, Jared Cook should have never been paroled.

Chris returned. He fell into the driver's seat and tossed a medicine bottle into my lap. "Amoxicillin. Take three today and two tomorrow. Then you're going to the doctor. You find him?"

"He lives in a townhouse on South Reese Street."

"That's South Philly," Chris said. "Not the best area, but not the worst."

I was already one step ahead of him, logging into the NCMEC site and digging for public records. "It's owned by a Charles Cook, purchased five years ago. So he's living with a family member who probably believes he's done his time and can still be saved."

"Then unless this Charles is involved, we probably aren't going to find Kelly at the house."

I didn't want to admit he was right, but we didn't have any other option at this point. My head felt heavy as Chris made his way to the southern end of town. My shoulder felt as if a hundred needles had been jammed into it. Adrenaline triumphed over exhaustion. Kelly might be at Cook's house. I could save her and get rid of Jared Cook. Or I could walk into a trap.

The Cooks' two-story, faded brick townhouse appeared to be well taken care of. The neighborhood was typical Philly working class, with postcard-sized yards maintained and dotted with colorful annuals. The townhouse resembled most of the others on the street, with only two exceptions: a wheelchair ramp and the uncollected garbage can waiting at the curb. Everyone else had already claimed their garbage cans.

Sweat broke out across the back of my neck. Trying not to tweak my burning shoulder, I clumsily pulled my hair up and started to open the door.

"Wait." Chris's voice ghosted into my ear, making me jump. "You need to stay behind the tinted windows and let me go first. If her stepfather sees you, he's going to run."

I hated to admit he was right. "You need to take something for protection. And exactly what are you going to say?"

"I've got my SIG Sauer. And I'm his new parole officer checking in. I'll need to sweep the house and make sure he's keeping his nose clean."

"What if he argues with you? He's not just going to let you inside."

"He's a convicted sex offender. He has no right to privacy," Chris said. "I can go in without a warrant."

"Parole officers can't do that unless they're also a cop. So unless you're going to pull a fake badge out of your ass, you can't just go inside and snoop."

"Then I'll improvise," Chris said. "I'll text when it's safe for you to come inside."

My insides fluttered. It was supposed to be me going up to

that door, not Chris. Then again, I doubted I would be able to stop myself from going for Jared Cook's throat. But Chris had a point. Cook would be watching for me. But wasn't my arrival part of his grand plan?

"Stay here." He stepped out of the car and winced. "Ouch."

"What's wrong?"

He made a face. "My foot. It's healed but sometimes I still feel the pain if I step just right."

His toe. I'd completely forgotten his mother had chopped it off in her efforts to escape last winter. I couldn't think of anything to say.

"It's all right." Chris knew exactly what I was thinking. "You've got a lot on your mind right now. And it's only a toe."

"I'm sorry." I glanced toward the house, dread pooling in my chest. "Be careful."

I watched him saunter unevenly up the walk, his head tucked down against the rain and his blue shirt stretched tightly over his broad shoulders.

He'd jammed the SIG into the back of his jeans. He didn't look like he was getting ready to face a sexual predator and probable kidnapper. He could have been going up to a friend's house. Thinking of how jittery he'd been when we broke into Brian Harrison's house last year, I wanted to take credit for his confidence. But that would have been too presumptuous. Chris's changes resulted from something far more compelling than me.

He knocked on the door; my stomach knotted.

Although the rain had slowed to a light mist, I still struggled to see through the drops on the window.

What if Cook attacked Chris? What if he got shot before he had the chance to defend himself? Was he really prepared for this?

I can't let him take the risk. This is my problem.

My hand fisted against the handle, but something held me back.

No one answered the door. Chris kept knocking, but the house remained quiet. He glanced back at the car, holding his hand out flat as a reminder for me to stay inside. I gritted my teeth as he hopped down off the short step and made his way to the front window and peered inside. He shrugged his shoulders and moved around toward the side of the house.

Panic mounted in my throat. He shouldn't lose sight of me. Hadn't he learned anything from being on the run with Mother Mary? I started to open the door and then slammed it shut. If Cook was watching, he probably had eyes on the Audi. My appearance could mean trouble for Chris.

I grabbed my phone and called his cell.

"Just be patient."

"I can't see you," I said. "You don't know who is inside that house. Cook is ruthless, and prison's only honed those skills. He could be leading you into a trap."

"I'm just going to knock on the back door. If there's no answer, then I'll come back to the car."

"Keep me on the line."

"You just can't give up the control, can you?"

"This has nothing to do with control. I actually give a damn if something happens to you."

"A conscience is a terrible thing." His rapping on the back door accompanied his words.

"I'm not getting into a philosophical conversation with you."

"Of course not," he said. "There'll be time for that later."

"Is anyone answering?"

"No. But the back door is unlocked."

I clenched the door handle, desperate to sprint to the house. "If you're going in, you need to take the gun out and have the safety off. Cook could be trying to lure you inside. He's obviously not working alone."

"But how would he know I'm a threat?"

"If they can find out about Shannon, they might know about you." The thought brought a fresh round of fear. I should have never asked for Chris's help. "Just come back here and let me do it."

"Too late." Chris's gagging suddenly made my stomach roll. "Oh hell. I don't think you need to worry about a trap."

TWENTY

I shoved my face into the crook of my elbow and tried not to dry heave. Crowbar from the Audi's trunk in hand, I stood shoulder to shoulder with Chris in the townhouse's kitchen and stared at the two dead men. One of them had died in his wheelchair, his reedy body helpless to the attack on the back of his skull. It looked as if a single blow to the head with an extremely blunt object had done the job. His chin rested on his chest, his neck having snapped forward with the blow. Dried blood stained his shirt and the chrome handles of the wheelchair.

The other man lay face down on the floor, his head bashed in so badly it resembled a busted watermelon. More congealed blood pooled around him. I had little hope of recognizing his face, but that didn't concern me, because Jared Cook was the man in the wheelchair.

Thank God for the air conditioning. It hadn't slowed decay, but it saved us from humidity making the horrific odor even worse. I searched for something to protect my hand. The kitchen was suspiciously clean. No blood spatter on the white, laminate countertop or aging oak cabinets. No drying dishes in the sink and no clutter on the counter. I used the hem of my shirt to open the drawers until I found a couple of dishtowels. I wrapped them around my hands, gently grasped both sides of his jaw, and then carefully tried to lift Jared Cook's head.

I might as well have tried to lift a centuries-old boulder. His neck muscles had completely stiffened into rigor mortis, and it would take more strength than I possessed—and probably more fortitude—to move his head.

Nausea swarming my stomach, I knelt down and looked up into his face.

Jared Cook's smile looked exactly as it had in the picture on Kelly's phone. Now that I saw him in person, I noticed the way his entire left eye socket seemed to sag, as if the bone structure had been affected. I thought about checking his face to see if I could tell if the break had happened during the attack, but his muscles were so far into rigor I wouldn't be able to.

"Is he still warm?" Chris asked.

"Cold."

"But he's still in rigor," Chris said. "That starts two to four hours after death, and the body starts to cool. I'd estimate he's in the middle of it, but I can't tell much more without taking a body temperature. The bugs haven't started yet—I suppose because the air conditioning's on. Closed windows have slowed them down. Then again, the room temperature affects everything too. But I'd bet he hasn't been dead more than ten to twelve hours. The bugs would have found him."

I stood up. "How do you know all that?"

He shrugged. "I've been reading up on pathology. Thinking about going back to school."

Why he'd want to spend his days in a morgue was beyond me, but whatever. Chris's intelligence meant he became easily bored, so he probably needed a new challenge.

"All right. So I think it's safe to say Jared Cook didn't take Kelly."

Chris nudged the wheelchair with his toe. "Yeah, but he

was in the picture. So one of the other guys hires someone, and Jared is just having fun?"

Something didn't feel right. I couldn't stop comparing the way Jared smiled for the picture and the way he looked now. They were too similar. Plus the way his face was drooping, and the wheelchair...

"We should still check the place," Chris said. "See if there's any sign Kelly was here."

Too old to be the popular open-concept style, the town-house had a small hallway leading to the dining room, which had been turned into a bedroom, with an adjustable hospital bed butting up against the wall adjoining the kitchen. I opened the small dresser sitting beneath the dining room window. Its gleaming, black pressed wood had been recently dusted.

"Adult diapers and cleansing wipes." Worry latched on like a malignant growth. How much time had I wasted chasing the wrong people?

"Christ," Chris said. "What happened to this guy?"

"I'm willing to bet in happened it prison." And it might have something to do with his parole. His wouldn't be the first case of a violent offender being paroled because he'd been injured so badly he couldn't physically repeat his crime. Over-crowded prison hospitals were happy to outsource if a family member was willing to offer care. And all on the taxpayer's dime.

We found no sign of Kelly in the small living room or upstairs. Both bedrooms were sparse, and only one appeared to have been used.

"No basement," Chris said.

I'd returned to the makeshift bedroom, drawn to Jared's hospital bed. Probably provided by the state, it was the kind designed to blend into the home. The side rails were a clean beige, and the espresso-colored frame fit nicely into any furni-ture set.

But the headboard was missing.

Making sure the towels still covered my hands, I examined the bed more closely. In addition to the remote control on the nightstand, it had buttons on the side. I pressed one, and the head of the bed gradually began to move up.

"Where's the headboard?" I asked.

"Maybe it doesn't have one," Chris said. "If the patient had seizures, the headboard could be a hazard."

I ignored him and looked at the carpet. It was still new enough to absorb an object's weight, meaning that moving furniture around left indents in the carpet.

"The bed wasn't here before."

"What?"

I pointed to the long, parallel lines running next to the bed. "Look at the bed frame—its feet are square. But these marks are long lines. This is where the dresser was."

"So? Whoever took care of him moved the bed, probably for a better view of the window."

I looked at the window. Nothing special, a standard vinyl window with dirt inside its frame. No curtains on the window, but a black, roller-style blind drawn all the way up. I grabbed the dresser and started pulling it away from the window.

"Let me do that." Chris took the opposite end of the dresser and lifted it away from the wall.

Two square indents rested beneath the window. The other two marks were probably beneath the bed's current position.

A sound made me turn. Chris had started playing with the remote, and the headboard of the bed suddenly rose up. "That's what I wondered," he said. "A lot of these beds have this option. But this is a pretty nice one. I wonder if the Cook family sued the prison or something. The state usually only provides bare bones for injured felons."

I pulled Kelly's phone out of my pocket and brought up the picture of her trapped. She lay in a bed with white sheets and a black headboard. I'd originally thought it was some kind of wall but this time I saw the sliver of space on the left side of the headboard. Whoever had taken the picture hadn't paid close enough attention. He hadn't zoomed in quite enough to crop out the beige wall. Just like the beige walls of the dining room.

But what about the black above her? I'd assumed it all meant she was in a basement or dark place but now...

I reached up and pulled down the black blind.

"Holy hell." Chris's voice ripped through my pounding head.

My entire body seemed to bottom out, and I suddenly felt as though I were floating along in some lucid nightmare.

Wake up, wake up!

But I couldn't.

Written in shiny, thick red marker was another message. No name attached, but clearly meant for me.

You're all wrong.

Say hi to Mac.

TWENTY-ONE

"I still think this is a bad idea." Chris gripped the wheel tightly as he drove. "Justin's not going to be able to tell you a damned thing to help find Kelly."

"I have to try." But Chris was wrong. Justin could tell me exactly what I needed to know, even if he wasn't aware of it. I just had to ask the right questions. And now Mac's life might be at stake. My options were eviscerated. "You didn't leave any fingerprints, right?"

Chris had used the Cooks' home phone when he made the anonymous call about finding the bodies. "Trust me. It's clean."

Part of me had wanted to leave Jared Cook to rot, but his caretaker hadn't done anything to deserve such a brutal death. He should at least be respected in death.

The fine hair on the back of my neck rose as we neared Justin's apartment. After Kailey Richardson's safe return, Justin had moved out of Poplar and moved two streets down from Todd's house.

The threat about Mac and the deliberate misleading—Kelly's abductor never intended for me to find her. He just wanted to screw with my head, and it worked. I should have called Todd already.

"What are you thinking?" Chris's voice bordered on pouting. It wouldn't be easy for him, but we had bigger things to worry about.

"How I'm going to get Justin to tell me everything." My feelings about Todd were my own.

"About that—"

"I think you should stay in the car." Problem easily solved. "Justin's plenty pissed off at you for shutting him out, and we don't have time for family drama. I've got a better chance of getting him to talk on my own."

"Fine with me." Chris pulled into the apartment complex and found a spot in front of Justin's building. I started to open the door, but he grabbed my arm. "Are you sure we're doing the right thing?"

"I'm not going to tell him anything. I just have questions about Jared's parole."

"I know you're not, and that's what's worrying me. I think you're in over your head." He released my arm, his hands falling limply into his lap. "Look, I know I gave you a hard time for letting my mother live."

"Chris, we don't have time for this conversation—"

He held up a hand. "Just hear me out. This comes back to Kelly. And you. Think about what happened last winter. About all of it. How badly did you want to come find me on your own? Wasn't there some part of you that wanted to ditch the police and the FBI and go full vigilante?"

"Most of me, until I found out you'd lied."

"Not a lie," Chris said. "Everything I told you was true. I just left out the part about Camp Hopeful."

"Whatever. I don't have time for this."

"My point is that you let the authorities do their thing because they were better equipped to find me. Because you needed their help. And let's be honest. Without their help, Mary and I would still be on the run."

"What's your point?"

"The point is you need the police on this," Chris said. "I'm afraid it's bigger than you realize, and you don't have enough time. First Tesla, and now Cook. You're running around in circles, and time is slipping away."

"You've changed your tune," I snapped. "Just a few months ago, you were still angry at me for letting Mary live. And now you're telling me to risk Kelly's life?"

"The situation is different now. And I was wrong." He looked embarrassed. "You have to understand how screwed up in the head I was. All that time with her, it messed me up. But I've been going to therapy, and things are better."

"Good for you. And you're right, it is different. I can't take the risk of Kelly's kidnapper finding out I've involved the police."

"You've got options," he said. "You don't think Todd Beckett would help, especially since his precious little brother is dating her?"

I wouldn't take the bait in Chris's tone. As much as I wanted Todd to be here, if only to have the calming influence of his presence, I'd already made up my mind. It was too late to go back. "I called you because I thought you'd be on my side."

"I am," he said. "Always. Even if you don't realize what's best for you."

"Don't worry about me," I said. "As long as Kelly comes home alive, no one else matters."

I had other reasons for not wanting Chris to come with me. Specifically, I didn't want him to know my plans after this. He wasn't wrong about my being in over my head. I was in way too deep, and I might have cost Kelly her life. Continuing to risk

Chris's was too selfish. And once I made the call, I'd have to bare everything. I didn't want Chris anywhere near that for fear he'd implicate himself.

Justin opened the door with bleary, nervous eyes. The dark shadows beneath them made it clear he hadn't slept much. I probably didn't look much better, especially since I was hiding a bullet wound under my shirtsleeve and I still had dried mud on my shorts. He made a lame attempt to block me from entering. "What are you doing here?"

I shoved my way past him. "I need information from you. No more bullshitting me. Do you understand?"

He glared at me, looking far from threatening with his too-long dark hair sticking up everywhere. He must have sensed this because he tried to stand up straighter, drawing his shoulders back to make his lanky chest seem wider. "You going to threaten to shoot me again?"

"I didn't exactly threaten to shoot you. I let you know I had a gun. But don't worry. It's in the car."

Justin shut the door, still trying to look tough. The flash of anger in his eyes reminded me of his mother. "Why don't you talk to Todd? Or are you going to keep blowing him off?"

"I don't have time to talk to Todd right now. I need information from you."

"Not until I get to talk to Kelly."

I gritted my teeth. "You can't. I told you the facility has a no contact rule."

"I don't believe that. Give me the name of the facility."

I wanted to slap him. "You're not in the position to give me orders. I promised Kelly I wouldn't give out the information, and I'm not breaking that."

"Yeah, well, I told you stuff I wasn't supposed to, either. But I trusted you. Maybe you should think about returning the favor."

His attempt at a guilt trip failed. I'd gone past the point of giving a damn about anyone else. "It's not a matter of trust. This is about finding a killer. And I don't think you told me everything Kelly shared with you." She had less than a day left now.

"Why does it matter? Do you think she's in danger?" His eyes searched mine, their sincerity almost cracking my resolve.

"Not while she's safe in the hospital, but when she's released? Who knows? That's why I want to find out who did this."

"I told you everything," Justin said.

"What about Kelly's stepfather?"

He paled and then swallowed hard. I shook my head. "You didn't think the fact that he was paroled was important?"

Justin flinched. He crossed his arms over his chest. "Kelly didn't know that."

"Stop lying to me!" I didn't care how loud my voice got. "She's his victim—she's notified of his parole by law. She would have also been given the chance to speak at the hearing. Did she omit that from me too?"

Justin's shoulder's fell. "The hearing was right after you left for Alexandria. I didn't know her then. She didn't go. She spoke to the parole board over the phone, and by then it was all just a formality. Once she understood the situation, I think she made peace with it."

I thought of Cook's smile in the cell picture and knew I'd been right. "What was the situation?"

"He was severely beaten in prison about a year ago. Multiple head injuries that left him mentally disabled. Couldn't say more than a few words, and it took him weeks to recognize faces. Couldn't feed himself, couldn't go to the bathroom. He didn't get better, and the prison hospital wanted him moved to a state ward. I guess his cousin volunteered to take care of him with state aid. He didn't want him wasting away in a home, even if the guy was a child molester."

"And there was no chance he'd recover?"

"'Severely mentally disabled' were the words Kelly used. The guy didn't even know his own name. So she didn't fight it. I kind of thought it was karma." Justin shrugged.

I couldn't muster any remorse for Jared Cook. Every so often, karma was a beautiful bitch. "What about his cousin, Charles Cook? The state would have done a full background check on him. And so would Kelly. What did she find out?"

Justin didn't seem surprised I knew the name. "He was a CNA at a nursing home for a long time. No record, good job history, religious. He spoke at Jared's original sentencing and apologized for not being as much of a part of his cousin's life as he should have been. He claimed if he'd been around, he might have known what was going on."

That's why the name had sounded familiar. Charles had cried when he spoke, his sincerity obvious. So he'd probably taken in Jared as a way to alleviate the guilt he'd taken on.

Charles had zero reason for attacking Kelly.

Jared couldn't have.

But Kelly had been there. Her kidnapper had taken a picture with Jared to mislead me. And then he'd killed both Jared and Charles.

And Kelly? Had he killed her and dumped her somewhere for me to find? My fear threatened to devour me, but I dredged up the next question.

"How long has he been out?"

"Just a couple of months," Justin said. "I didn't meet her until after he'd been released, and like I said, she seemed all right. The whole thing with Tesla's picture showing up in the investigation is what she focused on." Justin narrowed his eyes and stepped closer. "But I don't understand why any of this matters. I get that you're trying to figure out who killed Shannon, but I don't see how it's related to Kelly's investigation. You said Shannon was killed as some kind of revenge against you."

"And Tesla made it look like his son was the one trying to

buy kids from Jake Meyer—or so Kelly believed. Either way, it's my involvement that brings his possible involvement to light." Except Tesla had nothing to do with what had happened to Kelly. This was someone else altogether, someone who wanted to strike out at me for whatever I'd done to him.

"That doesn't mean Tesla's the one who killed Shannon or that he had her killed." Justin looked sheepish. "You have a lot of enemies."

More than you know, and more than I want to admit. But I have no choice now. Neither does Kelly.

"Thanks for the reminder. Is there anything else you haven't told me?" I searched his eyes, feeling a wave of guilt. But if he knew the truth, he'd want to help. And I'd put someone else at risk. If I hadn't already done that by coming here.

"No," Justin said. "If I think of anything else, I'll call you."

"Thank you." I turned to go, but Justin cleared his throat. "What?"

"You know I really care about Kelly. I never meant for anything like this to happen."

The small piece of humanity I hadn't permanently scrubbed away longed to hug him and tell him it would all be fine. Instead, I jerked around and headed for the door. "I know you didn't."

TWENTY-TWO

My feet dragged on the gray carpet as I made my way toward the building exit. Chris waited outside, and I had to make my decision before I went back to the car. If he sensed weakness, he'd never leave me alone. And then he'd keep talking until I broke, and he'd never let me make the call.

I knew the ramifications. But my own life didn't matter. I'd been screwing it up for so long I didn't deserve more chances.

A few feet from the car, I stopped cold.

Your penance is that you've convinced yourself your own life isn't worth much because you didn't save Lily.

Mac was right.

Kelly had replaced my sister. All the love I would have showered on Lily had been given to the abused girl from the rotten basement. All of my decisions were emotionally driven because I couldn't fathom the idea of failing both of them, especially when I seemingly had all of the pieces to find Kelly. I just couldn't figure out how to put them together.

I wasn't compartmentalizing a damned thing. Kelly and Lily and my anger and need for revenge were all twisted together in big knot of misery. If I couldn't separate one situation from the other, how could I possibly know what to do about Kelly now?

God, Mac. If this bastard went after him... After all this running in circles trying to convince myself I could handle anything, I had to throw away whatever hope I had left of forging a future. I had to give Kelly a chance.

Resigned, I reached for my phone. My stomach bottomed out. I'd left the phone in the car. I couldn't call until I got rid of Chris.

He got out of the Audi, shading his eyes. "What's wrong?"

"I don't know what I'm doing."

"We never do," he said. "But we'll make it up as we go along."

"That's just the thing. I can't involve you anymore. Or Mac. Or Justin. I can't pick one life over the other, and I'm clearly not capable of finding Kelly."

He leaned against the car. "So you're calling the police?"

"I am. Todd, specifically. I just hope he can fix this before it's too late."

Chris opened the door and grabbed the phone I'd left lying in the console. "For what it's worth, I think you're doing the right thing." His lack of argument surprised me. No doubt it was coming.

"Thanks." I took the phone and raced through the contacts, hoping Chris remained near the car so he couldn't read the screen. Todd would be hurt that I didn't call him, but I needed someone who could move quickly. And I wasn't ready to face Todd just yet. As soon as the line began to ring, I stepped back, pretending to walk and think. I just didn't want him to be able to hear the person answering.

"Agent André Lennox."

Something like hope flashed through me. "Hi, it's Lucy. I should have called you earlier, but I thought I could handle this on my own."

"What's going on?"

Like a pent-up kid with a confession, the truth burst out. "I came back to Philadelphia to see Kelly. She's been kidnapped, and the person left a message for me. I was supposed to find her on my own, with no help from police. He said I had forty-eight hours before he killed her. And I tried to follow the clues, but I screwed up and am now down to less than twenty hours. I need your help now, and I need it in secret."

Lennox blew out a hard breath. "I'm in DC, but I can get a jet chartered within the hour."

"Thank you so much."

"Who else knows?"

"Chris, but no one else so far."

"Listen to me," Lennox said. "You don't want him involved. Or anyone else. This needs to stay between us. Is he with you?"

I glanced at Chris still leaning against the Audi and checking his phone messages.

"Yes, but I've already told him I don't want to put him at risk. And I'm afraid for my stepfather, Mac. A message was left for me. There's been a threat against him."

"Get out of earshot."

I obeyed, trying to nonchalantly walk away and pace in a different spot. "I don't understand."

"Just listen to me. There's a lot you don't know, and you're right on not involving anyone else. It's too dangerous. Give me your stepfather's address, and I'll send an agent over there."

I rattled off Mac and Joan's address. My mother was going to love this.

"I'll assign an agent to watch him until we figure this out," Lennox said. "Now I want you to go back to Kelly's apartment —alone—and stay there. Lock the doors. Trust me. He's not going to kill her."

"How can you know that?"

"Because you're the one he wants. You have been from the start, and you're playing right into his hands."

I sat back in the Audi and tried to think of the best way to get Chris to step back.

"What did Todd say?" His probing eyes made me feel certain he knew I was about to lie to his face.

"He reamed me out for not telling him. After Tesla's call, he'd already suspected something was going on."

"He understands he's got to be quiet about this, right? He can't just show up at Kelly's apartment with badge blazing."

"I made that clear. He's pissed about it, but he understands. He's going to meet me there with a CSI in an hour, hopefully as undercover officers." That was a good one.

Chris started the car, his head bobbing up and down. "Good. I know it's scary to give over control to someone else, but this guy is different than anyone else you've dealt with. We don't know what his full deal is, but he's obviously in the business of mind-fucking you, not to mention out for revenge. The fact that he's been watching Kelly and knows so much about your life scares the hell out of me."

"Me too." I could have said more, but anything else would pique Chris's interest and end up doing the exact opposite of what I wanted. "Look, I shouldn't have asked for your help, but I really appreciate what you've done. I think it's time for you to step back."

"And just leave you alone?"

"He's going to find out I called the police," I said. "And he's going to flip. He's already made it clear Mac's a target. I'm sure you will be too. And I can't have any more on my conscience. It's overloaded."

He sighed, staring ahead at the rain drizzling down the

windshield. "It goes against my nature to just walk away from a friend when she's in danger."

"I know. But I won't be alone. Todd will take care of that."

He grimaced. "Bet that makes you happy."

"I don't even know what to say to that," I said. "All I can think about right now is Kelly and Mac. Todd's going to send an officer over there, but still."

"Todd will do anything for you." Sadness crept into his voice. "You realize that, right? You could give him the name of every person you've killed, and he wouldn't turn you in. He's too far gone."

Too bad I didn't plan on telling Todd. But I liked Chris's words.

"And that makes you happy." He let the engine idle, making no attempt to drive out of the parking lot.

"Why does it matter to you?" I said. It shouldn't matter to me, but no matter how hard I tried to shake it, the idea of Todd's loyalty gave me a spark of hope. Maybe I could salvage the rest of my life.

He turned those eyes on me again. "Are you kidding? All this time now? You can't be that clueless. Everything I've risked for you, everything I've worked on. Do you think that's just because I wanted to be buddies?"

An embarrassed sort of heat spread down my neck and over my face. "You and I, we could never make it. Not like that. There's too much darkness between us."

"And you and Todd are a perfect match?"

"I didn't say that."

"You didn't have to." He finally merged into traffic, jerking the wheel. "You know, when I first talked to you that night at Chetter's, I had this stupid plan that we would eventually get together and become unstoppable. I knew it would take time, but you'd see it too. And for a while, I thought you did. But then you just changed."

My mouth refused to work. I'd always been attracted to Chris, but I'd never been certain about how he felt about me. And now that he had laid it all out, I felt as though I'd been splashed with freezing, muddy water. "I'm sorry."

"It is what it is," he said. "I just have to accept it and move on."

"Do you really mean that? Because Todd will go ballistic if you're at Kelly's apartment when he shows up." More like Lennox would find a way to arrest us both.

Chris traced the fine leather on the Audi's steering wheel. "Do I have a choice? I'm not going to beg to be included in your life. You called me out of necessity. I get it."

A slap in the face would have stung less than the hurt in his voice. "It's not just that. Of course I feel a bond with you. We've experienced things together other people could never understand. But that's also why we can't be together."

His smirked. "We bring out the worst in each other."

"We'd end up getting killed. Or in jail." I didn't want Chris to pay for my bad deeds.

"I don't agree, but I'm too tired to fight with you anymore. Still, I have one condition."

My nerves wanted to implode. "What is it?"

"I'm going to take you into the ER and have someone look at that wound. I've got connections, so it'll be quick, I promise. They'll get you on the right antibiotic."

"And if I say no?"

"Then I'll be ready for Todd."

TWENTY-THREE

Chris kept his word, getting me in and out of the ER in less than two hours, bringing Kelly's time down to eighteen hours. The wasted time burned like a picked scab, but I needed Agent Lennox. I'd used up every other option. We picked up the Prius at Mac's secret house, which now sat empty. Mac had probably slunk home to Joan and had to spend the whole day making up for his absence during the night.

I braced for another argument, but Chris stood by while I got into the Prius and left for Kelly's.

Her apartment felt cold and foreign, as if whatever life Kelly breathed into it had been extinguished. With Lennox's impending arrival, I realized the apartment would be investigated as a crime scene. I'd already contaminated it, but I felt like I needed to be inside a bubble.

Without thinking, I sat down on my usual barstool and dropped my head into my hands. I'd thoroughly mucked this up. Every ounce of my being still screamed for Kelly's safety—to the point my muscles still twitched with the urge to act—but I'd fallen headfirst into the trap her kidnapper had set for me.

He'd known about Kelly's work for me—at least to some

extent. Whether he found out by spying or forcing her to tell, I didn't know. But he'd counted on my searching out the laptop and being able to access her information. He'd deliberately misled me because he'd known exactly what I would do with the information. Had he killed Shannon for fun, or was she simply a pawn in his larger plan?

Because that's exactly what he'd executed: a master plan that had likely been weeks if not months in the making. Which meant he not only knew my habits and routines and the few people I cared about, but he also knew exactly what motivated me.

I suddenly saw him in my mind's eye, as if he were some kind of disfigured cast-off of my own making, like a twin that had never fully developed and instead became consumed by me. Somehow he'd managed to escape and grow until he was big and strong enough to destroy my life.

My entire body quaked. Christ, I needed some real sleep.

But sleep meant bad dreams, and Lennox would be here soon.

Numb and yet feeling the ache of every move, I eased off the stool and set about making coffee. Instead of waking me up, the rich scent only made my eyes water with anger.

I'd done everything possible to keep my imagination from running wild about Kelly. I'd willed the image of the cell phone picture out of my head. But now I summoned it, remembering the terror in her eyes, the way the muscles in her arms strained, and how she tried to pull her body away from Jared Cook's.

How had the kidnapper managed it? Had he propped Jared up next to Kelly? Or forced the cousin to do so before he killed them both?

I guess it had been the latter.

Had Kelly cried at the sight of Jared? Did she feel a disgustingly pleasant feeling of karma when she saw how destroyed he was? That he couldn't even go to the bathroom by himself or speak his own name? I would have smiled at the sight, reveled in it. But Kelly probably felt pity.

Because that's the kind of person she was. She somehow found the decency in people no matter their bad choices.

If Lennox managed to save her, I hoped she'd be able to visit me in prison.

The coffee had steamed to the top of the pot.

My rubbery arms moved to the cabinet. I automatically reached for my favorite coffee cup: the one with the rainbows and the inscription "Go to hell."

Something jingled inside.

I turned the cup upside down and a shining silver dollar fell out, hitting the counter with a muted clang.

We left you a clue, though, didn't we, Kelly?

I reached for the cup, ready to slam it to the floor. Rationality stopped me just in time. Lennox would want to test for fingerprints. This had been the clue.

And the bastard had known all along I wouldn't find it until it was too late.

But what was the clue? What was the point in these coins? *So I know it's the same person who sent me the spoons and the one who sent the coins to Alexandria. The one who killed Shannon. That tells me it's all connected, that he's been tracking me for a while.*

There had to be more. Something crucial I was missing.

I searched my memory, suddenly struck with the feeling the answer was inside my head and would be heartbreakingly obvious once I found it.

Nothing.

Lennox would arrive in less than an hour, and I couldn't sit around drinking coffee, not after this.

I was going to find out how a stranger had gotten inside Kelly's apartment.

Time for the super to meet Lucy Kendall.

. . .

The maintenance office was basically an old closet in the basement. The door stood open, and a man with slicked-back gray hair sat at the desk, his eyes on the computer. Plump fingers tapped the same key, and I wondered if he was looking at porn or cat videos.

I banged my fist against the open door, and he jumped. He made no move to hide whatever he'd been watching, so my bet was for cats. Deep wrinkles lined his forehead, and he had the kind of sagging jowls that resembled a hound's. "Help you?"

"Who stole your keys and when?"

He blinked, and the thick mole on his right eye seemed to swallow half his face. "Pardon me?"

I closed the door with a bang. I had nothing but my anger as a weapon, but I could be incredibly persuasive when I wanted to. "I don't have time for your embarrassment. Someone took your keys and made a copy. When did it happen? Do you have any idea who it was?"

A jowl quivered. "Lady—"

"Not a lady." I positioned myself on the other side of his desk and leaned over, hoping my physical fatigue and emotional exhaustion could be mistaken for dangerous psychopath. Or maybe they were all the same thing. "I'm not a nice person, and I need answers. If you don't give them to me, I'll be forced to make you. And that's not going to be a fun experience."

He looked as if he didn't know whether to laugh or cry. His gaze drifted to the bandage on my arm and then over the rest of me. I knew he saw a dirty, glittery-eyed woman who could easily be someone off the street looking to cause trouble.

"Kelly Swan called you earlier about someone trying to get into her apartment. You checked the tapes for a stranger trying to get into the building. You got angry when she asked about you misplacing your keys. Cut the shit and tell me what happened." I should have been nicer, tried to sweet-talk him. But I'd lost that ability today.

"I'm telling you—"

"I don't care if you screwed up! I'm not going to tell your boss. Just tell me what the hell happened."

He swallowed. I kept expecting to feel some sliver of compassion for him, but that ability seemed to have been executed as well.

"Look," he said. "I made a mistake of being compassionate with you drug addicts before. I don't know what you're after from me, but I'm not giving in this time. You need to get out before I call the police."

Drug addicts coming off the street in Rittenhouse Square? Not impossible, but unlikely. "What are you talking about?"

"You tell that damned Preacher I know he took those keys last week. He's not welcome here, and neither are you." He held out a jingling key ring. "They went missing for just a little while, and it's him that did it. But no one's place has been broken into, so I don't see no point in reporting it. But I ain't making the same mistake with you."

Preacher.

Who I'd killed and dumped in a state park last winter.

My head spun like an out-of-control wooden toy. I expected it to fly off and land in the middle of the maintenance guy's tiny desk. Bet that would freak him the hell out.

"Preacher." The word choked me. "A tall, lanky black man?"

"Hell no. Some white guy wearing a baseball cap and looking like he needed a fix in the worst way. Jittering like hell—more than I've ever seen anyone. I was too scared not to let him use the bathroom. I still don't know how he lifted the keys. If he did," he added lamely. "Like I said, I only lost them for a little while."

I backed up and grabbed the doorknob for support. "Did you see anything on him? Anything that stood out?"

He shrugged. "Not really. He had a beard. Not real thick, but enough to cover his face. Scruff, I guess they call. Tall and white. Junkies all look the same."

"Was he thin or muscular? What kind of clothes did he wear?"

"I don't know! I don't notice that sort of thing on a man. He wasn't skinny, I know that much. I remember thinking he looked too healthy to be an addict. But people can fool you. And I wanted him out of here."

"He was shaking like he needed a fix?"

"Crazy like. Damn near epileptic."

Acting or did he really have a problem? No way a drug addict that desperate could pull off something this organized. If the thief had really been a user, then he would have been a pawn. And lost to the streets now.

"If he used the bathroom, how did he get the keys?"

The maintenance guy looked down at his hands. "I think I left them in the bathroom. But I don't know. They might've been lying around somewhere else." He seemed to realize I'd gone from belligerent demands to cold questioning. He looked me over again, and the widening of his eyes told me he was seeing something else this time around.

"You ain't no addict, are you? What's going on?"

I ignored his question. "You're sure he said his name was Preacher?"

"Yeah. I remember thinking it was stupid. I even asked him about it, and he said he was in the business of making things right."

How could this man know I'd killed Preacher? The only person who knew that was Chris. But that idea was crazy.

Nearly manic, I searched through the pictures on my phone. Chris didn't like his picture taken, but I had a couple.

One of them was taken near Christmas, and he had a few days' beard.

"Look at this." I held the phone out to the man. "Was it this guy?"

The super took the phone and squinted. "No. Too young. And much better looking."

Right. I knew it wouldn't have been Chris. But beyond him and Kelly, no one else knew. But rumors flew... was I looking for a cop? None of my victims had relatives on the PPD, state or county police, but that's as far as Kelly had checked. What if I'd killed some child molester who had a brother in law enforcement somewhere else? Just the credentials would give him access to a lot of information, if he played his cards right.

But that all sounded too complicated. I was missing something.

I left the super guy muttering in confusion and started climbing the steep stairs to the first floor.

My phone rang, and I eagerly glanced at the screen, stupidly hoping to see Kelly's number.

It was Joan's.

If I talked to my mother now I would lose it. I couldn't afford to waste the last bit of composure I had on that wretched woman.

I sent the call to voicemail.

She called again. And again.

Rage filled me. Who in the hell did she think she was? That I had to bend to her every whim? I supposed she was calling to go on about the police questioning her. She might have even heard about my involvement with Shannon by now; I had no doubt it would reach the news. How did Mac stand her?

My heart jerked to a stop. I called Joan back, feeling as if I were falling backward on the stairs. But Agent Lennox had sent someone over.

That's probably why she'd called. To complain about the intrusion and embarrassment to her.

"Lucy." Her high-pitched voice sent me stumbling down several steps. "Come to the Thomas Jefferson University Hospital right away. Mac had a heart attack."

TWENTY-FOUR

I had no memory of the drive to the hospital or the race to the nurses' station for directions to the cardiac unit. I only knew that the remaining shred of my heart had been yanked out.

The waiting room on the left, the nurse said. My shoes squeaked against the floor as I ran into the room in search of my mother.

Joan sat on the edge of a chair in one of the waiting rooms, staring out of the small window. She didn't acknowledge me, seemingly focused on the trees outside. But I saw the reflection of her eyes flickering back and forth, on high alert.

"What happened?"

Her narrow shoulders rounded, the tissue at her mouth now. This was the sort of moment a drama queen like her dreamed up. She needed to be trussed up and coddled, to be the belle of the pity ball. She probably envisioned me dropping to my knees in front of her and offering my life in exchange for her happiness.

"Mother. Talk to me, or I'll get a doctor."

In the window, her gaze hardened. She slowly turned to

face me. Mascara blotted beneath her right eye, foundation caked into the lines of her face—she looked properly aggrieved.

"He had a massive heart attack."

"From the atrial fibrillation?" That wasn't supposed to happen. Atrial fibrillation usually caused stroke, and Mac took his Coumadin religiously. Patients on blood thinners lived with AFib for years.

"A clogged artery," Joan said. "Something about a widow-maker." She grabbed a fresh tissue and pressed it to her face. "I'm too young to be a widow."

Hell if I'd soothe her. "People recover from massive heart attacks all the time. It'll take a while, but he'll be all right."

Joan's head wagged back and forth. "We didn't have any warning. He just slumped over in the chair talking to that agent." Her expression twisted. "Which you sent, didn't you? Asking those questions. This is your fault. And look at you! How dare you show up here looking so disgusting!"

I'd forgotten about my dirty shorts and stringy hair that couldn't seem to remain in its knot. Combined with no sleep and desperation, I looked like hell. As if any of that mattered right now.

"How long was Mac without oxygen?"

Joan started to cry again. A better daughter would have comforted her, but I needed answers. Thomas Jefferson's cardiac ward teemed with busy nurses and the occasional solemn doctor. I grabbed the first person I encountered. "Mac Kendall. I'm his stepdaughter, and I need to talk to his doctor."

The petite nurse gave me the once-over but appeared unfazed about my tattered appearance. She patted my hand. "I think the attending is with another patient, but I'll tell him you're here. I'm sure it won't take very long for the doctor to speak with you." She gestured toward the waiting room where my mother sat.

Shoulders sagging, I started for the room while the nurse

disappeared around the corner. The doctor could take forever to get to us. I couldn't sit in that room with Joan. She'd keep whining until I felt so guilty I'd have to say something nice, and I'd be damned if I wasted that kind of energy on the woman.

I sat down on the floor and prepared to wait.

A woman in a smart navy pantsuit approached me, a cup of coffee in her hand. "Lucy Kendall?" Her honey-colored hair hung in a bob that softened the sharp angles of her face. Her lips shined with some kind of clear gloss, but she wore no other makeup.

I gazed up at her. "You don't look like a doctor on call."

She smiled. "I'm Agent Williams. Agent Lennox sent me to keep an eye on your stepfather."

"Right," I said, getting to my feet. "My mother said you were there when it happened?"

The agent's smile faded. "I'd just arrived and had introduced myself. My orders were to pretend I was there to question your mother about photos of her daughter that appeared online."

"Lily's death."

"Yes."

A deep-rooted energy began to course through me. How would Lennox have known about that without speaking with Todd?

"How did Joan take that?"

"About like you'd expect," Agent Williams said. "Your stepfather came into the room, and I introduced myself and explained why I was there. I got the immediate impression he didn't believe it."

"He knew Kelly was missing and that I was trying to find her." The scenario began to limp together. "He was afraid for me."

Williams must have anticipated the guilt beginning to work its way through me. "I assured him you were in absolutely no danger. He seemed pacified, and your mother and I spoke. Mac sat in a chair and listened. He suddenly shook and then went limp. I called the ambulance right away."

While my mother prattled and did absolutely nothing for him.

"How long did he go without oxygen?"

Agent Williams hesitated. "I gave him CPR while we waited. The paramedics got his lungs working again but..."

"Too much time had already passed."

"I'm not a doctor," she said. But her sudden unwillingness to meet my eyes said enough.

"Is Agent Lennox here?"

"He's on his way," Williams said. "I'm supposed to meet him out front."

"Did he tell you what was going on?"

"Only the bare minimum." She waited until a nurse had gone by and then stepped closer. "I can't imagine what you're going through. But Agent Lennox believes Kelly is alive."

I stared at her. "Why?"

"He didn't give me details. He just said he thought this was all part of a big endgame and that Kelly's kidnapper wouldn't harm her before you played your role."

"My role?"

Agent Williams shrugged. "That's all he said. But I take him at his word. He's not one to sugarcoat."

Drained, I leaned against the wall. Something much bigger was at play here, and I had the very distinct feeling of being a pawn.

"Do you want to sit with your mother?"

I choked out a bitter laugh. "You met her. What do you think?"

TWENTY-FIVE

Fifteen minutes later, a tall doctor wearing wrinkled scrubs and carrying a model of the heart arrived. Agent Williams excused herself, and I almost begged her to stay. Inside the waiting room, Joan leapt from her perch and into the doctor's personal space. "What's going on with my husband? I've been waiting over two hours, and I can't get any real answers."

"I'm sorry for that." The doctor motioned for her to sit down. I shook my head and remained standing.

The doctor glanced between the two of us. "The major artery in Mac's heart was completely blocked. Has he been having any headaches or chest pains?"

"A few," Joan said. "He promised to go to the doctor."

The doctor held up the model of the heart. Far larger than I'd have expected, the model opened in two pieces. He pointed to the left side. "This is the main side of the heart, and the left anterior descending artery runs down the front. It basically runs this entire side of the heart. When it becomes blocked and isn't treated, the artery goes down followed by the front wall of the heart. It's a major heart attack."

"But people survive heart attacks all the time," I said.

"They do," the doctor said. "But Mac went without oxygen. Between the CPR and the paramedic's procedures, he was down over forty minutes. That's a very long time to go without oxygen."

I read the truth very clearly on the doctor's face. His careful expression and soft, steady voice the sort of things doctors reserved for the worst-case scenarios.

"He's brain-dead." My voice cracked. "That's what you're saying."

The doctor grimaced. "No one knows where that nickname came from, especially since some people do recover. But Mac's case is severe. We've taken several different measures and performed various tests. There's no brain function."

My mother's childish wailing made the entire scene feel like a terrible soap opera. She paced back and forth, clutching a wad of tissues, alternating between dabbing her nose and her eyes.

"But can you really tell this soon?" I asked. "It's only been, what, four hours? Couldn't brain function return?"

Kelly only has fifteen left now. Or maybe less. What the hell did I do?

The doctor sat his heart on the table. My mother continued to cry. He patted her shoulder but kept his eyes on me. "In some cases, but not this one. Going without oxygen for so long simply destroyed his brain."

"Well, we're not giving up hope," my mother said. "There's always a chance for a miracle."

The doctor shook his head. "I understand. But I've consulted with the other cardiologist on staff as well as the attending neurologist. We're all in agreement."

"Then you're wrong," Joan said. "Mac's strong. Give him a couple of days on life support, and you'll see."

The doctor gave me a compassionate smile. "Lucy?"

A memory whispered at me. "It's my decision."

"Excuse me?" Joan glared through teary eyes. I caught the warning in them: how dare I try to usurp her.

Finally, I had the control to break my mother, and it meant the hardest decision of my life. "Two years ago, when that guy on Mac's roofing crew fell and had a brain injury, Mac came to me about his medical directive. He wanted me to promise not to leave him on life support."

Joan's face reddened, the jackal sneaking through. "Well, you're going to break it."

The doctor cleared his throat. "It's a legal document. Mac designated Lucy with his power of attorney. She has to decide."

Mac and I, sitting in our favorite breakfast spot. Our little secret from Joan. Mac asking me to pull the plug if it ever came to it.

"So, what about it? If I ever needed it, would you snuff me out?"

Now I looked between the doctor and my mother, whose grief was being superseded by her need to control the situation. She glared at me over her fist of tissues.

"You're sure he's not going to recover?"

The doctor nodded. "You're free to take your time with the decision. Your stepfather believed you had his best interests in mind, and I assume you two discussed what he'd want done in this sort of situation." He glanced back at my mother as if he could sense her bitterness. "But I realize it's not something you can resolve lightly. I'll leave you to discuss it."

Joan pounced as soon as he left.

"You cannot kill Mac."

Her choice of word almost made me laugh. "Kill him? You can't seriously mean that. He's gone." The urge to cry welled up from my chest. I wouldn't give her the upper hand.

"There's always hope."

I gritted my teeth. "Mac didn't want to live this way. He told me that."

She glared at me. "He was distraught. He didn't know what he was saying."

"He signed the medical directive weeks after he asked me. We discussed it more than once, especially after he was diagnosed with AFib. Even though we knew the chance of a stroke from it was small, he was still scared. He didn't want to live on a machine." My resolve strengthened as I remembered the heartfelt way Mac talked about the directive. "He knew what he was doing. I won't let you take this away from him."

"You're the one who will be taking his life." Her shrill voice made a passing nurse jump. "You realize that, don't you? If you tell them to shut off the machine, you will have killed him. Is that what you want on your conscience? Taking a life?"

Instead of bursting into tears, hysterical laughter bubbled from my chest. The sound ricocheted off the walls of the small waiting room, and I heard myself sounding like a wild person. Joan stared back, her expression caught between shock and humiliation. I laughed until my sides throbbed and my throat felt raw.

Wiping the tears from my eyes, I started for the door. "I'm going to see Mac."

"You will not take him off life support."

We stared at each other. She dropped her chin, her expression as sinister as I'd ever experienced. I didn't flinch. "Face it, Mother. This is one thing you can't milk. But don't worry. I'm sure you can find online sympathizers even if you don't have horrific crime scene pictures to post."

Joan's mouth opened, her eyes wide. She looked like a fish out of water, tossed into the boat and gasping for air.

Too bad she was still breathing.

I didn't know what I expected when I went inside the hospital room. The cardiac unit had a different feel to it, a frenetic sort of energy accompanied by the various noises from machines I didn't understand. Instead of a private room, curtains separated the beds. A nurse moved from one patient to another.

The ventilator breathed for Mac, forcing air into his lungs with a sound that made my skin crawl. He still wore the shirt he'd been wearing when I left his secret place.

Now the hot tears came, spilling down my cheeks and soaking the bed linens. He might not have come into my life until I was a teenager, but he'd saved it in a lot of ways. Without him, I probably would have run away from Joan. I might have ended up on the streets and been one of the statistics I now fought for. My knees buckled, and I dropped into the chair beside the bed.

He and Kelly were the only family I really had. I was about to lose them both, and I couldn't stop it.

All the things I'd done to save other people amounted to nothing. I couldn't save Mac or Kelly. Or my sister. And I would be stuck with Joan.

I sobbed harder, drawing my knees to my chest and wrapping my arms tightly around them.

"Mac." I kept my lips close to his ear. "I just want you to know I love you. That you've been better to me than I deserve. And I don't want you to go. Because I need you." My throat felt as if it were going to split in two. "Normally, I'd find a way to get what I wanted. I'm good at that, you know. Learned from the best. But this is different. There's nothing I can do except let you go. A decent person would be grateful to have that option, but I'm not one of those. I'm angry. Not at you, but at the world. Lily's gone. Kelly's damned near gone, and now I'm going to lose you. I guess there's some truth to cosmic payback. Maybe God decided to punish me for all the bad things I've done." I wiped my eyes. "It's too late for me to do anything but bring you peace, but I swear to you, I'm going to do the right thing about

Kelly. I'm going to tell Agent Lennox every bad thing. That's Kelly's only chance."

Mac's breathing didn't change. The room remained exactly as it had been when I entered it, and yet I sensed a shift, as if he were somehow sitting next to me and prodding me.

"And Joan. You said I've convinced myself my life isn't worth anything because I didn't save Lily. You weren't wrong, but I think there's more to it. More than I ever allowed my brain to process. But now all these things are fighting to be heard, and I don't think I can ignore them. So Joan and I... well, you were the one person who kept us together at all. And it should be her lying here right now. God knows I'd have no trouble pulling the plug. But instead it's you, and it's just not fair."

I could almost hear him laughing, reminding me how life wasn't fair. That was the fun of it, he always said. Fairness is boring. What's a day without some challenge?

His hand felt strangely cold in my own, as though the machine didn't make his body create any warmth. The essence that made up Mac had gone somewhere else, and I could only hope it was a better place than this world.

I stood and leaned forward to brush my lips over his forehead. "Tell Lily I love her."

My feet dragged the floor as I left the room and flagged down the nearest nurse. "I'm Mac Kendall's stepdaughter. Please tell his doctor I'm going to honor his wishes and end life support."

TWENTY-SIX

Inside the waiting room, Joan paced, a rattlesnake ready to strike. I braced myself for her tirade. "I'm going to have him taken off the ventilator."

"You can't do this to me." Joan's fists balled up like a toddler's during a tantrum.

"Mother." I felt the darkness soaring in my chest. For as long as I could remember, my mother had caused nothing but hurt and anger. I never measured up to her standards. Lily didn't either. We spent the early part of our childhood trying to please her even though her standards changed with the seasons. Lily occasionally made Mother happy, but I couldn't remember a time Joan had praised me without an agenda. I'd been the second child, the one she couldn't afford and didn't want, and she saved her best manipulation tactics for me. "This isn't about you. It's about Mac. It's what he wanted, and I'm going to honor his wishes."

Her lipstick had smudged, making her frown look even more twisted. "He's loaded with medication. He won't feel any pain. But *I* will! I'll know he's gone, and I couldn't do anything to stop it. Because of you."

The irony devoured the last of my resolve, and I burst into hysterical laughter. Joan's gaping mouth and stretched-open eyes made her look ridiculous. I laughed harder.

"Stop it," she hissed. Clenching her tissue in her bony hand, she stepped toward me, her grieving expression changing into murderous rage. "You quit embarrassing me, or I'll make you sorry." She subtly raised her fist. The laughter evaporated.

I narrowed my eyes, my jaw muscles clamped so tightly pain shot up my skull. I recognized the sensation. I experienced it just before I killed the trucker last winter. Before I gave Cody Harrison the fatal dose of heroin. Before I injected Preacher with ketamine and then smothered him. All of my victims had realized the look meant something terrible was about to happen to them. Joan was no different.

She stiffened, the cords in her neck taut. Her fist dropped. Fear glittered in her eyes. "I just don't think we need to draw that sort of attention."

"I don't care what you think." The words seemed to rip out the last stitch. "You can't do anything to stop Mac's passing because he didn't want you to. He knew you would drag out his life for your own selfish benefit. You'd have done the same thing to Lily."

"What? Don't bring her into this."

"She *is* this!" I waved my hand between us. "She's always been this. You didn't listen to her, and she killed herself. Her death was your fault, and you never acknowledged that. You never took any accountability. You just sucked up all the attention you could, and when that died down, you put her death photos online so you could revel in that attention. How could you?"

Her face pinched like a rubber doll's, turning the wrinkles between her eyes into craters.

I felt breathless and yet charged with energy. Two steps forward, and I could put my hands around her throat. Choking the life out of her would be easy enough. She wasn't strong enough to fight me.

"How dare you!"

"How dare *you*?" I cut her off. "You're her mother. You were supposed to put her first. To protect her. Your boyfriend raped her for months! I knew something was going on, but I was young and innocent enough my mind didn't go there until she finally told me. But you were the adult. You had to know he snuck out of bed at night. Where did you think he went? For a fucking snack?"

Joan's smeared mouth trembled, her flinch brief but enough. I'd never allowed myself to go down that horrific road because I knew if I found out Joan had known before Lily told her, I wouldn't be able to handle the reality of it.

My system burned as though I just consumed fire. Pain struck the back of my head, reaching around my skull as if I'd put it into some sort of torture device. Two steps, and I closed the white space between us. Joan tried to stand her ground, but she coiled into herself so she appeared even shorter. Fear glistened on her forehead and upper lip.

The words came out in a hate-filled whisper. "Did you know before she told you?"

"I don't want to talk about this."

I looked around the small waiting room. We had it to ourselves, but the door stood wide open. Rage coursing through me, I quietly shut it and turned the lock. When I faced Joan once again, all the color had drained out of her face.

"Listen to me, Joan." My tone flat-lined. Whatever emotion for Joan I'd once clung to finally evaporated. She was just like Riley, turning a blind eye to a child's suffering. Except this time, the child had been her own flesh and blood. "Answer the question."

Her eyes traveled over me as though she were seeing me for the first time. And she was. I no longer needed the facade I forced in her presence. She didn't even qualify for the socially acceptable version of me.

"I didn't want to lose him," she finally choked out. "He provided for us, and if he'd left, I would have had to ask my parents for help or get a second job. I couldn't do either of those things."

I blinked against the throbbing of my head. "So you allowed him to use your child?"

"He said he was just talking to her." Joan's chin jutted defiantly.

"You knew he wasn't."

"Not at first, but then I heard... noises." She glanced between the door and my shaking form. "You know how Lily was. She *knew* she was beautiful. And so willful and always against me."

I bit my tongue until I tasted blood just to make sure I hadn't slipped into a sick trance. Once again I stepped into Joan's space, breathing her minty breath. "Are you blaming her?"

"It's complicated."

"It's not. He was a sexual predator, and you prostituted your daughter." My spittle landed on her cheek.

"I never—"

"You just said he provided for you financially, so you allowed it. That's prostitution. You sold your daughter for material things, and you killed her."

Joan slapped me hard enough my head twisted to the left. The sting made me smile.

"Do you know why I came in from Alexandria yesterday?"

She shook her head, her shoulders nearly pulled to her ears. "Because I found out about the message board. Do you know why Detective Beckett was so interested in your posting those photos?"

"I didn't post anything."

"Stop lying to me." The guttural tone had much more impact than shouting. She snapped her mouth shut. "You somehow conned the police to give you copies, and then you posted them online for attention. You wanted people to feel sorry for you. Those pictures were used to stage a murder victim's body."

"What do you mean?"

I soaked up the shock on her face. She deserved everything I was about to deal her. "A young girl in Alexandria was killed and posed to look like Lily's death scene. The message was for me."

"You? Why?"

I smiled, feeling the power work its way through me. "I have enemies, Joan. Someone wants to settle the score."

Her gaze again darted toward the door as she shrank back from me. "Why would you have enemies?"

"Oh, I've done bad things, Joan." I felt crazed, a schizophrenic energy eclipsing everything else. "Ever since Lily died, I've blamed myself because I didn't do enough. I should have stood up for her. I thought if only I'd tried to talk to you, things would have changed. But I was wrong. You made sure she never had a chance."

A bead of moisture trickled from Joan's temple. "You're not thinking clearly. You just need to sit down and process, and you'll see."

"I see very clearly now." My hands reached toward her, my fingers long and pale and wicked. I had no other thought but extinguishing her miserable existence.

"Lucy! What are you doing?"

"You ruined our lives." My fingers wrapped around her neck. No pressure yet—I would take my time, breathe in her fear. She grabbed my wrists, but I barely felt her scratching fingernails. "I hate you."

A loud bang made both our heads whip to the left. Todd's

face in the tall, rectangular window. His eyes locked with mine. He mouthed my name, his hand on the glass.

I wanted to kill Joan.

You can't do that to Mac.

I dropped my hands, and Joan staggered back, falling into a chair dramatically.

The same numbness that accompanied every kill enveloped me as I unlocked the door and pulled it open. Todd stared at me, his hands outstretched as if he didn't know what I was about to do.

I took both of his hands and then pulled him to me, wrapping my arms around his waist. "She knew Lily was being molested. Is there a statute of limitations?"

"You know it's more complicated than that. Lily's not here to accuse her." He held me stiffly, his heart pounding in his throat.

I pulled away and looked into his shocked face. "I would have killed her."

"I know."

Agent Williams's knowledge of Lily's pictures came back to me. "Why are you here?"

"He's with me." Lennox stood in the hallway, leaning against the wall. "I'm sorry about your stepfather, but we don't have much time."

Todd took my hand. "Lucy, we need to talk."

The insidious worry that sprouted at the Cooks' house bloomed larger. "All right, but I need to be with Mac first. I don't think it will take long."

I've never relied on anyone else for anything, but I needed Todd to go inside Mac's room with me. I didn't expect to fall into a crying heap, but I wasn't sure how I could handle watching Mac take his final breaths with Joan's theatrics—not after what I'd just found out. I didn't trust myself not to attack her again.

Todd stood on my right side, his arms crossed and his face drawn into an unreadable expression. Joan positioned herself to Mac's left, clutching his hand and simpering. The hospital chaplain flanked her, his black uniform making me think of the raven waiting to swoop in on the dead. Joan didn't look at me.

If the doctor noticed the dynamics, he didn't comment. "Once the machines are off, Mac's body will begin to shut down. Because he suffered a great deal of brain trauma, I think his organs will stop quickly."

Joan wailed. "What am I going to do without him?"

I went rigid, staring at her. Todd's hand closed around my elbow. I breathed deeply, forcing the murderous thoughts to their normal corners. "Will he suffer?"

The doctor shook his head, touching one of the tubes that ran into Mac's IV. "He's getting a steady dose of morphine. He won't feel any pain."

I swallowed over the rock in my throat. I still couldn't grasp how quickly this had happened. Hours ago, Mac had waved goodbye as Chris and I drove off in search of Kelly. If I'd known that would be the last time I spoke to him, I would have said so many other things. I would have thanked him for being a good father and for showing me there are still good men in this world. I would have made sure he knew his influence on my life, and that he was loved. I would have done so much more.

But now he was gone. "You're absolutely sure?" I asked the doctor one more time. "There's no chance of any recovery? Not even a tiny percent?"

The doctor nodded, no sign of impatience or frustration on his plain face. "His brain will never work again. It can't tell his heart to pump blood or his lungs to breathe. It can't do anything. All the things that made Mac a person have already died. His body is just a machine that needs to be turned off."

Joan threw her head against Mac's unfeeling arm. The chaplain patted her shoulder.

"I'm sorry to be so blunt," the doctor said. "I can't imagine your pain, and I'm sorry for your loss. But I don't like to mislead anyone."

"I appreciate that." I looked again at the shell in the bed. Mac's face looked peaceful, as though he was caught up in a deep, blissful nap. I smoothed his bushy eyebrows, and then took his hand, almost smiling at the missing finger. His silly story about losing it in his nose had been so long ago, and yet I could remember it clearly, watching his eyes sparkle and hearing his big belly laugh.

He didn't want to live this way, and he'd counted on me to do the right thing.

I kissed his forehead, feeling the hatred burning off my mother.

My gaze shifted to her. She still refused to make eye contact, and I still wanted to squeeze the miserable life out of her.

But this was about Mac.

"Have you finished saying your goodbyes?"

She jerked her head up at the question as though she were about to argue. Finally, she looked my way. I watched her take everything in, from my clothes to the man by my side and finally my face. With the mask gone, did she see the monster?

Joan shivered. "Yes."

I looked at the doctor. "Go ahead."

He nodded again and then began turning off the machines. They stopped quietly, with the morphine drip being the only thing left. Mac coughed, his body failing.

Death had been on my mind for as long as I could remember. Even as a small child, I was acutely aware of the life cycle. Graveyards both terrified and fascinated me. Until Lily died, I believed my grandmother when she said death was a peaceful transition to the next phase of our existence.

Lily showed me the truth, and fascination turned into fear.

As Mac's body died, I waited for that fear to sink its teeth in and for the panic to ensue.

We're all eventually nothing.

But the feeling never came. Instead I saw a wrecked body stop fighting a losing battle and felt a peculiar feeling descend: calmness.

If anyone would make it to the place Christians called Heaven, it would be Mac.

The doctor pronounced time of death, and Joan started her show all over again.

I took Todd's hand and left the room.

His grip felt strong and comforting. We didn't speak as we left the cardiac ward, taking the northeast elevator to the first-floor cafeteria.

The option of denial died with Mac. No matter how selfish or cruel I might be, I needed Todd in my life. I wanted him by my side. Eventually I would have to tell him how I felt. A tremor of fear raced through me at the prospect. And then I glanced at Todd's watch, and the reality of the situation crashed over me.

I leaned against the side of the elevator, defeated. Evening approached. How many hours did Kelly have left? Lennox said she wouldn't be killed, but how could he know?

And why had he brought in Todd?

As the elevator ground its way to the first floor, my eyes drooped. I forced them open and tried to find something to focus on. A poster on the opposite wall advertised a class at Penn State for paramedic training. The course promised to bring in current Philadelphia paramedics to talk about the rigors of the job.

The photographer had positioned the best-looking paramedic in the center, making him the focal point.

The camera certainly loved Chris.

TWENTY-SEVEN

The pub across from the hospital was nearly empty, and I thanked God for that small blessing. I sat down at the table across from Lennox and Todd and waved at the college kid loitering between tables. "Rum and Coke, two shots, no ice."

Neither man spoke as we waited for my drink. The bar was mostly empty this time of day; a few doctors and nurses had come in to grab something after their shifts, and a sketchy guy hung out in the back corner, but our section remained empty.

The waitress returned with my drink and offered food. I waved her off as I slugged down the alcohol. It hit my throat with pleasant warmth but did nothing for my nerves.

"All right." I set the glass down and looked at Todd. "I'm happy to see you, but why are you here? And how did Agent Williams know about Lily's pictures?"

He scratched his ear and shifted. "There are some things you don't know."

"I gathered that. Thanks for sharing."

His nostrils flared. "Like you shared with me about Kelly? You couldn't trust me? Or do you just think I'm not a good enough cop?"

"It's got nothing to do with that." I hated that Todd was going to hear the truth about me—or rather, I hated I was going to have to watch his face and see the disappointment.

"And thanks for breaking Justin's heart," Todd said.

"You think I enjoyed that? I was trying to save Kelly's life. You didn't say anything to him, did you?"

Lennox finally stepped in, waving his large hand between us. "Justin still believes Kelly is in the hospital. Can we skip the lovers' quarrel and get to it?"

Todd's head dropped to his chest. I took a long drink. Might as well get it over with. The sooner I spilled my guts, the sooner Kelly could be found.

"Fine." I drained the glass, wishing I'd taken the time to appreciate the liquor. "Like I said, I originally thought whoever took Kelly was out for revenge over the sex trafficking ring. But I was wrong. It's much more personal."

"You called Lennox because you thought he could maneuver faster?" Todd rested his elbows on the table, his hands close to mine.

"I called Lennox because I didn't want to hurt you. But you're here now, so you might as well hear it all too. It's nothing you haven't suspected. I'm just going to share names so Lennox can start investigating. If it's not too late."

Todd's hands jerked. "Lucy, don't."

My head snapped back and forth fast enough to hurt. "This is Kelly. I would do anything for her. If it's the end of me, then so be it." I looked at Lennox. "I guess you'll get the credit for breaking the case, if there is really one. I'm sure someone cares, but since we're talking about the bottom of the barrel in society, who the hell knows." I knew I was rambling, but I had to work up to admitting to killing over half a dozen men in less than two years. Throwing my life away wasn't easy, especially when it might be too late to save Kelly.

"Don't say anything else." Todd slammed his fists on the

table. "For once in your life, let someone else talk. Agent Lennox, tell her what the hell's going on."

Lennox loosened his bright red tie. "I'm going to say I don't know what you were just referring to and move on to the case at hand, because while I think Kelly is still alive, we don't want to mess around too long."

"The case at hand is what I was going to talk about."

"Lucy, please." Todd looked ready to leap over the table. "Don't talk anymore."

I pointed at Lennox. "You said this was about me. So I'm doing the right thing."

He took off his blazer and carefully folded it on the back of the booth. "It's about you, but you're way off. Have you ever heard of the Silver Stalker?"

I shrugged. The name sounded familiar, but my brain verged on mush.

"He's a serial killer who leaves a coin with his victims—who are all female. Stupid signature, but Kelly said silver has a lot of symbolism," Lennox said. "I've been tracking him for over two years. The media thinks he's relatively new, but that's by the FBI's design. We don't want another serial killer sparking national attention."

"That's thoughtful of you," I said. "How are women supposed to protect themselves if they don't know he's out there?"

Todd made a noise that sounded like agreement. Lennox glanced at him, the tension in the air growing thick. The FBI didn't always share with the police and vice versa. Egos on the rampage. I had no time for it.

"He operates primarily in Pennsylvania, but we've confirmed other victims in Delaware and Maryland, and we're currently investigating an older case in eastern Ohio," Lennox supplied. He took off his glasses and rubbed his eyes. I gave him a few moments. Chasing a man like the Silver Stalker had to suck the life out of him. My own victims weren't bloodied or broken or innocent. The only time I'd come close to experiencing some of the revulsion of Lennox's job was during the winter when the teenage girl had been found in the hunting cabin. Mary Weston's work, and the image of the tortured girl would stick with me for the rest of my life. Lennox had dozens of those images to live with.

He put his glasses back on with a sigh. "The Silver Stalker doesn't discriminate, which is unusual for a serial killer and makes him especially hard to track. He's meticulous in his planning, and he kills every victim the same way. But he doesn't care if they're black, white, Hispanic—you get the picture. Some are tall, some short. Thin or heavy—again, no preference."

"So what does he get his kicks from?" Todd asked.

"Every confirmed victim was missing for a minimum of two weeks before she was found. They were starved and dehydrated, given just enough sustenance to survive. None were sexually assaulted. And all were strangled."

"Isn't that supposed to suggest a personal killing?" I tried to remember the criminology classes from years ago.

"It can, but stabbing is more so. The penetration can be seen as a sexual replacement. But these women..." Lennox paused and looked at the table, his neck muscles tight. "They all showed signs of being strangled multiple times."

"So he kept reviving them?" Todd's voice dropped.

"Either that or he knew the right moment to stop. It's another way to control and terrify. And then there's the signature: he always leaves a piece of silver, usually a coin, but not one that's circulating. Those aren't true silver. He leaves a collector's type of coin. Sometimes a dime, sometimes a quarter or silver dollar. They're all at least 90 percent silver."

Something clicked in my head: the silver spoons; the Lady

Liberty silver dollars delivered to me and left with Shannon; the same silver dollar at Kelly's. How long had the Silver Stalker been watching me?

Todd spoke before I found my voice. "Why the silver?"

"It's got a lot of symbolism," Lennox said. "In mythology, it's viewed as cleansing. So I suppose it's this jerk's way of saying he's cleansed the women of their sins. Who knows what the hell this guy is thinking."

"The Silver Stalker is doing this?" Just saying the words made me feel sick. How could Kelly survive against that kind of predator?

"This winter in Maryland, Kelly's computer and research skills impressed me. I needed someone local in Pennsylvania, and she agreed." Lennox crossed his arms on top of the table and gave me a purposeful look.

"Kelly was working for you?" I could no longer hide the betrayal, slumping down in my seat. How many things had Kelly kept from me?

"She was doing online work regarding the Silver Stalker cases," Lennox said. "Shortly before she was taken, I gave her a name to research. She called and said she had something but didn't want to leave it in a message. She thought her apartment might be bugged. She didn't say why. She sent me an encrypted email, and it took my team a couple of days to break it. Kelly was taken late Thursday night—the same day she'd sent the email."

"You put her in this danger." I wanted to come across the table at Lennox. "You knew she lived alone and was trying to rebuild her life. Why would you do this?"

"Because I needed her help." He didn't appear to be fazed by my anger. "And you still don't know the entire story, so simmer down."

I felt feverish. The drink hadn't helped.

Kelly's apartment had been bugged. It made sense. That's

how the Stalker knew so much about me, how he managed to track Kelly's and my movements.

I finally had information to add. "The super's key was stolen by a drug addict who called himself Preacher."

Todd sat up straight. "A white guy?"

"White and stocky. Obviously not Preacher. I'm thinking he got the key to the Stalker, who made a copy. The guy pretending to be Preacher returned it. Kelly's super is an older guy. He didn't want to admit his mistake." I turned back to Lennox. "What was the encrypted message?"

"Hold on," he said. "Beckett, why did you ask if the drug addict was a white guy?"

Todd's voice sounded even wearier than he looked. "Earlier in the week, a homeless man was discovered in a dumpster a few blocks away from Kelly's apartment. It's not Major Crime, but I keep an eye on her neighborhood. He didn't have any identification, but he had a note in his pocket. Preacher's name was scribbled on it." Todd balled up the cocktail napkin and threw it against the wall. "It was weird, but I didn't think anything about it. Not with the search for Shannon going on."

Lennox was nodding, his fingers tapping on the table. "Makes sense. We know he knew about Preacher. Obviously." His eyes flashed to mine.

"She gave you a name in the encrypted email," I said. "Who is it?"

"Rich Hasel." Lennox's neutral voice only spurred my feeling of unease.

"I don't know anyone by that name."

Lennox and Todd glanced at each other. What were they building up to?

"Rich Hasel owns the land north of Philadelphia where the first Silver Stalker victim was found nearly two years ago," Todd said.

"So? That's hardly enough to make someone a murder suspect."

"You're right," Lennox agreed. "But the DC Park Police are checking all the rental cars in the Alexandria area for the week prior to Shannon's murder. Process has been slow, but guess whose name came up this morning?"

"Rich Hasel." I still couldn't figure out why they were talking to me as if they were trying to cushion a blow.

Lennox nodded.

"But I don't understand why the Silver Stalker would target me. Because that's what Shannon's death is about. If Kelly found something on him, then fine. But it's all tied to me—you said so. Why would this Rich Hasel—if that's even the Stalker's name—be after me?"

"It's an obsession," Lennox said. "Something I believe started years ago. You encountered each other at a place that put you both on common ground. You may not have been aware of him, but something about you called to him. He never forgot it, and over the years, it built until he envisioned a special kinship between you. All while you never knew he existed."

An acerbic taste invaded my mouth. My stomach turned rancid. I waited for the hammer to come down.

Lennox sensed this. He leaned forward until his barrel chest bumped the table. "Shannon was enrolled in the paramedic program at Penn State. This person had a connection to that program. And he knew Kelly is your lifeline."

"Rich Hasel is a Philadelphia paramedic?" I felt slow, like I'd been climbing uphill for days and still couldn't reach the top. Whatever I was missing teased my subconscious, warning me of an impending disaster. "How do you know? Are you watching him? Do you think he took Kelly?"

"Rich Hasel doesn't exist," Lennox said.

I dropped back against the booth. "Please stop talking in riddles and tell me."

Todd finally put an end to my misery. "Rich Hasel is an anagram for Chris Hale."

TWENTY-EIGHT

I felt as though I'd been thrown off a cliff and plummeted toward an angry ocean, its waves slashing against the rocks, eager to suck me into their depths. My lungs filled with imaginary water until I felt ready to burst.

"Breathe," Todd said. "You're turning purple."

I inhaled, my throat stinging.

"Say something." Todd's fingertips brushed against mine.

Shaking my head "no" took a monumental effort.

Lennox's flashy red tie suddenly seemed like the flag bullfighters waved. He played with the soft material, the red blurring until I saw nothing else. "It's true. Kelly traced the credit card Rich Hasel used to rent the car."

"It was in Chris's name? How could that be? Why would the rental company allow him to use someone else's card?" My hysterical voice caught the attention of the bartender. I tried to calm down.

"The account is in Rich's name," Lennox said. "But Kelly recognized the account number as one Chris had given her last year."

Oh my God. It couldn't be. But I remembered that day

clearly, when Chris had been determined to earn Kelly's trust. He'd given her a paper with the account number to his trust fund.

There's almost a million dollars in there, and that's all the information you need to get into my account.

"But that was to Chris's trust fund." My lips stuck together; I wiped them with a cocktail napkin and took a drink of Todd's water. "Kelly verified it."

Lennox didn't seem to be concerned about why Chris had shared the account number in the first place. "She verified the account existed. But did she verify the name on the account? The bank certainly didn't tell her that. She would have to go pretty deep into a bank's records to do that, and it's risky. Did she really think it needed to be taken that far?"

I couldn't remember Kelly actually tracing the account. My head had been too full of desperation for little Kailey Richardson. "She just said the account was good."

"Her email said that she recognized the account, and she could prove it was one and the same. She referenced the 1986 silver dollars you received, as well as the coin found with Shannon's body. She also said the crime scene was staged to resemble your sister's suicide. She was adamant Chris Hale was the Silver Stalker."

"Why did she tell you and not me?"

Lennox continued to mess with his stupid tie, smoothing it this time. "I told her to keep any communication about the Silver Stalker between us. That included you."

So what? Kelly broke law enforcement rules all the time. Maybe she thought I wouldn't believe her. Or she didn't have enough time before she was attacked.

She did it to protect you from Chris.

I pinched my lips together. Sobbing in front of Lennox wouldn't help the situation.

"She said it comes back to Camp Hopeful," Lennox said.

"Chris admitted to you he remembered you from the camp—after you found the pictures in his apartment."

I grabbed my hair, digging my fingernails into my scalp. I didn't want to remember, but it was too late. I saw the classroom at Camp Hopeful, the chairs arranged in a circle, occupied by faceless people. And me, boiling over the way my mother had treated Lily.

Lily's hair. I told them about Lily's curls.

"I told the group about how Lily's hair was done to mock my mother. Chris was there." It hurt to say the words out loud. All these years later, the spouting off of a broken, angry teenager had sealed my fate.

"Last winter, during the search for him," Lennox said, "his uncle told me about Chris—habits, hobbies, that sort of thing. He mentioned he collected coins and that his favorite was the 1986 silver dollar with the Statue of Liberty. Do you know why?"

Chris's closet, where I found the pictures. He had a drawer full of coins. Did he have silver dollars? I couldn't remember. I had to take another drink of Todd's water before I answered. The liquid did nothing to ease the gritty dryness. "Chris was born in 1986."

"Mary Weston collected coins too." Lennox's tone never changed—he never sweetened the news, but he also didn't showboat. He just laid out the facts. "She had a 1986 silver dollar with her when she was booked. There's no way to tell if Chris gave it to her or if she had it on her, but I've had a couple of conversations with her since then. She collected coins."

"So he picked up the habit from her." The rum was going to come back up. Lennox hadn't put Kelly in danger. I had when I allowed Chris into our lives.

And he warned you from the very beginning.

My hands shook. I clenched my fists.

"Do you remember when Mary was going to shoot you?" Lennox asked.

I was going to let her. "Yes."

"Her right hand is permanently damaged, so she had to use her left. Which meant her shot would have been unnatural and possibly not a very good one. You told me later she held it awkwardly, and you didn't think she'd kill you."

"So?" The shaking in my hands had spread to the rest of my body and turned me into a quivering mess of rage.

"Her cousin was shot by a right-handed person, at a distance of at least fifteen feet, by a single gunshot to the head," Lennox said. "No way could Mary have done that. Both she and Alan were left-handed. Chris is a righty."

The memories assaulted me like jabs from a knife: Chris's lie about why he originally sought me out; his ease with handling Preacher's body; the coins; the family history; the damned poster at the hospital.

"Lucy." Todd's tone teetered on the brink of anger. He'd never trusted Chris, and he'd warned me. "I know it's hard to believe, but you've got to step back and consider this from an outside perspective. His family history, the things he witnessed as a child. The lies he told you. And Kelly is the one who put it all together. You know she wouldn't have accused him if she wasn't sure."

I had no answer. No argument, and I couldn't say the words out loud. Not yet.

"You said yourself that staging Shannon's body to look like your sister's was personal. How much more personal does it get than Chris?" Lennox's dark eyes were so intense I had to look away.

A scream built in my throat as the betrayal began to set in. I'd talked to Chris about Lily. He knew the pain and the guilt. He'd even said her death was my real problem. Nothing but a carefully orchestrated act. He'd manipulated me from the beginning, just like my mother.

"But I called Chris early this morning." I clung to the last shred of hope. Surely Lennox had dreamed this all up—his involvement in Mary Weston's case clouded his judgment. Just because Chris came from two generations of madness didn't mean that he had to be evil too. "He came to help me look for Kelly after I got shot at Tesla's. Why would he do that if he was testing me?"

"What?" Todd twisted to glare at me. "You didn't say anything about being shot. Did you get it treated?"

I raised my shirt sleeve. "It's a flesh wound. Chris treated it." The irony made me sound ridiculous. I left the part about Mac out. No one else needed to know how he'd helped me. "And the picture of Kelly." I took out Kelly's phone so they both could see it, even though I'd already emailed it to Lennox. "This was taken with Jared Cook last night sometime before I found the phone. We found Jared Cook and his cousin dead earlier today. Chris said he was on shift last night, and he would have had to have killed them before he came to help me because we were together until I called you." I leaned forward eagerly, like a child trying to convince her father she hadn't been caught stealing the cookies.

"He wasn't on shift," Lennox said. "I checked."

"You were the anonymous call on the Cook murders," Todd said.

"Chris was." And he'd been so adamant the police were called. That Jared's cousin be treated with the respect he deserved. Chris had said those words right to my face, his tone dripping with compassion. Could he really have played me that well?

"All part of his game," Lennox said. "He's been leading you on from the moment he met you. He's got some grand scheme in mind."

"What?" The answer came to me before either man could speak. Chris had given it to me months ago at Chetter's.

"I think he wanted you to kill with him." Todd spoke the words I didn't have the courage to. "He fixated on you at Camp Hopeful. Years later he becomes a killer. He sees you on the news when Justin was going to be released and decides to track you down. You tell him your thoughts on pedophiles, and he sees the opportunity to groom you." His gaze slid past me to the wall. "Maybe he even hears a few very bad things about you. Somehow he sees you as an equal."

He watched me.

And he knew me. He knew how to pull my strings until I did exactly what he wanted.

"But then you changed the game," Lennox said. "You took a job on the good side. You decided you were going to stop your..." He searched for a word. "We'll stick with 'private investigating,' and leave your old life behind. That wasn't what he wanted, and you messed things up."

"And who was the catalyst for all of that?" Todd asked. "Who made you believe you could really start over?"

"Kelly." I felt as though I were still stuck in the raging ocean waves, my head trapped under water, Lennox and Todd's words not quite making sense. This couldn't be. I would have sensed it at some point.

But you did.

You just explained it all away.

Even after he told you.

This is all your fault.

You could have stopped Shannon's death and Kelly's kidnapping if you'd only listened and tried harder. Just like Lily. You could have saved her too.

I dragged my fingernails across my scalp, coming away with strands of my dark red hair.

"I know it's hard to accept," Lennox said. "And everything we've given you is circumstantial. It could all be coincidence."

Everything in my vision appeared distorted. Lennox's head swelled to the size of a balloon, his mouth moving without making a sound. Todd's drooping cheeks seemed to sag all the way down to the floor.

The final gauntlet was about to drop.

"But," Lennox continued, "we do have physical evidence."

I tried to remember what he actually looked like, focusing on his dark eyes. Lennox never revealed anything until he was sure he'd get the most bang for his buck.

I swayed on the seat. "What is it?"

"Hair was recovered from two of the Silver Stalker victims. Testing revealed both were foreign hairs from a male's head. Dark blond."

A woman's hysterical laughter doubled my irritation. I realized it was my own and clamped my mouth shut.

"It wasn't much," Lennox admitted. "But we kept them in evidence storage. Last month, I finally got a court order to test Mary Weston's DNA against the hairs found on the Silver Stalker victims."

As though I wandered onto the fringe of my memory, I saw Chris and me sitting in The Coffee Bar the day of Kailey Richardson's disappearance. I'd conned my way into her mother's apartment and had my first verbal scuffle with Todd. While I licked my wounds and planned how to find Kailey and finally nail Justin Beckett, Chris appeared out of nowhere, just as he'd done at Chetter's. I remembered his words that night as clearly as if he were sitting beside me once again.

The father was arrested, the mother too damaged to raise her son. The little boy was adopted by his aunt and uncle, who changed his name from Weston to Hale. He never stopped having the nightmares. And now he's pretty sure what he saw as a kid made him a sociopath, and he's desperate to find some sliver of humanity inside him.

"And the hairs were a matriarchal match to Mary Weston." My voice sounded like someone else's—a fool who'd been played. All of this could have been prevented if I'd only been able to get past my own ego and listen to Chris.

"They were a match," Lennox said. "So was the hair taken from Shannon's crime scene. If we hadn't caught Mary, we might not have ever been able to put it all together."

"He wanted me to find her. He said he wanted to kill her." The confession bubbled out. What did it matter now? "I told him we'd search for her but we should give the information to the police, because he didn't want that on his conscience."

How fucking stupid I'd been. Chris never wanted me to kill his mother. He'd convinced himself the three of us could have some kind of twisted family. That's what Mary had been talking about that night in the parking lot. He must have bared his soul to her during their family reunion.

"I don't think he wanted to kill her." Lennox echoed my thoughts. "I think he got tired of waiting and reached out. I think he went willingly with Mary and staged his entire kidnapping. Including cutting off his own toe."

He'd struck out at me because I didn't do what he wanted. He'd changed the game. And instead of suiting up for the role he'd intended for me, I opted out and left him with no one to play with.

"So..." I tried to grab hold of the shock and channel it into something useful. "You're telling me that Chris had a plan for me. And when I didn't follow it, he struck out by taking Shannon."

"Yes," Lennox said.

My own breathing roared through my ears, loud as a wind tunnel. I looked at Todd, half wanting to see a smug expression so I'd have someone to lash out at, but I saw only sincere worry. "And he has Kelly. He's put Kelly through a personal hell."

Because you told him how to do it. You told him what happened to her.

Both men nodded.

My hands vibrated in time with my nerves as I pulled up the picture of Kelly.

She was so damned scared and helpless.

Shannon dead, my sister used as a pawn.

Kelly tortured.

I'd been played from the beginning because I'd allowed it. Because I'd been so full of ego I couldn't see what was right in front of me.

"Lucy." Todd's warm fingers rubbed my chin. "Your lip is bleeding."

I tasted the blood; I welcomed it.

Chris wanted me to play his game. He thought he was smarter than me—and so far, he had been. But he underestimated the lengths I'd go to protect the ones I loved. And he didn't realize how willingly I'd throw my life away for them.

I looked at Todd, knowing he would be the one to put up the most fight. "Then it's time Chris and I had an honest chat."

TWENTY-NINE

"No." Todd said exactly what I expected him to say. "You're not taking this any further. It's too dangerous. He cut off his own toe to fool us. Can you imagine what he'll do to you? This is what he wants!"

A smile crept through my disgust. After all this time and all the suspicions I'd essentially confirmed, he still wanted to protect me. He should know better by now.

Agent Lennox's reaction was distinctly the opposite. He leaned forward like an eager puppy. "Tell me what you're thinking."

"Chris wants me. So I'm going to trade. Me for Kelly."

"You can't do that," Todd said.

"He expected you to call me sooner, I think." Lennox's voice brimmed with fresh energy. "He's incredibly organized and smart. And he's also educated enough to know that no matter how careful a person is, some shred of physical evidence is always left behind. When we arrested his mother, I told Chris we would be getting her DNA to match to unsolved crimes. He probably knew then his time might be limited."

"And then I decided to leave him." I had a clear purpose

now. It was just a matter of execution. Literally. "So everything escalated."

"Right," Lennox said. "You're his endgame."

"To what extent?" Todd glared at Lennox and then returned his attention to me. Worry filled his eyes. "What's he want with you?"

What did he see when he looked at me that way? Surely he saw my true personality—the one I'd tried so hard to hide from Todd. "For us to kill together. Just like you said. He told me that last fall."

Their surprised faces barely registered. I continued to spill my secrets. "It was the first night we met. He thought I killed pedophiles and wanted to team up. He said he was a sociopath. I laughed him off and got the hell out of there. He kept coming around, and I convinced myself he was really a victim of his parents. He even broke down and told me he'd never killed anyone but was afraid he was destined to do so." It all sounded so ridiculous now. How could I have been so blind?

"This was October?" Lennox asked.

"Yes."

"He was killing long before then."

"I realize that now," I said. "But I didn't want to believe it then. I thought I was smarter, better. And he played it better than any Oscar performance I've ever watched."

"He's had years to plan it all," Lennox said. "And let's face it: our society's obsession with serial criminals is a huge benefit to the intelligent ones. He's been able to study everything others did to appear normal and fine-tune it."

He glanced at Todd. "I spent a lot of time speaking with Chris after his supposed kidnapping. By then I had some suspicions, but his performance was incredible. He's able to emulate the gamut of emotions. He didn't slip even once." The hint of admiration in Lennox's voice mirrored the grudging awe I felt at Chris's ability. "But he doesn't feel a single one. He's a shell."

"Which is what makes him extremely dangerous." Todd drummed his fist on the table for emphasis. "Whatever you're planning, forget it."

"It's the only way we're going to find out where she is." I didn't have any other choice, and Kelly was running out of time. She was lucky if she had twelve hours left. And Chris was probably counting the minutes until I put it together and came calling. "He's way too many steps ahead of us right now. I have no idea where he'd hide someone. Agent Lennox, you know his anagram, and I assume you've checked into his financials. Did you come up with any place he might stash Kelly?"

Lennox shook his head. "Nothing, but just to be sure, I sent agents to check all previous crime scene locations. Nothing."

"She's somewhere close," I said. "She has to be, because he wants to be able to be my buddy and still keep an eye on her. And he wouldn't have time to drive that far." Another thought occurred to me. "What about traffic cameras? Have you checked for the Audi?"

"That's an enormous process," Lennox said. "We have asked for the shots, but we don't want to clue in the Philly PD. No offense, Detective Beckett. But with his uncle being the assistant district attorney, there's no reason not to assume Chris doesn't have contacts on the police force. We can't run the risk. And going over those tapes takes hours we don't have."

"Which means I need to confront him." I directed my words to Todd. "That's what he wants. He's got to believe he's in control, or we'll never save her. It's the only way."

"If you think you'll be able to wear a wire or some kind of tracking device, you're crazy," Todd said. "He's too smart for that. That's the first thing he'll check for."

"So you guys are going to have to figure out a way to track me without Chris knowing it." I glanced at Lennox. He looked as ready for this fight as I felt. "That's your thing."

"It'll have to be boots on the ground, old-fashioned police

work. We can't put anyone new in his building—too obvious. We moved an agent into the vacant apartment on his floor shortly after Chris was rescued in Maryland." Lennox's jittery movements matched my own frenetic energy. Revenge—it's what I excelled at.

"Our agent's very familiar with his routine, and we don't believe he's made her," Lennox said. "But we haven't risked trying to approach him or putting any sort of listening device in his apartment. However, we can coordinate so that she knows when you arrive and when you leave."

"And then what?" Todd still remained unconvinced.

"As soon as I got the DNA match, I put another agent in place at the sandwich shop adjacent to his building," Lennox said. "He's on shift now and will be able to follow Lucy if she leaves with Chris. You and I will be in position nearby."

"I don't like it." Todd eyes stayed on me. "You're not thinking clearly. He's planned this all out. He's played all of us. He's going to be a step ahead of you no matter what we do."

I felt sluggish, yet my thoughts raced. "Until I catch up. And I will, because he made a mistake in involving Kelly." I lowered my voice in an effort to stay in control of my emotions. "He's underestimating me."

Todd's jaw muscles tightened. His eyes bored into mine. A silent communication passed between us. He knew what I would do if given the chance.

"I can't let you." His soft words carried a dual meaning. "Not over him."

"Over Kelly," I corrected. "And I have to." Impulsively, I reached for his hand. "Please. If I don't do it, she'll die. I can't live with that."

His tight grip made my fingers ache. "What if he kills you first?"

"He won't. He's got to put on a show for me."

"I agree," Lennox said. "Detective, I realize you have

personal involvement. I brought you in for Lucy's moral support. But I don't need you on board with the decision. It's mine to make, if she's willing."

I looked at Todd once more, silently pleading. I wasn't backing out, but I wanted him to agree.

He held up his hands. "Fine. But if something happens to her..." He pointed to Lennox. "I'm holding you personally responsible. And I won't keep quiet."

"Fair enough," Lennox said.

Todd sighed. "We need to be in separate vehicles. That way we cover more ground."

"Agreed," Lennox said. "The Audi is the only vehicle registered to him, and we know the makes and models of his aunt and uncle's vehicles. As of noon today, there were no rentals under his anagram."

"Doesn't mean there won't be now," Todd said.

"We'll check again before she moves in."

I was really going to do this. Fully aware of what I was capable of, Agent Lennox was going to let me face off with Chris.

He knew I didn't have any drugs or poison left. In his mind, I would be completely helpless.

Let him continue to underestimate me.

"I can have everything in place within fifteen minutes," Lennox said. "The sooner we move, the better. I think Kelly's still alive because he wants you to see his work in person, but his patience may run out."

"Then you'd better get started."

Lennox excused himself. As soon as the agent disappeared around the corner, Todd grabbed my hand again. "You can still change your mind."

"You know I can't."

"Why didn't you tell me about Kelly?" He asked the question I'd been waiting for. And I gave him the answer I owed him.

"Because I was going to kill the man who took her. I didn't want your morals interfering." I saw absolutely no reason to keep pretending Todd wasn't aware of the things I'd done.

"Please, stop," Todd said. "I can't hear any more of this. If you start telling me things—"

"Isn't this what you wanted? You've always believed it."

"That was before." His face reddened; his words came quickly. "I blamed you for not helping my brother when he was a kid, and then you came barging in on Kailey's case. You were so cocky and bullheaded and determined to destroy Justin. The idea of putting you away for the rest of your life was intoxicating. But then you admitted you were wrong. And you tried to fix things."

"I did a bang-up job of that, didn't I?" I leaned against the booth and took another long drink of water. Rum would have been better.

"The point is, you wanted to make it right. And I could tell that you really believed in what you were doing. And you cared." Todd interlaced his fingers with mine. "Somehow, the line between right and wrong started to blur, and now I can't even see it. If you tell me the truth, I'll have to find it again. I don't want to do that."

"But I'm no better than those men," I said. "Shouldn't I be held accountable?"

"Probably," Todd said. "I don't want to do that. I didn't want you to move to Alexandria, but I knew it was your only hope. I had this dream—I still do—of you realizing that in spite of all the bad choices, you're still a good person. That you have people who care about you and need you in their lives. Who want you in their life."

His heartfelt words should have invoked tears or some brief glimmer of happiness. But my emotions were stuck on the task ahead. I couldn't rest until Kelly was safe and Chris exactly where he deserved to be. "You're worthy of so much more than me," I said.

"I want you," he said. "And you don't get to change that."

I should have told him to figure out a way. He needed to accept the chances of me coming out of this situation unscathed were slim. I had no right to tether us. But I really needed him to know I felt the same. "I don't want to change it." I squeezed his hand, knowing that I had to offer him something honest. "If I don't come back, you need to know I feel the same way."

He smiled grimly, his eyes bright. "You're coming back. We aren't going to let Chris kill you."

My smile felt as twisted as my soul. "I'm not worried about that. But his uncle might not accept I killed his precious nephew in self-defense."

THIRTY

Lennox wanted me to park in the street, but since blue skies and oppressive humidity had triumphed over the storms, Center City swelled with activity. The parking garage presented a whole new level of complications, but I didn't see any way around it.

Chris had happily accepted my phone call to talk after Mac's death. Getting into his apartment posed no issue.

"Keep your phone on as long as possible." Lennox used an unregistered phone in case Chris decided to check my caller ID. "I'm sure he'll force you to give it up, but we might get lucky and be able to track the GPS for a while."

I doubted it. "All right." I maneuvered the Prius into an end spot. "I'm on the second level, east side, near the elevator. Any last words of advice?" I double-checked my pockets to make sure my identification was still there. After we left the bar, I'd run to the nearest thrift store and bought a change of clothes. Nothing more than an old T-shirt and cutoffs, but least I no longer wore shorts caked in mud.

"Don't kill the guy unless you have to," Lennox said. "I've got a lot of questions for him."

I wondered if he could see me smiling. "I'll do my best."

"Once you leave his apartment, you need to stall him. Stay aware of your surroundings. And if he does take you to Kelly, keep your cool. We need as much time as possible to find you."

"You're not going to be able to stay on our tail," I said. "You won't be able to get that close. He'll lose you near the end." I shut off the ignition.

"I know," Lennox said. "But I'm hoping things will be narrowed down enough that my people can figure out a search grid. That's why you need to stall him. Let him think he's won. I don't think you need coaching on how to deal with him. Your biggest issue is going to be your temper."

"Or I could just kill him and bring Kelly home." I had no idea how I planned to defeat Chris since he had every advantage. But I'd improvise.

Lennox grunted. "The thing is, I know you're not joking. You really think his uncle won't find a way to throw you in prison? Self-defense won't matter this time."

"Maybe I don't care," I said.

"You better start caring. Kelly's going to need you."

Score another one for the agent. The man missed very little.

"Look," he said. "You're one of the strangest people I've ever encountered. We both know I could have hauled you in a long time ago. But I don't think the world is a better place with Lucy Kendall in prison."

"But I'm a danger to society."

"I'm betting you've learned the error of your ways," Lennox said. "Like I said, you're an enigma. And I'm taking a risk on you."

"So much for the FBI being on the straight and narrow." He probably wouldn't feel that way if I killed his star criminal. He wanted to study Chris, analyze him. I couldn't blame him. But did the man deserve to live? I didn't think he deserved to be provided a place to sleep and three meals a day on the state's dime.

"Life isn't that easy, and you know it. I've got too many psychos like Chris Hale running around to worry about you."

I stepped out of the car, welcoming the humidity. "There's something else I need to tell you. In case I don't get another chance."

"Go ahead."

"I found your sister."

A beat of charged silence passed. "What?"

"I wanted to pay you back for the recommendation to NCMEC. So Kelly and I started looking. It ended up being a stroke of luck after a big investigation into another trafficking ring. The pimp kept a photo collection of his girls. Her picture was old, but I recognized her tattoo from an old mug shot."

"She's dead." He spoke flatly.

"I'm sorry. She's an unidentified in a morgue in Chicago."

"Thank you." Lennox's tight voice gave me my first breath of peace in days. "I knew she was gone, but to have closure..."

"I know."

He cleared his throat. "Lucy. Watch yourself."

"Don't worry about me." I ended the call and stepped into the elevator.

THIRTY-ONE

I stared at Chris's door, a bitter mix of fear and adrenaline tainting my mouth. The gold number seemed to tease me. My shattered ego threatened to ruin everything before I even got started, but I found a way to shut down the voices. None of it mattered now. The playing field had finally been evened.

I knocked once. He answered the door with a wary smile. Did he know Agent Lennox had arrived and that I'd been with him? Or had he bought the story that I needed to vent about Mac and my mother?

"Hey." He stepped aside so I could walk into his apartment. What once appeared pristine and rich now looked stark and terrifying. "I'm sorry about Mac."

"Thanks." How long did I keep up the charade?

I walked to the large window that overlooked the neighborhood. Several stories up, I doubted any of the undercover agents saw me. But I still felt a tiny bit of comfort. "My mother and I finally had it out."

He stood a few feet away, leaning casually against the table. His mouth dropped open. "Really?"

"It was cathartic," I said. "Telling her what a miserable bitch she was opened my eyes to so many things."

"I'm glad," he said. "I know it's hard, but it'll get better from here. She was never a parent anyway. You won't miss her. Mac, on the other hand. That sucks."

"It does." I wouldn't tell him how I felt about Mac. No way in hell.

"What about Kelly?" The concern is his voice sparked a feral rage. "I assume Beckett's working on it?"

"He sent a crime scene crew to her apartment," I said. "He's got forensic people reviewing the video, and everyone in the building's being questioned. He thinks the super might have some information."

"Really?" Not a shred of worry in Chris's voice. "Hopefully he's right. The problem's going to be narrowing down suspects."

"No. The list has been narrowed significantly."

"How?" Finally, a teensy falter, a little hiccup in his smooth voice.

"I gave him the names of all the men I've murdered. Including Preacher."

Perverse excitement washed through me at the astonishment on his face. "Are you serious? Why would you do that? You'll go to jail."

"I don't care. Kelly's all that matters."

Chris's hands went to his hair, dragging through it until it stood on end. "There had to be another way. Beckett's been waiting for this. You just handed over your life."

"Don't you mean 'our' life?" I hadn't planned on exactly how I'd get to the real heart of things. But there it was, hanging out there like a giant elephant we couldn't ignore.

"What?" Chris's voice turned sharp. "Did you tell him I helped with Preacher?"

"Of course not. You're safe. Just as you intended."

He cocked his head, those penetrating blue eyes searching

mine. Now I understood why they'd always unsettled me. It wasn't attraction. It was the beast hiding behind them.

"It's time to stop playing games," I said. "I'm here. That's what you want."

A smile played on the corner of his pretty lips. "I don't follow."

"Do you want me to explain it? Is that what you'd prefer?"

"I would."

He wanted to be praised. To hear how he'd fooled me from the very beginning. His arrogance would be his undoing.

Admitting my mistake to him stung worse than accidentally stepping onto a hornets' nest. But it had to be done. "I should have listened to you that night at Chetter's. You told me exactly who you were, and I was too cocky to believe it. Surely I had no equal. And yet there you were. The sociopath in shining armor."

Now the smile broke wide. "Go on."

"You wanted us to be partners. That was the truth. Did you expect me to say yes right away, or did you anticipate my thinking you were just a poor boy whose parents had done terrible things?" Part of me really wanted to know the answer. His mind was like nothing I'd ever encountered. I couldn't blame Lennox for wanting to bring Chris in alive.

A kind of swagger took over his movements as he crossed his feet in front of him and leaned back against the table, his broad smile reminding me of a jack-o-lantern. Nothing on the inside. "In a perfect world, you would have accepted my offer right away. But I didn't expect you to. So I had a plan B. And C. That's the key to success, you know. Anticipate every possible outcome and plan accordingly."

"But you didn't anticipate my moving to Alexandria."

A shadow rose in his eyes. "No. That's when I had to change course."

"Shannon."

"A nice girl," he said. "She hadn't been on my radar. But when she showed up at the paramedic class and I realized who she was, how could I resist? It was all too perfect."

"That's how I figured it out," I said. "I saw a poster in the hospital. You were on it. Everything clicked."

"Finally." He threw up his hands. "I've given you so many hints. I really thought you were smarter."

"I'm sorry I disappointed you." I kept my voice even, trying to squash the hatred. "So since Kelly's down to less than eight hours, let's get down to it."

He crossed his arms, his grin on the verge of maniacal. "Go ahead."

"You want me as a partner. I'm here. I'll do whatever you want. Just let Kelly go."

"Really?"

"Yes. You want to be a killing team, I'll follow. I'll give up everything."

"And Kelly goes free," he said.

"Yes."

"Then she tells the police."

"Not if I ask her to let us go. I'll make her understand."

Chris's boisterous laugh made me want to attack him. "Sure you will. The second you get the chance, you'll call your cop boyfriend and turn me in."

I shook my head. "I won't."

"Why should I believe you? I know you, Lucy. It's not in your nature to just roll over."

I had to make him believe he'd already beaten me. He needed to see the defeat on my face. I thought about Mac, watching his last breaths—of the realization my own ego had done this to Kelly and to Shannon. "There's nothing left for me," I said. "Mac's gone. Kelly's hurting. I don't have the willpower to keep fighting. And she means more to me than my own happiness."

His amusement turned to disgust. "Of course. I'm always last. Yet I'm the only person who understands you."

His earlier words in the car took on new meaning. He wasn't talking about love. He meant the destiny he imagined for us. "I can't argue that. You do understand me. You made me feel like I wasn't alone in my head. I owe you for that."

He jammed his hands into his pockets and started to pace. "You owe me for everything. I've done so much for you, and you see nothing."

"I'm sorry. But I'm trying to make it right."

"You're trying to save your precious Kelly." Spittle bubbled on the corner of his mouth. "That's it. You don't see why we are so good for each other. Why we should be together."

He couldn't hide the longing in his voice. Sociopaths weren't supposed to love, and I wasn't deluded enough to think Chris felt that way. But he'd attached himself to me in a way that was more than just partnership. I represented something to him. I just needed to figure out what.

"I promise I'll stay with you," I said. "Just let Kelly go."

"This isn't how it was supposed to be." He moved like a cat, languid and fast at the same time. Every muscle in my tired body tensed, anticipating the strike. But he was still too fast. I raised my hands to block him, but the needle sank into my bicep with enough force my knees buckled.

"The thing is"—Chris's lips moved against my ear—"you almost found her. You just didn't look closely enough."

THIRTY-TWO

He'd injected me with something. The drug invaded my bloodstream, its effects immediate. The beating of my heart accelerated to the point I thought I could reach out and grab it. I stumbled backward, the entire room spinning as though I'd taken multiple shots of alcohol all at once.

My fingers numbed. Coordination abandoned me, and I hit the floor hard. Something snapped, and on some level I realized it must have been my arm. But I didn't really feel pain. Just an uncomfortable tingling sensation.

Giant blue orbs appeared in front of me and then blinked.

"Feel good?"

"What did you give me?" The words felt stuck to my tongue.

"One of your favorites." His white teeth were dazzling. "Ketamine."

A voice in a far corner of my mind shouted a warning. I couldn't understand it.

The blue orbs continued to stare at me. I felt serene on the surface, but fear crawled beneath my skin, trying to escape.

"Who knows you're here?" Chris's voice sounded like silk: a black, silk scarf stretching out as far as I could see.

I wasn't supposed to tell him. But the drug stripped away all the confusion. Why not tell him? Keeping secrets took so much effort and caused me pain.

"Agent Lennox and Todd."

"Good girl. And are they going to follow us?"

My head felt like an inflated balloon escaping into the wind. I couldn't figure out how to answer him.

His hand floated in front of my face. "I didn't give you as much as Preacher. Too dangerous for the first time. Unless you want to go through the K-hole?"

What was that again? Out of body? Slipping away from the conscious?

"No."

"I don't blame you. Not the first time." The silk scarf changed. A deformed head with red slits for eyes appeared at the end, its jaws open and coming straight at me. "But I think we could give you a little more, just to make things easier on me."

I saw the needle, and I heard myself say "No."

But he injected me anyway.

My body became liquid. I danced across Chris's apartment, as graceful as a ballerina. He danced with me, all smoke and silk. I felt weightless. No more worries, no more guilt. Finally free of every fear that had dragged me down. I jumped high, arms outstretched. Chris caught me around the waist, and we waltzed through his bright apartment.

So bright. Like a floating room in the clouds.

Words on the tip of my tongue, but my mouth couldn't work. I felt the muscles straining, but nothing.

The room in the clouds disappeared. Everything became very dark, with lights streaking in the distance. I wanted to reach out and capture the lights. I looked down; where was my body? Chris had taken it away and left me with only my floating head.

Suddenly the lights buckled into a green corridor, the walls flashing like static.

And then I saw the shadow. Two arms and legs. A definite head.

Someone was there!

I cried out but only in my head. My mouth didn't work. I'd been thrust into a well of tormented souls, millions of tangled rubber bands all forming one giant mass. I couldn't see the creatures, but I felt them. They stroked my hair, touched my face. Whispered into my ear.

One of them started screaming.

"Murderer! Murderer!"

The shadow started to move away. I couldn't let that happen. He had to tell me how to get out of this place.

Please. Please help me. This isn't what I want.

The shadow turned. I strained to see its face.

"Why should anyone help you?"

Blank space. I couldn't muster a single reason why I deserved to be pulled out of this strange dimension.

"You're a killer." The shadow was talking again.

I know. I'm sorry.

"You don't get to be forgiven. Murder is murder." The shadow moved closer. I saw almond-shaped eyes and a circular mouth.

You're right. I have no excuse. I deserve to be trapped here forever.

The static turned luminous, until the tunnel became so bright I had to close my eyes.

"Why did you kill us?"

Who was the shadow? His face still consisted of only eyes and mouth.

Because I thought I could make up for not saving my sister. I thought it was my fault. But my mother knew Lily was being molested. She knew the whole time.

"That doesn't make your actions right." His voice—if that's what it really was—appeared to soften.

I know. But I have to get out of here. I have a reason.

But what was it? I couldn't think of anything but the freakishly bright white and the static and the weird shadow man. My body or whatever existed on this plane curled up in a pugilistic stance.

I'm done.

THIRTY-THREE

I became aware of my surroundings gradually. The heady scent of urine and feces struck first, so pungent I started to gag. Darkness flashed several times before I realized my eyes were trying to open. The lids felt glued to my skin. A wretched tingling pierced my feet, as though I'd been sitting on them too long, and they were finally coming back to life. Something soft and firm surrounded me, its distressed material warm against my fingers. An armchair.

I tried to sit up, but a sharp jerk against my midsection stopped me cold. The rope burned the flesh on my arms. Carefully, I wiggled my hands until I figured out exactly how I'd been tied up: arms trapped to my sides, rope wrapped tightly around the chair. My ankles were bound with some kind of wire that cut into my skin.

My chapped lips struggled to speak; my mouth stung.

A burning sensation struck my right wrist and then a dull, consistent pain. I vaguely remembered falling in Chris's apartment. I must have broken it.

Something else lodged in my conscious: a soft, choked whimper, followed by several sharp intakes of breath. A woman crying for her life. Her rapid, retched breathing elicited a terror I'd never experienced.

"Hello?" I sounded as though I'd been eating gravel, the effort of speaking tearing up my throat. "Kelly?"

The woman cried out something I couldn't understand. The language didn't matter—her high-pitched anguish said enough. And she wasn't Kelly.

Where am I? How far away from the city has Chris taken me? I had no way of knowing how long I'd been unconscious, and my head still felt foggy from the drug.

Get it together.

After several more attempts, my eyes finally remained open. I searched for something to help get my bearings, my mind racing faster with every passing second. A house of some sort, I finally decided. Did Chris own other property? Had he used his alias? Was the place really pitch black or just blocked out like the Cooks' house?

My eyes adjusted to the lack of light. I made out shapes—or rather, the lack of them. No furniture. Just the chair I sat in and a metal folding chair. Was that a rickety end table next to me? I shifted, hoping to get some blood into my limbs and loosen the rope. But my efforts only made me sink deeper into the chair I'd been tied to, the cushion broken down into a perfectly shaped butt spot. The chair seemed familiar, but I couldn't figure out why until I caught the scent of Old Spice and cigars.

"Oh my God."

"Very good." Chris's soft voice sent spasms of fear up my back. I squirmed against the rope as light suddenly filled the sparse room. Sorrow dragged over my throat with the burn of hot coals. The pain of the day sucked away any remaining resilience.

The place looked just as it had when Mac had taken the bullet out of my arm, less than twenty-four hours ago.

And now he's gone.

The tears squeezed out of my eyes before I could will them away.

"Mac's little hideaway." Chris stepped into my line of sight, looking exactly the same but still entirely different. He still wore his hair strategically messy, his clothes unremarkable—the same black shirt and jeans he'd worn before he injected me with ketamine. His face had become a caricature of the man I thought I knew.

It was as though Chris had suddenly stepped off the pages of a blank coloring book and become three-dimensional. Rosy-cheeked and slightly out of breath, eyes shimmering like blue topaz, he reminded me of a man who'd just had a satisfying round of sex. Everything about him seemed larger, more potent, and absolutely barbarian.

"I thought it would be the perfect place for us to take the next step." His voice had a singsong quality, or maybe that was just the lingering effect of the drug. "After all, you're the only one who knows about it."

"That's not true. I told Todd."

Chris's once charming smile was more suited for a sadistic clown. "Now, now. Don't lie to me."

"I'm not."

"Lucy. Have you forgotten how the ketamine works?"

It's like a truth serum.

He laughed at my obvious panic. "You gave Preacher enough to make him tell you everything. I didn't go quite that far because I didn't want to hurt you. But you told me enough."

Chris grabbed the folding chair and placed it in front of me. He sat down, crossing his legs, his hands around his knee. "I'm confident Lennox's plans to tail us failed. How's the wrist? It's broken. I set it the best I could, but I don't have the materials for a proper cast."

He'd used an Ace bandage and a plastic brace, but I could feel the awkward position of the bone.

"At least I had a splint at my apartment," he said. "But it's not going to heal straight unless you go to the hospital and have them re-break it. We can't do that until things are worked out."

I dropped my head against the soft back of Mac's old chair. Now that I was aware of the break, the pain doubled. I gritted my teeth and tried not to show the weakness.

In the darkness to my left, the desperate mewling came again. Instinct demanded I look for the sound, and I instantly regretted it.

Chris's hum of appreciation scared the hell out of me.

I asked the question I knew he wanted to hear. "Who is that?"

He still sat with his legs crossed—the doctor assessing his patient. "We'll get to her eventually."

Fear rose up in my throat, my pulse hammering. I tried to slow down, taking deep breaths. He had the upper hand, just as he wanted. If I could keep my head, I could still use his arrogance to my advantage.

Before I could speak, he stretched his legs out, hands on the back of his head. "Shannon was afraid of the dark. Did you know that?"

"No." How was I going to prevent him from breaking me down? He knew how to strip away my control.

"Her mother was an alcoholic," Chris said. "You knew that. When Shannon was little, she used to put her in the closet so she could drink with her friends and not worry about the kid getting hurt. Hence the fear of the dark."

Shannon hadn't told me, but I wasn't surprised. I'd heard plenty of similar stories throughout my career.

Chris continued, obviously happy to have my undivided attention. "Personally, I love the dark. That's when my grandfather and I used to go hunting."

He laughed at my surprise. "Yes, I remember him. Before everything went south, he took me out to find the girls. I even picked one of them out. I thought her hair was pretty." He looked at his fingernails. "I don't remember her name. But I remember how she cried in the barn. She was afraid of the dark too."

I felt lightheaded, but I needed to keep him talking. Make him think I still cared. "So you knew your parents were killers?"

"I knew they were people on a mission. I knew fun things went on in the barn because I heard my mother and grandpa come back laughing. I thought I was missing the party."

"And what about your father?"

Chris rolled his eyes. "He tagged along. Did whatever my mother said, but he didn't have the same passion as her or Grandpa. It's his fault they got caught, by the way."

I waited.

Clearly enjoying his audience, Chris chattered on. "I wasn't allowed in the barn because there were things in there that could hurt a little boy. But Grandpa was going to show me the family trade soon. He'd promised. My father didn't like that, and one day he told me to go into the barn and decide for myself. So I did. And you know what happened after that." He laughed, rubbing his hands together. "At least he's the one who went to prison. Talk about karma."

I saw the opportunity and took a shot at getting him off kilter. "But your mother abandoned you. She left you to your uncle and went on to a new life."

His face changed again, tightening in anger. Just like that, his pretense disappeared. The real Chris appeared, eyes as dead as any body lying in the morgue. He was the scariest thing I'd ever encountered. "She was supposed to come back. But she changed her mind. I'd planned to kill her. And then it seemed perfect if you were the one to kill her—your initiation into my real life."

"Why didn't you kill her?" I needed to know the answers. He'd played me for so long, and I hadn't had any real clue. Even when I caught him in lies, I never thought past his just being generally screwed-up. Now that I realized the extent of his deception, a tiny part of me was tantalizingly curious. How had he done it?

"My grandpa is the one who met me that day outside of Jarrettsville," Chris said. "He thought I was an imposter and shot at me, but when I started talking, he knew I was really little Chris. And he brought me back into the family."

"He helped you and your mom make amends."

Chris didn't confirm or deny my assumption. "I'm glad I got to see him before he died. I just wish he could have been buried with the rest of the family. He wanted to be put in the crypt, even if it hadn't been used in decades. His ancestors were war heroes, and so was he. So he thought it was fitting." He drew his legs back and sat up straight. "But, oh well. And now you know why I keep the girls in the dark. So they can truly appreciate it."

"You keep them in the dark because it heightens their fear."

"That too." Admiration briefly crossed his face. "I've got so much to tell you. But we've got some things to work out first."

"So let's get down to all of it."

Chris cocked his head, pursing his red lips as though he were considering a purchase. "Just like that?"

"Isn't this what you've been building toward all these months?"

"You already know what I want." He didn't blink as he watched me, his eyes seeming to burrow into mine.

He wants to consume me.

"A killing partner. That's the easy answer." Survival instinct begged me to look anywhere but at his deceptive gaze, but I maintained eye contact. Why had I ever thought I could see into the depths of his soul when I looked at him? He was empty. "But I think you want me to know why. To understand. Because isn't that part of what bonds us? That we're the only ones who understand our actions?"

He regarded me for a moment. The woman in the other room cried harder. I wanted to scream at her to shut up—that I was trying to save us both—but I couldn't concentrate with her constant yowling.

"I understand you." Chris pointed a long finger at me. "I have from the moment I realized you were a killer. After Jake and Riley, I thought you were coming around to understanding yourself." Chris inhaled, eyes briefly closed, his expression turning dreamy. "I had so many plans for us, and we were so close. But then you just crashed."

"Jake and Riley were about self-defense."

His shoulders bounced with a silent laugh. "Don't lie to yourself. Those kills were about self-preservation, not defense."

I needed to change the subject. Get him talking about himself. Let the arrogance flow. "I won't pretend to know you."

"You couldn't possibly. I told you who I was, and you kept making excuses."

"I was too cocky." Lying would only get me into more trouble. "I thought I was the teacher, and you were the pupil."

"You assumed you knew better than me." His voice grew louder with every word. "I eventually believed you'd come around, so I let it ride. That's not to say I didn't make things happen along the way—keep you on the right path."

He patted his chest, and I drew back in the chair. Whatever he was about to say was going to be awful.

"Sarah, of course. The owner of Exhale Salon, remember? And her boyfriend." His blasé way of speaking—like we were talking about something as boring as the weather—turned me ice cold. Chris cared about nothing, and yet he made everyone he encountered believe his intentions were pure. He blended into society like the rat living in the sewers. And he planned every meticulous moment.

As he watched my internal struggle, I swore he'd somehow managed to crawl inside my skin and infiltrate my mind. I wanted to flee, to be anywhere else but here. My mother's house suddenly seemed like heaven.

"Why?" I choked.

"I thought—mistakenly—that being the center of a murder investigation would make you snap and embrace who you really are." His posture slumped. "But it didn't, and I had to frame her ex-boyfriend. That was a depressing time. I had to start all over. But fortunately my mother answered her email."

I'd thought as much when Lennox told me everything, but to hear it all now only confirmed the depths Chris went to. He was even smarter than I'd imagined. "You knew your mother was Justin's mother before we even went into her basement, right? It was all an act."

A smirk danced at the corner of his mouth, but the girl's intensified pleading drew his attention. He stared in her direction like a starving animal on the hunt. When he looked back at me, the lifelessness of his gaze almost stripped me of the last bit of courage. "Let's get back to you. I saw your face after you killed Preacher. You liked watching him die."

He knew about Mary all along.

Keep playing the game.

"Because he was a bad person who deserved it." I didn't want to think of the rush I'd experienced smothering the life out of Preacher, even though I knew that's exactly what Chris wanted me to admit.

Another laugh from him, this one loud and boisterous. "There you go, playing judge and jury again. You know that's all bullshit, Lucy. You just needed to find a way to justify your need to completely dominate another human being. To control them to the point of saying whether they lived or died."

He dropped his crossed leg, his boot landing hard on the floor. The light played off his face as he leaned forward, making him look even more effervescent. "Tell me you don't think about it every day. Maybe when you're driving in a parking lot and some ungrateful prick cuts you off. Or an old woman is walking in the middle of the aisle, oblivious to anything around her."

His voice lowered to a husky tone that had once given me chills of desire. "Admit it. You've imagined grabbing them by their hair and cutting their throats. Or yanking the selfish driver out of his truck and beating him until he was so scared he pissed himself and begged for mercy."

I shook my head. It didn't matter that he had a point. I would never do those things just for kicks. I had remorse. Chris didn't even know the meaning of the word.

"Oh yes," Chris said. "See, those are the everyday urges we both have to control. Such a pain in the ass. Let me tell you, I've come close so many times in the ambulance. Some of the thugs and worthless human beings I have to haul to the hospital. Who would miss them? But there's no fun in any of that. Controlling the urge, denying yourself. That makes the real fun so much better." He licked his lips.

The girl whimpered again for help. Chris's hands twitched.

I felt trapped inside my own skin. "What do you want me to do?"

The smile again—the child-killing clown. "You said you would stay with me. Kill with me."

Sweat saturated the back of my neck, my arms burning from the pressure of the rope. "If you let Kelly go."

His eyes closed briefly, his shoulders slowing raising and then falling again. And then an inhuman, cold blue stare. "You have to prove yourself for me to even consider your offer."

THIRTY-FOUR

The girl's bare feet dragged against the floor as Chris pulled her in from the bedroom. Twine bound her wrists and ankles. Her short, denim skirt barely covered her small thighs; her halter top fell just beneath her pushed-up breasts. Fresh welts covered her long legs.

Chris shoved her onto the floor in front of me. She fell into a heap, helpless with her hands duct-taped behind her back. More duct tape concealed her eyes.

The residue on Shannon's face.

He takes away their sight to amplify their fear.

The girl's head whipped back and forth. She must have sensed someone else in the room, as she slithered toward me until her head bumped into my leg. Her pitiful cry made my head hurt.

"Who's there? I heard you talking! Help me."

I jerked at my restraints, fighting the pain of my wrist. The wire cut deeper into my ankles.

"I chose her for you." Chris sat back down. "Normally I'm not selective. But I know you like to pretend you have some kind of moral code, so I figured she was a good choice."

The girl continued to beg for her life, her words too nonsensical to understand.

"I can't do this." The argument was futile, but I had to make it. I raised my voice over the mewling. "Not like this. I need to prepare."

"Kelly's life is at stake," Chris said. "What more preparation do you need?" He kicked the girl's hip. "Shut up. You know you need to be punished."

"I don't," she sobbed. "I didn't do anything."

"Oh yes you did." Chris wagged his finger at her, exuberance lighting up his face. "You stood by while that piece of shit molested your little girl." His gaze slid to mine. The reflecting light made his eyes glow like the beast's who waited in the closest. "Just like someone else we know. Right, Luce?"

My insides froze. How could he possibly know about Joan? I'd never told him.

"I do my research." As usual, he knew what I was thinking. "And my uncle's got some connections. Did you know the police who questioned your mother suspected her of knowing all along? They threatened to charge her with neglect, but in the end didn't have enough evidence. That's why the social worker visited you for several months after Lily's death. Do you remember?"

That social worker had been my only sliver of light back then. Joan claimed she was checking in on us to make sure we were coping with Lily's death. My mother lied to me. Imagine that.

"See," he said. "I know more about your life than you do."

Chris's cartoonish smile and his arrogance stoked my anger. Maybe I had some fight left after all. "Actually, I already knew about Joan. She admitted it to me. I just didn't tell you."

He struggled to keep his expression passive, but I saw the twitch between his eyes. "You're lying."

"Am I? You know me too well for that." As long as he didn't

ask when I discovered the truth, I could cling to the minuscule advantage.

"Whatever. It makes no difference to me. The point is this woman is just like your mother." He got up and thrust his boot into the woman's side. "She allowed her daughter to be raped by her live-in boyfriend."

She shrieked in pain. Still flailing like a fish about to be gutted, the woman on the floor continued to plead for her life. "I didn't know. That's what my boyfriend told the police, but he's a liar. I turned him in the second my baby told me. If I'd known, I would have killed him!"

Tears dampened the duct tape over her eyes, and mucus oozed from her broken nose. "Please."

Chris stood up and stretched. "I call bullshit. Do you really think it's possible for her to live in the same house and not know what was going on?"

"I worked nights," the woman cried. "He was taking care of her. I trusted him."

"Nights." Chris made quotation marks with his fingers, dancing around the sobbing woman. "That's code for being a hooker. She was out spreading her legs while her daughter was violated."

He stepped over her, his foot using her back like a stool. She screamed in pain. Chris knelt in front of me and put his hands on my thighs. I fought not to recoil. I should have slammed my knees into his chin, but I was injured and bound. And he would have only gotten angrier.

"Lucy, we've discussed this. You can't have it both ways. If you're going to hold the boyfriend responsible, then you have to hold this poor excuse for a mother responsible too." He ran his hand down my legs, stroking my calves. "Unless you want to be a hypocrite."

"You said you wanted to be partners." I decided to try again. "That means equal say. I didn't choose her. I haven't confirmed your story. You know my code. If you want me to kill with you, then you need to be fair."

He let go of my legs and moved closer until his face was only inches from mine. "Fair? Are you seriously saying life should be fair?" He didn't look away, didn't even blink. He just kept staring at me.

An acute fear unlike anything I'd ever experienced seized me. I felt as though I'd been yanked out of my body for a split second and then thrust back in, but without the exact fit. The protective layer of my flesh dissolved. My brain completely unhinged. Tremors attacked, and my body stretched to the point of snapping.

Chris smiled, and the first sign of real emotion flickered in his eyes. But it wasn't compassion or even arousal.

It was sheer glee.

"Do you know why I kill?" His whisper amplified the assault on my senses. I couldn't even figure out how to shake my head. He traced my cheek and then my mouth, and finally his hand slid over my eyes. "For this. The fear." He inhaled; his head dropped back in ecstasy. "It's like a drug. I swear to God I can smell it. All I've got to do is breathe it in, and I'm flying."

I'm going to die.

So is Kelly.

"So here's the deal." Chris pulled his gun out of his pocket as he stood up. "Either you kill her, or you'll never see Kelly again."

The woman let loose a fresh wail. "My name is Maura. I have a seven-year-old daughter. I'm all she's got. Please."

Chris ignored her. He reached into his pocket and pulled out a shining, silver coin. "This is my last 1986 centennial coin. It's kind of symbolic, don't you think? Our first act as true equals."

Unable to speak, I forced a nod.

With his dead eyes focused on mine, he stepped close to me,

his breath in my face. He slipped the coin into the pocket of my cutoffs. "You can put it on her when she's dead."

Keeping his gun on me, he slid a knife out of his pocket and began cutting the rope. "If you try to run or fight back, believe me when I say I'll shoot you. Then I'll kill Maura here, and then Kelly. And before I kill Kelly, I'll make sure she knows you chose yourself over her life."

The pressure of the rope eased. I started to rise from the chair, and Chris pulled the magazine off the gun, the muzzle less than three inches from my face. My wrist and forearm throbbed with pain.

Maura rolled onto her back. "Please. Your name's Lucy, right? Don't do this. Think of my little girl."

"I don't want to hurt you." I kept my eyes on Chris. "But I'm trying to save my family too."

"You're going to have to be creative," he said. "No poison here. And I'm certainly not giving you my gun."

Was I really going to do this? How could I take this woman's life?

How could you have taken anyone's life?

And what's one more? For Kelly?

"I'm getting bored," Chris said. "You won't like me when I get bored."

I didn't have a choice. This would be the one thing I'd never be able to forgive, but it was for Kelly. I grabbed the seat cushion of the armchair with my left hand. The cushion felt like an anchor.

Holding my right arm close, I dropped to the floor next to Maura. Chris drew closer, his gun ready to fire.

Could I tell her to fight? What if I whispered where to kick, and she could get the gun out of his hands? Where had the knife gone?

The twine dug into her skin. Her calves had gone blue from

lack of circulation. My right arm was useless. If he shot me, Kelly had no chance.

And I'd never see her again.

I put the cushion over Maura's face.

"Please don't do this!"

This is your punishment for all your bad deeds—an innocent life.

I couldn't use both hands, so I lay across the tattered cushion until I had all of my weight behind me. Maura fought, writhing and begging, her tied legs flopping up and down. I closed my eyes and pictured Kelly's face.

Disappointed. The word ghosted over me as though Kelly had stepped into the room.

She wouldn't want this. And Chris was going to kill us both anyway.

Damned if I wasn't going to put up some kind of fight.

THIRTY-FIVE

Maura's movements slowed, but she remained conscious. I couldn't fake anything this time. It all had to be real. I took a deep breath and rolled over to my right side, dumping my weight onto my broken wrist.

Indescribable pain shot up my arm and into my shoulder. I instinctively curled up against it as my body tried to protect itself. Maura jerked again, and I tumbled off her, the cushion still in my left arm. I ended up on my back, teeth gritted against the pain and trying to catch my breath.

"Jesus Christ." Chris stomped over to me, the toes of his boots close enough to touch. "What the hell was that?"

"It's my arm." I looked up at Chris through very real tears. "She pushed back, and I lost my balance. I can't kill her this way. I don't have the strength."

"Well, you better figure out how to get it done, Lucy, because the river is rising. Kelly doesn't have a lot of time." He leered down at me, an angel of death so high off his own ego he'd missed his mistake.

You almost found her. You just didn't look closely enough... the river is rising.

Where had I been with a rising river?

The cemetery.

Something feral took over. I didn't stop to think. I raised my bound legs and slammed them into Chris's kneecap. He stumbled back, his boots connecting with Maura's heaving form. As soon as she felt the contact, she raised her own legs and blindly kicked. The impact was enough to send him off balance and make his grip on the gun perilous. As she rolled behind me, I managed to get on my knees. I dove forward and crashed my head into Chris's groin.

"You stupid bitch." His body went rigid, but he didn't drop the gun, instead bringing it down hard on my head. I saw stars, but I didn't stop. I reared back and drove in harder, sending him toward the folding chair.

Chris grabbed my hair and yanked my head back. He'd gone rabid, eyes wide enough to explode from their sockets and white spittle foaming around his mouth. He looked at me with more hatred than I imagined possible.

"Lucy, we could have been so good together. But you had to screw it all up. And now I've got to pay the price." He stuck the muzzle of the gun beneath my chin. I wouldn't give him the satisfaction of being scared now. At least I wouldn't have Maura's death on my conscience. And Kelly would have been proud of me.

"You're just like my mother," he snarled, his spit splashing onto my cheek.

I didn't see the knife until it drove into his neck.

THIRTY-SIX

The duct tape still hung from Maura's temple. Her tears must have made the glue wear off. She'd cut the twine off her ankles. Chris had been so absorbed in me he didn't even realize she was escaping.

His arrogance had been his demise after all.

He stood motionless, hands going slack. I wrenched the gun away and got to my feet.

The knife stuck out of his neck, blood pouring down his chest and arm. His eyes flashed around the room, his expression frozen in disbelief.

Maura staggered away, some of the shredded duct tape still tangled in her fingers. Her terrified eyes met mine. "He wanted you to kill me."

I nodded.

"It sounded like you've killed other people."

The gun felt awkward in my left hand, but I could probably hit her from this close distance. If she talked... no. I wouldn't become Mary Weston.

Chris collapsed onto the floor with a loud thud, gasping for air. I edged closer for a better look at his neck. I didn't think she'd hit the carotid artery, but he was going to bleed out if we didn't get help. Lennox wouldn't be happy, and if I turned out to be wrong about Kelly, I'd need Chris.

"Maura, get his phone out of his pocket."

She shook her head.

"It's fine. He's not going to pull the knife out. He's a paramedic. He knows it's the only thing keeping him alive." I smiled down at him.

Chris's glazed eyes met mine. "Just kill me."

"I'm not giving you the satisfaction. Maura, get the phone."

With her hands still tied, her efforts were clumsy. But she still managed to pull the smartphone out of his pocket. She started to dial 911.

"No," I said. "People are looking for me. I want you to call Detective Todd Beckett of the Philadelphia police." I gave Maura the number and then rattled off Mac's address. "Tell Detective Beckett to get here now and to send EMS. And then give me the phone."

Wide-eyed, Maura did as she was told. She never stopped looking at me.

"He's on his way." She hadn't ended the call. I could hear Todd shouting over the line.

"Give me the phone," I said. "Go into the kitchen and find another knife to cut your hands free. And then bring all the towels you can. We need to try to slow down the bleeding."

"You want him to live?"

I looked at her disgusted face and wondered if she could distinguish between Chris and me. Or did she just see two depraved killers?

"He's kidnapped my best friend. I need him to live. Please, give me the phone."

Maura hesitated. Todd kept screaming. Chris gulped for air, his blood staining the floor. His eyes closed. Finally, she handed me the phone and started for the kitchen.

"Todd."

"Lucy," he shouted. "Thank God. Are you all right?"

"I'll live. Chris is touch and go, and we don't have much time. I know where Kelly is, and I need your help."

"I'm on my way."

THIRTY-SEVEN

Chris's pulse slowed and became almost nonexistent. His blood soaked the towels Maura scrounged up from the kitchen. My left hand hurt from keeping pressure on his neck. Touching him felt repulsive, but I had to try. There were stories only he could tell.

"Why don't you pull the knife out and let him bleed to death?" Maura sat in the open doorway, her long legs blocking the entrance. Great purple spots about the size of a man's fist lined her leg. Her jittery hands gave me the impression she would very much like a cigarette. She rubbed at the duct tape residue on her forehead.

"He's a serial killer," I said. "The FBI has a lot of questions for him."

Was that the only reason? Was there still some part of me that felt connected to Chris and would mourn his death?

"What about you?" Her hoarse voice bothered me more than the bruises. I couldn't explain why. I just knew that the sound of it dug into my nerves like a rusting needle.

I looked down at Chris. His face had lost all of its color, his lips tinged with blue. His breathing was sporadic. "I have questions too."

"That's not what I meant." She stared at me with no sign of fear, only curiosity. "It sounded like you kill men like the one who hurt my little girl."

I wasn't about to answer her. She might feel a kinship with me now, but a few hours could change everything.

"I didn't know." Maura's hoarse voice cracked. "I swear to God, if I'd caught him in the act, I'd have cut his dick off."

Chris's blood soaked through the towels and dripped onto my knee. "I believe you. I'm sorry about your daughter. Get her therapy, make sure she knows it's not her fault and you love her."

"It happened to you?"

I pressed harder against the towel. "My sister."

"I'm sorry." Maura tugged at her top, suddenly self-conscious. Lit up by the porch light, her disheveled blond hair looked like a broken halo. "I don't have the best job prospects."

"I'm not judging you."

She grunted something that sounded like appreciation, but her gravelly voice made it impossible to tell. "He took your friend. You were going to kill me to save her, which I totally get. What stopped you?"

A haggard moan came from Chris, and I enjoyed a flash of satisfaction at his suffering. "Knowing that if he actually let me see Kelly again, I'd have to tell her I'd killed an innocent mother. She'd never forgive me."

"Tell her I said thank you."

A wave of urgency made me feel like I was slowly turning inside out. "I hope I get the chance."

Emergency lights streamed into the doorway. Maura got to her feet. "Oh look. EMS brought friends."

Two armed patrol officers approached the doorway, guns at the ready. Maura's hands immediately went into the air. "Look,

I'm the one who got kidnapped." She jerked her head toward me. "So did Lucy. The piece of shit who did it is bleeding to death on the carpet."

A female paramedic pushed past the officer. She had a sapphire stud in her nose, and I dully wondered if she ever worried about a drunk trying to yank it out. An intricate ivy tattoo on her neck stood out against her ashen skin. Her gloved hands shoved mine away and applied new pressure.

"Chris!" The tattooed medic glared up at me while her partner began to pack gauze around the blade. Removing the knife would be up to the emergency room doctors. "What the hell happened?"

"He's the Silver Stalker," I said. "He kidnapped Maura and then me. We got lucky."

The woman looked at me as if I'd just started speaking a foreign language. "Are you kidding me? Chris Hale? You're nuts."

She'd find out soon enough. Lennox would have his hands full with the media. Chris's story had it all: generations of evil, a handsome hero, and a series of brutal murders that probably spanned years. "Talk to the FBI agent when he gets here. By the way"—I pointed at Maura—"she needs medical attention, too, if you hadn't noticed. He abused her pretty badly before he started in on me."

The tattooed medic ducked her head and began to assist her partner. "She's stable. Get her out to the other rig."

My emotions tangled. "You know she saved my life. She's not someone to just throw away."

Blue-gloved hands flying, the female paramedic ignored me. I had no reason to be angry. Critical patients were treated first. Medical professionals didn't base their standards of care on someone's vocation. And I needed Chris to live. Yet I couldn't stop the indignation.

"You're just going to ignore me? While you try to save

someone who is pure evil? Do you realize that? Is it because you think you know him? Or he's got a pretty face? That means nothing, lady. He's a killer!"

A steady hand touched my shoulder. Maura. "It's okay," she said. "Let's just go outside and get away from him."

My throat burned as I tried to catch my breath. What was I doing?

"Come on," Maura urged. She walked outside, aided by one of the patrol officers.

I didn't move. Part of me wanted to witness Chris taking his final breath. I deserved to be there.

"Lucy!" I hadn't noticed Todd's arrival. Flashing his badge, he cut by the patrol officers and hurried toward me, stopping at the sight of my splinted arm. He cradled me close, examining the arm. "How badly are you hurt?"

I finally managed to look away from the carnage on the floor. "I broke it when I fell at his apartment. Chris splinted it. But I'll probably need surgery." Seeing Todd's pale, scared face reminded me of what was still at stake. "Doesn't matter right now. We need to get to Kelly."

"You should get checked out." Todd's gallant tone was wasted. We didn't have time.

"I'm fine." I headed for the door. "Let's go."

"We need to question her," the responding officer said.

"She's my witness," Todd said. "I'm working with Special Agent Lennox on the Silver Stalker case. He'll be here momentarily."

He took my uninjured arm and led me toward the door, ignoring the other officers. He spoke quietly into my ear. "Lennox is going to stay here and deal with this case. You and I are going after Kelly. I've already sent a squad car to Monterey Cemetery and told them to look for any disturbed areas that aren't already underwater. I've got a second team in the abandoned building. Agent Williams is digging up everything she can about the place's history. No pun intended."

He kept a gentle hold on me as I walked down the steps and toward his car. I toddled like a child, stress and the ketamine still disrupting my system. "I told you on the phone, Kelly's not in the building. She's in the cemetery."

Additional police officers had arrived. I turned my head, hoping none would recognize me. We passed by the ambulance where Maura sat, attended to by another med. She raised her hand, and I nodded.

"This way." Todd steered me to the right. "Kelly being in the cemetery makes no sense," Todd said. "That place has been underwater for years."

"Not the vaults on the hill. I've seen them."

We'd almost reached Todd's car, but he stepped in front of me. "You said Chris drugged you with ketamine. That stuff messes with you pretty good. I think you're confused."

"I'm not confused." I brushed past him to the car, wincing as my arm bounced against my chest. "Just drive, and I'll explain it."

Todd grumbled something about my being stubborn, but he got in and started the engine.

The dashboard clock said it was 1 a.m. "What day is it?"

"Sunday morning," Todd said. "You disappeared yesterday evening." He looked disgusted as he put the car in gear and pulled onto the street. "Chris had Cook's car. We realized it after we checked security footage and ran the plate."

"It's my fault," I said. "The ketamine makes you lose your inhibitions. I told him you guys were watching."

"We should have been prepared. I'm sorry."

"It's fine," I said. "I just want to get to Kelly."

Todd took the first freeway exit toward the northern part of town. "Tell me why you think she's in the cemetery."

I tried to remember the last few hours. Much of it was just a blur of fear and desperation. Part of me still believed I would wake up from this terrible nightmare. "Chris never forgot his grandfather," I said.

"Big surprise," Todd grunted.

The pain in my arm seemed to ramp up with every second, and no matter how hard I tried to remain motionless, I felt every jolt of the car. "During the Westons' killing spree, Chris used to go with him at night, looking for girls. He even picked one out."

Chris had been so proud of that detail. Would he have turned out differently if his mother and grandfather weren't sadistic killers, or was he predisposed to evil?

"Last winter, I think Chris planned to kill his mother, but his grandfather prevented it," I said. "They had some kind of fun family bonding time. While he shared his life story with me, Chris mentioned his grandfather should have been buried in the family crypt. That he was a war hero, and so were his ancestors. That's where his grandfather had wanted to be buried."

"Okay." Todd didn't seem to be impressed. "But there are a lot of family vaults in this area. Most of them probably have a crypt since they're all old. How can you possibly narrow it down to Monterey Cemetery?"

It took me a minute to remember the answer, and when I did manage to speak, my mouth moved in slow motion, as though the muscles forgot how to work. "Because right after he injected the ketamine, Chris told me I'd almost found Kelly. That I'd looked in the wrong place. And then at Mac's, he said Kelly didn't have much time, the water was rising. The cemetery is the only place that makes sense."

"Maybe. The river is rising fast thanks to all of the rain, and the ground has got to be saturated. But"—Todd's voice grew gentle—"this guy spent nearly a year playing with your head. How do you know he's not doing it again?"

"I don't. I'm just hoping that he was too far into the heat of the moment to lie." I refused to give up hope. "But why do you think I didn't pull the knife out of his throat?"

"You're not going down for that," Todd said with finality. "I don't care who his uncle is. The guy's a killer, and he had two women held hostage."

"I didn't stab him. Maura did."

Todd glanced at me. "Really?"

"I was going to kill her." I felt no shame in telling the truth. "Chris said the only way I'd see Kelly again was to kill her and prove to him that I'd really be his partner. I didn't think I had a choice. And I came close. But Maura kept fighting, and then I thought about Kelly and what she'd say if she knew what I'd done."

I hoped Maura and her daughter got the help they needed. Maybe the entire experience would give her the confidence to turn her life around.

"You did the right thing." Todd laid his hand on my knee. "I always knew you had it in you."

The praise made me feel like I needed a shower. "Maura saved us. I fought back, but I was too injured and couldn't get to my feet. She got loose enough to get the knife. I didn't even know he'd put it down."

"He got cocky," Todd said. "I have to admit, seeing him like that gave me a lot of satisfaction."

I closed my eyes. "Me too. I just hope we aren't too late."

THIRTY-EIGHT

I hated industrial areas. They were never as shiny and futuristic as movies portrayed. Instead most were gray and worn, with big smokestacks polluting the area and parking lots with giant cracks from the abusive weather. Add in the element of darkness, and an industrial area could pass for a post-apocalyptic refuge.

"You need to do something to stabilize that arm." Todd unbuckled his belt and slid it out of the loops. "We can use this."

Arguing only wasted time, so I allowed him to secure the belt around my neck and carefully place my arm in the loop. He grimaced at his handiwork. "Better than nothing."

I climbed out of the car and was immediately struck by the fishy smell of the river. Even at a distance, I could tell the current was faster tonight. The water sounded like an out-of-control waterfall hell-bent on destruction.

Heavy cloud cover made the night sultry black. Flashlights danced in the empty apartment building and the power plant as Todd's officers continued their vain search for Kelly. I shut the door and started for the vaults. "Who's searching the remaining graves?"

"Agent Williams," Todd said as he caught up with me. "The only places left are the vaults, and the ones not completely destroyed are locked up. We've also got a K9 searching, but the elements are messing the dog up. There's a lot of human decay and debris around here, even if the water has buried it. Those dogs can smell it."

We crossed the long-forgotten parking lot into the thatch of land that led to the small remaining section of the cemetery. I forged ahead, my shoes sinking into the wet earth. "They're looking for a live human being. Do they have Kelly's scent?"

"Yes." He took my good hand and laced his fingers through mine. "You need to be careful before you break something else. And the vaults are on the southeast side."

His hand provided a small comfort, but I couldn't focus on anything but Kelly. "I remember seeing them yesterday. What about the other side of the river? Did the cemetery go that far?"

"Not according to the historical map," he said. "We'll know more once we catch up with Agent Williams."

Waterlogged weeds clung to my bare legs as we raced along the slick riverbank. My ribs hurt, the humidity making every breath a chore. Despite the belt, my arm still jarred with each step. The river bent sharply left, and the vaults loomed in the hillside ahead. Broad and fairly level, the small hill was a logical spot to put a burial vault—if the river wasn't so close.

"It's not the river we need to worry about with these crypts," Todd said. "It's the groundwater seeping in over the years, combined with all this rain. Especially in crypts."

I refused to think about what that might mean for Kelly.

Moonlight seeped through a crack in the clouds and provided me with my first look at the vaults. There were four in all. No two were alike, and all of them were in various states of decay, with the far left reduced to a mound of rubble. How many people had stood where I was and walked the path to the vaults to bury their loved ones? Gray and ghostly, the vaults seemed aware of their power over me, their energy suppressing my courage.

Agent Williams jogged toward us, bolt cutters in hand. Her businesslike tone rose over the noise of the river. "I made some calls and finally got ahold of the former city planner." She wiped the sweat off her face. "Long story short, vault number three belonged to a family named Kent."

"Chris's family." I had no doubt it was true. His mother and grandfather had probably regaled him with family history. And he'd catalogued it all for future use.

"Follow me." Agent Williams led the way to the smallest vault. Weathered dark gray and covered with moss and dirt, the vault was built into the hillside with the pentagon-shaped entrance framed by four rows of rotting bricks. A modern padlock protected the iron gate.

Todd grabbed the bolt cutters from Agent Williams and quickly snapped the padlock. As lightning flashed in the west, Todd pushed the gate open. My heart dropped.

THIRTY-NINE

As Todd predicted, water pooled at the bottom of the steps. I didn't wait for permission and scrambled down the slippery stone. Seven steps later, my feet were wet and freezing. I pushed ahead, shuffling through the water toward the vault's inner door.

My left hand brushed against the walls, feeling the rough stone and centuries of deterioration. I needed to breathe and not worry about what I might find. I needed to get to Kelly first.

"What's the door made of?" Todd stood behind me, with Agent Williams and her big flashlight at the top of the stone stairs. "If it's stone, we might need help."

I touched the door, feeling the cold grain. "Wood. Give me one of your flashlights."

Todd handed me the flashlight, and I searched for some kind of latch. Closer inspection showed age had warped the door, preventing it from shutting properly. I reached for the gap between the door and the tomb and then realized my right arm was useless. "You go."

Todd and I squirmed in the narrow passage, his chest brushing up against my back. He stuck his flashlight in his mouth and grabbed the door and started to pull. It didn't give. "Something must be blocking it."

He cautiously moved his leg, testing the depths of the water. "There's something here." Todd reached down and pulled, his face twisting into a grimace. "It's heavy. Back up."

I gave him as much space as possible. Using both hands and most of his weight, Todd slid the heavy object away from the door. "It feels like a big piece of concrete. Probably broken off the vault somewhere."

My gaze landed on the etching above the door. A leaf, lined with what appeared to be silver.

"Get inside, please."

The door opened this time, albeit barely wide enough for one person to fit through. I moved to get past Todd, but he blocked my path. "Lucy, you should prepare yourself. He may have killed her right away. And if there's more water—"

"I know. Please, let me by."

He nodded and stepped aside.

My ears rang. My vision blurred. I felt overheated despite the cold sweat. I couldn't swallow.

Just get it over with.

I entered the tomb.

My eyes took a moment to adjust, even with the help of the flashlight. The putrid water was deeper inside, most likely flowing into a crack in the vault's foundation. I eased forward, water quickly going to my knees. I shined the light over the walls in search of the shelves that would hold the coffins. We'd entered an antechamber. Roughly 6' x 6', the internal entryway may have been meant as a mourning area or for storage of personal objects.

A second hallway lay directly across the main entrance, and from the looks of the water, I assumed another set of stairs.

So dark and dirty.

If our flashlights fell into the water...

"What do you see?" Todd asked.

Hell.

That single thought made me seize up with my old fear. This is where I would end up one day. Not this vault or even one like it. I might be cremated. It didn't matter—the end result was the same.

I would end up as nothing tangible, just evaporated energy. Like a star that finally died out, with no visible trace of its former existence.

Simply ending.

I lurched against the wall, my lungs refusing to work. My life was suddenly being squeezed out of me as if I were shrinking into some abnormal copy of Lucy Kendall. I wanted to escape my body and run far away from this place.

Todd's hands closed over my shoulders. "It's okay, just close your eyes and breathe. I don't like tight spaces, either."

It's not that, I wanted to scream.

It's death. The finality, the meaningless of our lives. The fact that with just one blink, we're gone. That I will end up just like the bodies in this crypt, and no one will ever know who I really was. That I hated myself and never got over my sister's death, or that my mother ruined our lives. That I did terrible things but still kept going. No one will know I was here!

This is where Chris would have put me.

I collapsed against the chamber's filthy wall. My fingernails raked against the stone in my effort to stay steady. The ancient, jagged surface snagged my index fingernail. It ripped off and remained stuck in the rock.

"That's all you're getting of me, Chris." My voice fell flat in the tomb. "I beat you. And I won't quit."

"Lucy." Todd spoke louder. "I think the water's rising. It

rained again tonight while you were with Chris. The ground's overloaded. We need to keep moving."

"Right." I stepped through the water, trying not to think of the chemicals that might be in it—or what could go floating by. By the time I crossed the small chamber, my thighs were wet.

I'd never been in such a dark place. My hand trembled and so did the beam of light.

"Be careful," Todd said. "You're going to hit the stairs with no warning. I should go first."

"No. I need to find her." I inched forward, trying to feel the floor through my shoes. My left foot slipped over the edge of the stairs. I pitched against Todd.

"Easy," he whispered. "Use the wall for support."

I did as he said, pressing my left side up against the ragged wall. Four steps made this descent shorter. But much steeper. The steps were so narrow the toes of my shoes hung off the edge. I stumbled off the last step and water splashed onto my face.

We'd reached the crypt.

Disintegrating bricks made an arch over our heads. At least two feet larger than the antechamber, the crypt had shelving centered in the wall on each side of us.

"They're probably stacked on top of each other," Todd said.

Water eclipsed the bottom shelves.

Todd nudged me. "I'll go left—looks like there's still a coffin in that one—or what's left of it. You check the right."

Cold leached into my very bone marrow as I made my way to the shelf. I prayed I would see Kelly alive and breathing inside. I raised my left hand and shined the light into the cylinder-like shelf.

And it was empty.

I almost sank into the water as my hopes evaporated. But I couldn't stop. I braced against the wall and used my foot to feel for the drowned shelf. I kicked blindly and connected with nothing. Did that mean she was curled up farther in the shelf, or had someone's bones long rotted away?

Cold, stinking water splashed onto my neck. I jumped and pitched forward. More water struck my chin; my feet fought for purchase below the flood. My flashlight glowed against the murky, green water. A misshapen piece of wood floated by.

"She's here," Todd screamed. "Chris blocked off the end with that piece of wood. Her feet are cold."

"Kelly!" I flailed through the water. It pushed against me—Chris's final effort to steal Kelly away.

"Kelly, I'm here."

Todd shouted again. "Hold the light up so I can pull her out."

I stuck the flashlight in the air as high as possible. Todd's back muscles strained against his damp dress shirt as he tried to ease Kelly out of the opening.

What am I seeing? What's he done?

I saw her ankles first, and it hit me.

I drank her in with hungry eyes, cataloging every visible injury. Bites and lesions covered her bare legs. Her fingernails were shorn to bloody nubs. Layers of filth covered her clothes, and she had a nasty cut on her arm.

Duct tape covered her eyes.

But her mouth was open, gasping for air.

Kelly's alive.

FORTY

A paramedic tried to tell me I couldn't ride in the ambulance with Kelly. I told him to go to hell and climbed in while Todd pled my case.

A second medic carefully applied rubbing alcohol to the duct tape and then gently pulled off the adhesive. Kelly's eyes fluttered open and then closed. The skin that had been protected by the tape remained clean, a stark contrast to the rest of her body.

"Kel, can you hear me?"

As Todd brought her out of the vault, she dropped in and out of consciousness, her words making little sense, save for one: Chris. She kept saying it over and over, as though she somehow knew she'd been rescued and needed to make sure the name of her tormenter was known. She screamed blindly when Todd cut the ropes, her limbs jerking unnaturally, like she'd forgotten how to stretch them.

I smoothed back her grimy hair. In the harsh light of the ambulance, the bruises looked even more horrific. Chris had beaten her more than once, and the repulsive purple marks around her neck made it clear he'd strangled her.

What if she had brain damage or couldn't talk?

I took her cool hand in mine, careful not to disturb the IV. Her destroyed fingernails bothered me more than anything. I couldn't imagine the fear she felt trapped inside that tiny space, unable to move.

I would have absolutely lost my mind.

"You can ride with her." Todd stood at the ambulance's back doors. "But you need to stay out of Rick's way." He nodded to the paramedic attending to Kelly. "And you need to step aside at the hospital. Your arm needs to be X-rayed, anyway."

"Did you call Lennox?"

He nodded. "I let him know we found her."

Todd waited. The question sat on the tip of my tongue. Did I really want to hear the answer?

"We need to get going," Rick the paramedic said. "Her vitals are decent, but I want to get her to the hospital."

"Go ahead." Todd stepped away and started to shut the door.

I mustered up the closest thing to a smile I could. "Thank you."

"Always."

Rick stayed busy on the drive, watching Kelly's pulse and checking her breathing.

"Do you think she's brain-damaged?" The idea ate away at me until I had to ask.

"It's really hard to tell." His gloved hands grazed her bruised neck. "They'll have to run tests."

"But you said her pulse is strong, right? And her breath sounds are good."

"That's true," he said. "But when the brain is deprived of

oxygen even for a few minutes, a lot of bad things can happen. You'll just have to try to be patient."

Just like Mac.

I kept nagging poor Rick, even though I knew he didn't have the answer. "She said his name—the man who did this to her. That's a good sign, right?"

Rick sighed, obviously frustrated with my questioning. "It just depends."

I looked down at her again. Oxygen flowed through the mask, and her color appeared to have improved. Chris would have wanted her brain to work. He'd want her front and center while he annihilated me.

Feeling Rick's eyes on me, I glanced up to find the paramedic staring. "What?"

"Is it true what they're saying? That Chris Hale is a serial killer, and he kidnapped both of you?"

I nodded and braced myself for a barrage of disbelief: Chris was a nice guy, he was from a good family, a great paramedic.

But Rick only shook his head, a grim expression darkening his face. "He always gave me the creeps, anyway."

"How so?"

He tugged the back of his hair, revealing a Celtic tattoo on his forearm. "This is going to sound kind of stupid, but it was his eyes. They just looked right through me."

"It doesn't sound stupid at all." As though it had burned me, I remembered the coin in my pocket. I took it out and stared at Lady Liberty standing tall. Looking at the iconic symbol of freedom made me feel as if I'd been trapped in the vault all over again.

Kelly's fingers flexed in mine, a low moan escaping through her mask. Her eyes fluttered beneath the lids.

"Kelly." I shoved the coin back into my pocket. "You're safe. It's over. Chris is dead."

I decided she must have heard me because she immediately

calmed down. I patted her shoulder and told myself Kelly would be just fine.

"I guess you haven't heard." Rick checked Kelly's breathing again and then made an adjustment to her oxygen.

My heart dropped. "Heard what?"

"Chris Hale's expected to live. You saved his life."

FORTY-ONE

The orthopedic surgeon set my wrist. I was lucky, because the break hadn't really started to heal. But the process still hurt like hell. I stayed at the hospital overnight for observation. Doctors assured a worried Todd the ketamine shouldn't have any long-term effects.

And just like Rick the paramedic said, Chris Hale was expected to live. His aunt and uncle were already rallying around him. Lennox kept his room under guard. I didn't visit.

Kelly had no internal damage, and her brain scans were good. Her condition was the result of dehydration and lack of food. Her attending physician medicated her to allow her body time to rest before she had to be reintroduced to the shock of the situation.

I waited all night and well into the next day before her eyes finally opened. The moment they focused on me, I knew she'd been aware all along.

"Don't try to talk yet." I grabbed the water cup and carefully put the straw to her badly chapped lips. "They've been giving you fluids, so you can drink some of this."

She sucked the water down eagerly, her bright eyes taking everything in. When she finished, she breathed hard. I planned to let her rest, but she had other ideas.

"How did you find me?" Her rasping voice was a shadow of its normal self, but the sound was still beautiful.

"Chris told me."

"What?"

I smiled. "He thought he could outsmart me. And I guess he did for a long time. But he underestimated what I would do for you."

Her eyes filled with tears. "I knew you'd figure it out."

"I didn't, really. I ran around in circles. First I thought Robert Tesla Jr. had something to do with it, because he was a suspect in the sex trafficking case."

"Chris planned that." Kelly tried to sit up. I gently pushed her back down. "He made me write the file."

"I figured that out after I found out the truth. I ran into Justin when I was at Tesla's, and he told me what you found out about Tesla's father. Take another drink."

She did, groaning in appreciation. "That tastes so good. I'm sorry I didn't tell you I was looking into Tesla and his friends."

"It doesn't matter." I decided to get it over with. "But you should know, Jared Cook is dead. So is his cousin. Chris killed them after he sent a picture of Cook with you to your phone. He wanted to mislead me."

Kelly closed her eyes. "I know. When he took me there, and I saw Jared..." She shook her head. "He killed the cousin first. That poor man didn't know what hit him. Then again, I guess Jared didn't either. Chris went on about how Jared had gotten what he'd deserved. And Jared didn't have a clue what was going on. I felt sorry for him."

"I knew you would." Always better than me. Thank God.

"But you called Lennox?" She looked doubtful. She knew I would want to kill the person who'd put her through this.

"I didn't have a choice," I said. "When I saw Jared and realized what had happened, I knew it had to be something else, and time was running out. I thought whoever had taken you was related to some of... my people. So I called Lennox and planned to give him names."

Kelly tried to sit up again. "You were going to do that?"

"Of course I was." I eased her shoulders down. "Todd barely stopped me. But by then Lennox had decrypted your message." I looked at the clock and watched the black hands tick the seconds away. "I'm sorry I trusted Chris and did this to you."

"Don't be. None of us knew."

"I went to him and offered to trade myself for you. But he had ketamine. When I woke up, he told me everything. Including how to find you."

She looked at her hands. I'd cleaned her fingernails as best I could while she slept, but the tips were still bruised. "Is he dead?"

"He kidnapped a woman," I said. "A single mother, a prostitute whose daughter had been molested. He wanted me to show that I was serious about being his partner in exchange for your life and thought she was the perfect place to start." I felt tears building and willed them to stop. "I couldn't do it. There was a struggle; she stabbed him."

Her body relaxed. "So he's dead?"

"No. I saved his life."

"Why?" Unsurprisingly, there was no judgment in her voice.

"In case I was wrong about where you were. And because there are families out there who need closure."

A smiled played at the corners of her mouth. "I guess you do have a conscience after all."

I snorted. "Don't tell anyone."

"What happens now?" she asked. "To you, I mean?"

"Lennox said he'll let NCMEC know why I'll need a few more days off work. He says not to worry about it."

"And that's it? You're going back?" She was trying to sound brave, but I could see the worry in her face.

"Only if you'll go with me. I can't leave you behind again. And you don't have to decide now. I know there's Justin to consider." I glanced at the door. "Speaking of which, he's waiting. I should let him in."

She blushed. "Did he help you search?"

I swallowed around a lump in my throat. "I lied to him. He thought you'd committed yourself because you'd moved too quickly in your relationship. Needless to say, he's pissed off at me. But he'll get over it."

Kelly started to laugh and then winced in pain. "My entire body hurts."

I stood up. "I'll get Justin."

"Lucy."

"Yes?"

She reached for my hand. Her dry, broken skin felt wonderful. "Thank you."

"Don't thank me. Thank yourself. Your faith in me kept me going." I wasn't sure how to broach the subject, but I felt like I had to say something. "I can't imagine what you went through. I just want you to know that I'll be there in whatever capacity you need. And Todd's looking for a way to prosecute Tesla Sr. and the others."

"No," Kelly said. "Let them go. At least as far as I'm concerned. Investigate them for current stuff, but I promised myself while I was trapped in there that if I made it out alive, I would let all of that go. It's in the past, and I'm not going back."

"All right." She was a better person than I could ever be. "Whatever you want."

"You should try to do the same. With everything. Lily

wasn't your fault. Neither was Shannon or what happened to me. Or Mac."

I looked at her, unable to speak.

"Chris told me. He thought it was funny." She squeezed my hand. "I'm sorry."

The words wouldn't come, so I just nodded. "I'll get Justin."

Justin shot me a dirty look as he hurried to Kelly's room. I sat down next to Todd in the waiting room and leaned my head on his shoulder. "I wonder how long he'll be mad."

"Give it a few days," Todd said. "He doesn't burn long. How's your wrist?"

I held it up. My cast was pink. For some reason I'd chosen the color I'd always hated. It was bright and pretty. "Hurts like hell. But I kind of like it. Reminds me I'm still alive."

"I didn't think you would be after we realized Chris had taken you."

"Neither did I."

Todd took my hand, the gesture comforting and familiar. "What happens now?"

"Now we try to move forward. If Kelly is willing to come to Alexandria, I'll stay with NCMEC. Otherwise, I'll move back. I need to be close to her."

"And what about us?"

He worried his lower lip, making deep creases between his eyes. I smoothed them out. "Do you really want there to be an us after everything? In your line of work? People will talk."

"Let them." He brushed his lips against mine. The kiss was tentative at first, searching, and then more demanding. He pulled away first. "I want to be with you. So if it's Alexandria, then we'll figure it out. Maybe I can transfer to the DC Metro Police."

"And Justin?"

He grinned. "Justin will follow Kelly. He's smitten."

I kissed him again. "Maybe he's not the only one."

"Maybe he isn't."

FORTY-TWO

ALEXANDRIA, VIRGINIA, SIX MONTHS LATER

"Are you ready to leave?" I leaned against Kelly's cubicle in the call center at NCMEC, resting my chin on the edge. "And I think we should eat out tonight because I don't feel like pretending to be a decent cook."

She laughed and pulled off her headset. Her dark hair had grown out past her chin, making her look even more delicate. "Sure. Just let me get my stuff together."

I waited impatiently, my stomach growling. I'd spent my lunch hour organizing leads on a new case. "Is Justin working tonight?" As Todd predicted, Justin had followed Kelly to Alexandria. He'd found a job working nights with a janitorial crew and was taking criminal justice classes during the day.

"Until midnight." Kelly's recovery had been amazing. Her time in the tomb had somehow destroyed her fears and inhibitions. Instead of shuttering the world away, she'd embraced it, going so far as to volunteer at a women's shelter once a week. She slipped into her winter coat, buttoning it all the way to her chin, and then we walked toward the elevators. She rubbed her temples. "You know the white van legend that's basically in every neighborhood in America, right?"

"Of course."

"Well, this time it was real. Kirksville, Missouri. A guy jumped out in broad daylight and snatched a seven-year-old girl off her bicycle. It happened twenty feet away from her house."

"Jesus," I said. "I guess that'll be coming over my desk before too long."

"Maybe." She shivered as we entered the January air. "Too bad we had to park so far away. And I thought DC was supposed to be nicer in the winter."

"Come on," I said. "It's a lot warmer here than it would be in Philly."

"I still hate it."

"Me too. I heard from Todd."

She linked her arm through mine. "Bad news?"

"He can transfer to the DC Metro, but he'll have to start at the bottom of the totem pole. It'll be like being a rookie all over again." Todd had been trying to transfer to the metropolitan police for months. The process was long and arduous, and he'd finally gotten the final word this afternoon. "I told him to wait. He's still thinking about it. There's always the Alexandria Police or the National Park Police."

"He'll get here."

"I hope so, because weekend trips are exhausting." And expensive. Mac had left me a sizeable inheritance—much to my mother's disgust—but I wanted to save it to buy a house. So Todd and I were spending a lot of our money on gas, trying to see each other at least twice a month. But I wouldn't give the trips up for anything.

We walked quickly down Prince Street and then cut over a block. A snowflake landed on my nose. I hoped it snowed. As much as I'd complained about the bitter northeastern winter, I missed the snow.

Kelly cleared her throat. "Did you get another letter?"

The letters. They'd been coming every week since Chris

had been incarcerated, almost always on the same day. I dug around in my bag until I felt the familiar envelope and then handed it to her.

She didn't bother to look at the return address. We knew it by heart now. Chris was housed at the United States Penitentiary in Lewisburg, Pennsylvania, still awaiting trial. He refused outside communication but continued his weekly barrage.

"I don't want to read it." She handed it back to me and then tightened her scarf.

"There's no need." I stuffed the envelope back into my bag. "Says the same thing it always does."

I knew the letter by heart now.

"With every day, and from both sides of my intelligence, the moral and the intellectual, I thus drew steadily nearer to the truth, by whose partial discovery I have been doomed to such a dreadful shipwreck: that man is not truly one, but truly two."

— Robert Louis Stevenson, *The Strange Case of Dr. Jekyll and Mr. Hyde*

Dear Lucy,

You know this speaks to both of us. Mother was right.

I'll be waiting for you.

"He's wrong." Kelly said. "It's over."

I jammed my hands into the pockets of my wool coat. The Lady Liberty coin Chris had meant for Maura made the tips of my fingers burn. I took the smooth silver in my fist, letting its warmth slither over me. A reminder, not of the way I'd nearly ruined my life, but of the person I really was.

A killer. A woman who still struggled to accept life's cruelties and who had access to personal information about pedophiles all over the country. A killer who fought every day against the tantalizing urge to bring justice for just one more child.

I'd keep the coin.

Just in case.

EPILOGUE

Chris knew he was smarter than all of them. And maybe that's what screwed him in the end. His grandfather always said being cocky was only meant for roosters and stallions.

He should have listened.

Now he was stuck in a tiny cell, listening to filthy criminals live their filthy criminal lives. Men rooting and grunting and crying at all hours of the night. Men in anatomy only!

His grandpa never cried, even when he knew he was dying and his dumb daughter had waited too long to stop it.

These men were as weak as his father, simpering and following orders.

He wished Lucy would answer his letters.

Or take a phone call.

He had no interest in communication from anyone else. That stupid FBI agent drove him insane, always trying to get him to trip up and say something incriminating. But Chris never did. He was too smart for that.

But he needed to see Lucy. Had she learned her true purpose? Or had recovering Kelly further buried the killer inside?

Chris hoped it had. He hoped Lucy was lulled into a soft, snuggly cocoon and that she'd fooled herself into believing she could actually deny her basic instincts.

Her fall would be that much greater.

And she would fall down.

The great ones always did.

A LETTER FROM STACY

Dear reader,

Thank you so much for reading *The Lonely Girls*! I had a lot of fun researching and writing the entire Lucy Kendall series despite the dark overtones. If you read and enjoyed the book and want to get updates on my next release, just sign up at the following link. Your email address will never be shared, and you can unsubscribe at any time.

www.bookouture.com/stacy-green

As always, the best part of writing is the reaction from readers. If you loved Lucy and Chris as much as I do, I would love it if you could leave a short review. Getting feedback from readers is amazing and helps encourage new readers to try my books for the very first time.

Thank you so much for reading,

Stacy Green

KEEP IN TOUCH WITH STACY

www.stacygreenauthor.com

facebook.com/StacyGreenAuthor

twitter.com/StacyGreen26

instagram.com/authorstacygreen

ACKNOWLEDGMENTS

Ah, Lucy. Still my favorite character so many books later. I put so much of myself in Lucy, right down to her snarky personality and obsession with the truth. Lucy was also my mom's favorite character and series, and that makes her extremely special to me.

I've known the true villain of the Lucy series from a very early stage. My close friend and copyeditor Kristine Kelly had come to visit, and the two of us sat on my deck talking about all the ways to beef up a certain character. And I said, "Wouldn't it be great if..." Kristine looked at me, and we knew exactly where the series had to go. The idea of the perfect psychopath fascinates me. I wanted to create an antagonist so compelling readers couldn't believe that person to be any sort of evil, even if some instinct niggled away at them. I hope I've done exactly that with this series. So, thank you to Kristine for helping me to find the core of Lucy's story.

Those of you who know me are aware that research is kind of my addiction. I can easily disappear down that rabbit hole, and this book took my research to a new level. Many thanks to Staca Sheehan (Director, Case Analysis Division) at the National Center for Missing and Exploited Children (NCMEC) for allowing me to visit NCMEC. The tour of the Washington, DC offices, along with many interviews with Staca, provided vital realism to Lucy's new role.

NamUs is a very real program, and if you have a friend or loved one listed as a missing person, I urge you to check out the site. Todd Matthews (Director of Case Management and Communications) provided me with several screenshots so that I had a better understanding of how both law enforcement and civilians utilize the system. Thanks so much to Todd for his kindness and generosity.

When I decided on moving Lucy to DC, I hedged for a very specific reason: I had no law enforcement contacts in the area. Thankfully Sergeant Lelani Woods of the National Park Police stepped in to help, connecting me with veteran detective Robert Freeman. He's my eyes and ears in the DC area, and has been instrumental in helping me get the details correct. His description of the Consolidated Forensic Laboratory (where Lucy goes to identify Shannon) made those scenes much stronger. Without his candor, I wouldn't have had any idea the place existed, let alone its layout and design.

Thank you to Detective Jennifer Roberts of the Cedar Rapids Police Department for helping me to understand how an investigator can play nice with a sexual predator.

And thank you to Melinda VanLone for touring me around Alexandria to find Lucy's apartment and local hangouts.

To Rob and Grace: thank you for your patience and support. Words cannot express how grateful I am that you both put up with me.

Finally, to my amazing readers: what a ride we've had! Thank you for sticking with Lucy even when she grew darker than I imagined, and for your endless support online and in person. Without readers, authors have nothing. Thanks for the reviews and the tweets and the Facebook posts, and for being positive in the moments when I needed it most. You guys are amazing.

And now we come down to the final question. Is Lucy a true sociopath? I don't think so. Is she done killing? Never say never.

Until next time!

Stacy

9 781837 900435